Johanna Lindsey

SURRENDER MY LOVE

Johanna Lindsey

SURRENDER MY LOVE

AVON BOOKS ◆ NEW YORK

AVON BOOKS
A division of
The Hearst Corporation
1350 Avenue of the Americas
New York, New York 10019

AVON TRADEMARK REG. U.S. PAT. OFF. AND IN OTHER COUNTRIES, MARCA REGISTRADA, HECHO EN U.S.A.

Printed in the U.S.A.

For all the ladies who wanted Selig,
this one's for you

Chapter 1

Wessex, 879

HE ENTERED THE long hall of Wyndhurst and every woman in it stopped what she was doing to follow him with her eyes. There was nothing unusual in that. It happened every time he was in the presence of women; here, at home, it mattered not where, they couldn't help but stare at him. Here at Wyndhurst, it made no difference that he was a Viking and they were Saxons all, or that the two rarely mixed without bloodshed. It was only last year that their own men concluded yet another war with the Danish Vikings to the north.

It was not fear that held these women mesmerized, though this Viking could be fearsome when warranted, skilled warrior that he was. It was not awe for his towering height, which surpassed even that of their Lord Royce, who was an exceptionally tall man himself. It was simply that they had never known a man of Selig Haardrad's uncommon handsomeness.

He didn't just have a body the northern gods would envy, he had been blessed with a face likened to an angel's, with eyes that could be as dark as a summer storm or as light as polished silver, prominent cheekbones to frame a perfectly shaped nose, and brows subtly arched and as raven-black as his long, luxurious mane. He also had lips so sensual, every woman he met yearned to know the taste of them.

The women should have grown used to his looks in the six years since his first appearance, when he had come with his Norse Vikings to raid their land and nearly died for it. But familiarity made no difference either. And none were immune, not old Eda in the cooking area at the end of the hall, although she was the first to recall herself and snap at the women there to get back to work. And not young Meghan in the front of the hall, who sat sewing with her ladies before the open windows.

Meghan was no more than ten and four, but she still sighed dreamily and wished this particular Viking was not twice her age. Not that she wasn't old enough to marry. Babes could be married if the need for an alliance was strong enough. But Royce, her brother, had no such need and was already related to Selig by marriage. And besides, he loved Meghan too dearly to consider letting her leave his home for many a year yet, and she was perfectly happy to have it so.

On the left side of the long hall, at one of the tables set around a large barrel of ale, where the men were wont to gather, Selig's sister, Kristen, watched him approach. She didn't usually notice the effect he had on her women, but with the silence that greeted his appearance today, she couldn't help it. She noted the smile he bestowed on several women, and the winks he gave even more, those he knew intimately. There were too many winks in her opinion.

Sitting beside Kristen, her husband, Royce, rolled his eyes, seeing the same thing, and remarked in an aside to her, "He ought to get married and put them out of their misery."

. "What misery?" she snorted. "He spreads himself around too much to leave naught but happy sighs in his wake. The misery would come if he *did* marry. And why should he, when he has women of all ages throwing themselves at him in two countries, not to mention every market center he visits?"

"So 'twas the same in Norway?"

"Always." She sighed.

Royce chuckled, aware that she was not the least bit annoyed with her brother for his legion of conquests, including those in her own hall. They were too close, those two, for her ever to begrudge him anything. He knew Kristen had even set herself the task of avenging Selig's death when she thought Royce's cousin Alden had killed her brother in that raid that had brought both her and Selig to Wessex six years ago.

It was a time Royce didn't like to dwell on. How close he had come to ordering the deaths of the prisoners his men had captured that day, and almost lost his true love in the process. His wife had been one of those prisoners, though her friends had helped to disguise her so that she appeared no more than a boy. And the guise would have worked, for she was nearly as tall as they, and as tall or taller than most of his own men. It was the Vikings own forgetfulness, in still treating her like a woman, shielding her, aiding her, coming to her defense, that drew attention to her and finally to the truth the day Royce had her whipped.

He had separated her from her friends after that, moving her into his hall. He had thought her their whore, no other reason for her presence with them coming to mind. And she had let him think it, had been amused by it, and with her boldness unlike any he had ever encountered in a woman, she had tempted him from the first. If she had not, he could have resisted her, despite her beauty, despite the fascination she held for him, for he hated all kinds of Vikings with a passion.

Although he had fought wars against them for fifteen years, his hatred had only blossomed eleven years ago. In one horrific ordeal, he was forced to watch, impaled on a wall, while Danish Vikings killed his father and his only brother, and raped and killed his betrothed. Royce was left to die there, amid the corpses of his loved ones, and would have, if the Danes hadn't gone on to sack Jurro Monastery further inland, allowing those servants who had survived to aid him.

Aye, Royce had good reason to despise all Vikings. Yet he had fallen in love with one, and because of that, was even tolerant of her family. They visited en masse from Norway from time to time in their longships, but her brother Selig had been a more frequent guest, and in fact had stayed to live with them for three out of the past six years.

The first year of their marriage, Selig had stayed merely to be assured Kristen was going to be treated properly in her new home. He stayed the winter that time, though he returned to Norway with his parents when they left after their visit the next summer. And although their parents didn't come every summer after that, Selig did, with a new ship of his own (Royce had burned the first one), and usually with one or both of his younger brothers in tow.

At the next table, pretending to sharpen his short wooden sword as one of the men was sharpening a real one, five-year-old Alfred finally noticed his uncle's arrival and ran out to greet him. With a laugh, Selig swooped the boy up and tossed him a good six feet into the air, just short of touching the high ceiling. Kristen squeezed her eyes shut with a groan, but her son's delighted shrieks told her he had been safely caught. She looked again to see him up on Selig's wide shoulder, being carried back to her and Royce.

On Kristen's lap, three-year-old Thora put her arms out to receive the same treatment from her uncle, who was more than happy to oblige. But Kristen slapped his hands away when he reached for her daughter, saying, "Not if you value your life."

Selig merely laughed at her warning and knocked her own hands aside to snatch up his niece. But he didn't toss her. He held her up to kiss her baby-soft cheek so loudly, the smack of it was heard throughout the hall, as were the little girl's giggles. He then straddled the bench across from

Thora's parents, but he kept her in his arms, where she settled down comfortably, looking so tiny against his broadness. Kristen couldn't be angry with him when she knew how much he loved this child of hers who so resembled him.

One child was named for a king; Royce had seen to that. One was named for a god, a Viking god; Kristen had seen to that—to her husband's chagrin. However, it was a fact that neither child had Kristen's dark blonde hair or light acqua eyes. Alfred had his father's dark brown hair and green eyes, but little Thora had taken after Kristen's mother, just as Selig had, both with Brenna's raven-black hair and gray eyes, both looking more Celtic, as Brenna was, than Norwegian or Saxon.

" 'Tis done," were Selig's first words, given with a pleased smile.

Kristen and Royce didn't need an explanation for the brevity of that statement. Two years ago Selig had made the decision that he would like to settle here in Wessex. He was his father's heir, but his father, Garrick, wasn't so old that Selig would be inheriting his house and lands in Norway any time soon. In Norway, Selig still lived in his father's house. He now wanted a house of his own, and this he had started to build on land near Wyndhurst that Royce had sold him. It should have been completed last year, but last year the Saxons had been at war with the Danes again, and Selig had surprised everyone—except Kristen, who knew how much he loved a good fight—by joining the war to fight beside his brother-in-law.

Selig had been wounded in the major battle that year, severely enough that he had fallen unconscious for a time and had been unable to join Royce when the Saxons put the Danes to flight. The jest was, as he liked to tell it, that a Dane had saved him, pulling him to safety and binding his wound, the man assuming Selig had to be one of his own army since he in no way looked a Saxon. And as Selig spoke all the northern tongues, Danish included, the man had never learned of his mistake in aiding the enemy, and Selig was able to make his way to the Saxon side of the field before the battle ended.

The building of his house had had to wait until the war was over, and Kristen knew how much he had chafed at the further delay the weather had caused, for he had spent the winter with them. But the building was resumed in the spring, slowly, because fields also needed tending at that time, and Selig now had his own to plant.

Royce had loaned him his own builder, Lyman, as well as those serfs he could spare, though Selig had bought a half-dozen slaves in the Viking market centers of the north on his return trip that year, before he even told Kristen of his plans. He had bought men only—no Saxons, in deference to his brother-in-law—for the express purpose of building his house and working his land. His father, however, had given him a few more, which put his blessing on the venture, since Garrick wasn't at all adverse to having Selig live near Kristen to keep her safe; his opinion of his son-in-law was not so high that he cared to leave her safety solely in Royce's hands.

Selig was so obviously pleased by his accomplishment, Kristen was delighted for him. "So when is the celebration feast to be?" she asked.

He laughed. "Not until Ivarr returns with some women who can prepare it."

Ivarr was his closest friend who had been captured along with Kristen and the others. All of them had been enslaved and made to wear chains that summer, until Kristen's father and uncle had come to free them. It was their habit now that Ivarr would take Selig's ship to trade in the north each summer that Selig spent with Kristen.

"You sent him to buy women?"

He reacted defensively to the surprise in her tone. "I cannot come to you every time I need something sewed or a hot meal, Kris."

She was not upset with him. Slavery was a fact of life, and Christian and heathen alike saw nothing wrong with enslaving a defeated people. Her family had always owned slaves, some captured on raids, some bought. Her husband owned them, though his were mostly freemen who had been unable to meet the fines for whatever crimes they had committed, and so by Saxon law were enslaved as punishment. And his many serfs were not much different from slaves.

Her mother had been captured and given to her father as a slave, and so had Kristen been captured and enslaved by Royce for a time—until her father came to put an end to that. Though truth be known, Royce had already decided to marry her, so he didn't need the inducement of an enraged father and a hundred Vikings at his gate, nor her mother's dagger at his throat.

"Of course you will need women to care for both you and your home," Kristen said now. "But you should have let me choose them for you. Ivarr will pick only the pretty ones, if I know him, whether they can cook and sew a seam or not."

"You think so? Truly?"

The eagerness in his tone brought a laugh from Royce, but Kristen would have thrown something at her brother's head if he were not still holding her daughter. "You have more women available to you than you know what to do with, Selig. I would think you would want some with the skills to do what needs doing if you are going to pay good coin for them."

Both men burst out laughing, and Kristen added with a scowl, "Besides that."

Selig was still chuckling. "Let us hope, then, that they are skilled in all areas, or I will still be visiting your hall, sister."

"When did *you* get so particular?" she scoffed.

He shrugged, giving her the grin that could melt the stoniest of hearts, and said, "You know me too well."

She did indeed. Selig loved all women, just as they all adored him, and he treated each one the same. He didn't take advantage of a slave merely because she was a slave and couldn't refuse him, but wooed her as he would a free woman. The women Ivarr bought for him wouldn't mind in the least being owned by him, of that Kristen had no doubt.

"So when do you expect Ivarr back?" she asked.

"He was to sail to both Birka and Hedeby, so I do not expect him for a fortnight, another month at the most."

Kristen would have offered her women to prepare his feast, but knew he would want to wait until Ivarr and the rest of his men returned before he celebrated the completion of his new home. Seven of those men had elected to settle in Wessex as well, including her dear friend Thorolf. The rest of the men would sail home to Norway with Ivarr before the winter months stranded them here, to return again next summer.

She sighed, glancing around to note the number of women still staring in Selig's direction, their work ignored. Just about all. "I can see I will not get much done around here, now that you have idle hands again." She turned to her husband, jesting. "Can you not find another war to send him off to?"

Royce snorted. "You would take an ax to me if I did."

Which was more than likely. She had hated it when both her husband and her brother had ridden off to fight against the Danes last year.

She was about to admit as much when one of Royce's men ran into the hall. "Five riders approach, milord," he said, "one nigh dead by the look of him. They bear the king's banner."

And Kristen groaned inwardly, afraid war had again come to Wessex.

Chapter 2

IT WAS NOT war that was threatening again, as Kristen had dreaded, but a new plan devised by King Alfred and his advisors to strengthen the existing peace. The delegation of five that arrived at Wyndhurst from the west had been on their way to King Guthrum's court to do Alfred's bidding. They had not been attacked. The ailing man suffered no wounds, but some kind of natural affliction that was causing him severe pains, and limbs that would no longer do his bidding.

Kristen wouldn't learn what business the men were about until after she had seen the ailing one to a bed and summoned the healers, and even then word was brought to her before she returned to her husband that the man had died. That quickly, and of what the two healers couldn't say.

But it was this news she had to bring to the waiting men, and the four who had ridden with the dead one took it badly; not in grief, for they barely knew the man, but in the failure of their mission, which his death put an end to. They assumed the king would be furious. Royce had doubts of that. Knowing Alfred as he did, as a friend as well as his king, he imagined Alfred would chafe at the delay, then merely find someone else to replace the man who had died.

Of course, finding a replacement wouldn't be so easy, for it was their interpreter who had died, the one who was to speak to the Danes for the bishop in their party, who was the diplomat. The other three men were along as guards, since they had uncertain lands to pass through that were rife with thieves these days. The bishop could have easily been replaced, but there were not that many men in Alfred's kingdom who spoke the language of the Danes to make it easy for him to find another interpreter.

7

Selig also had to wait until Royce could explain what the problem was, but not because he had been busy elsewhere, as his sister was. He had simply not understood a word of what the Saxons had said.

Unlike Kristen, who had learned the different languages of all the slaves during her growing years at home, including her husband's tongue, Selig had learned only those languages he had thought would be useful to him in trading. So he could speak to any Dane and Swede with ease, could make himself understood to any Finn or Slav; and, of course, any Celt would think Selig was one of his own, for he spoke that tongue so well, thanks to his mother. But he couldn't speak to a Saxon unless like Royce, the man also knew the Celtic tongue, and fortunately, many of them did.

Selig had seen no need to learn the other languages that Kristen had learned, because he hadn't entertained the idea of raiding the southern lands as other Vikings were still doing, but had planned to follow in his father's footsteps and become a merchant prince. That one raid he and his friends had tried and failed at had been no more than a lark, their attempt to take some of the wealth from this land before the Danes conquered it all.

It behooved him, of course, to learn the Saxon tongue now, since he had decided to settle in this country, and so he was learning it. But he was no longer a child who had naught else to do but study, so he had not grasped much of it yet, was in no hurry to do so, and was still at a loss in situations like this when no one spoke slowly for his benefit. Actually, the Saxon words he was learning, he was learning from women, and those words did not exactly come up in conversations of this sort.

When Royce again joined him in the gathering area of the hall, next to the ale barrel, Kristen was also just returning from putting her children down for the night. They had shared their evening meal with the guests, but Kristen and Selig both had refrained from joining in the talk, which was mostly the lamentations of the four strangers. The hall still buzzed with activity, though, and the sky outside had yet to fully darken, it being well into summer.

After refilling their tankards with ale, Kristen was the first to speak. "Did I hear them aright? King Alfred actually wants some alliances made through marriages?"

Royce shrugged, not as surprised as his wife. "That is the gist of it. Three of his nobles have volunteered to sacrifice their daughters, all three ladies comely, all three richly dowered."

Kristen let that "sacrifice" pass, knowing he had not forgiven the Danes, nor ever would forgive them, for the slaughter they had done at Wyndhurst all those years ago. "Do those dowers include land?"

"Aye."

"God's mercy, Royce!" she exclaimed incredulously. "Your king and his brothers before him have been fighting all these years to keep the Danes out of Wessex, and now he will just *give* them property here?"

"His reasoning is simple," Royce explained. "Better three properties than the whole of Wessex when the Danish faction that is still greedy grows restless again. We know now that at least half of Guthrum's army is as tired of war as we are. They want naught more than to settle on the lands they have already taken for themselves. 'Twas the other half, the young men who came late to the war and so had not gained much yet, that started up the last war."

Which was the one that had so nearly succeeded. In fact, the Danes thought they had won, thought Alfred had died. And they were not the only ones to think so, with the Danes so firmly entrenched at Chippenham and ravishing the countryside around it.

Royce had first joined the fray again when Alfred's army had to chase the Danes out of Wareham in 876, then again at Exeter in 877. But after the Saxon army disbanded for the winter that year, as was the usual habit, the Danes made a surprise appearance at Alfred's court at Chippenham, where he was enjoying the holidays, and he and his family just managed to escape. His courtiers were scattered, the Danes ravished the countryside in triumph, and word spread that Alfred had been defeated. But he had not. With a small band of men, he hid deep in the Somerset marches, building a fort there from which he harassed the Danes and planned his strategies.

Royce had received word where to meet Alfred in the spring last year, at Ecgbryhtes-stane, and it was there that he, Selig, and his men joined the fight for a last bloody battle. They met the Danish army at Ethandune and put them to flight, but followed them back to their fortress, which they surrounded until the last peace was arranged soon after. It was a peace that no one really trusted; the Danes had broken it so many times in the past. Of course, this time there was a difference. This time King Guthrum of the Danes and thirty of his war leaders had been baptized in the Christian faith.

Guthrum had taken his remaining army back to Chippenham after all was settled, and had returned to East Anglia this year, where word was they were finally settling down in this area they had long ago conquered. But there were still those who doubted there could be a lasting peace, given the experiences of the past. Yet others were hopeful now, considering it was the first time that Alfred hadn't had to pay any Danegeld to get the Danes to depart Wessex. He had demanded hostages instead, as well as the baptisms. And there was one last difference this time. Alfred had finally acknowledged that the lands north of Wessex belonged to the Danes.

West Mercia was theirs, the people reduced to serfdom, and East Mercia under their firm control. Northumbria to the far north they had already settled, and East Anglia had been theirs from the start. It did seem, indeed, that it was time to give up the hope that they could eventually be expelled from all of the land. They were entrenched, there to stay, and Alfred was wise to recognize this fact and to take steps to assure that the existing peace would be a lasting one. Alliances through marriage was one way to do so.

"So Alfred is sending this delegation to King Guthrum," Royce continued. "They are few enough in numbers not to appear threatening when they begin passing through Danish lands, yet large enough to keep the bishop from being robbed on the way. He is the one who will negotiate the marriages with Guthrum, and 'tis hoped the three men Guthrum chooses will be high in his favor."

"So that they will advise against war if it comes to that again?"

"Exactly," Royce replied. "But now they will have to return to Alfred until another interpreter can be found, which could take months. And he is presently on the move, visiting his ealdormen west of here, so there could be further delay just in locating him."

"Why delay at all," Selig mentioned casually, "when I could take the man's place?"

Kristen snorted at the notion, but Royce grinned, saying, "Aye, you could speak to Guthrum easily enough, but who would interpret the bishop's words for you?"

Selig flushed slightly, having overlooked that pertinent fact. "The difficulties I am finding in communicating here are becoming a damned nuisance," he grumbled, and said to his sister, reproachfully, "why did you never insist I learn the Saxon tongue? You got Eric and Thorall to learn it."

Eric and Thorall were their younger brothers, and Kristen merely pointed out, " 'Twas easy to get them to follow my suggestions, for they were both much smaller than I was—for a time. You never were." To that he grunted, so she added, "Why do you want to involve yourself in this? 'Tis none of your concern."

"This . . . something else." He shrugged. "I merely have time on my hands now, with naught to do but amuse myself in your hall for the next fortnight."

With a half-dozen women still ogling her handsome brother, she turned to her husband and said, "Mayhap 'tis not such a bad idea."

Royce laughed. "Do you get the impression she does not like you underfoot, Selig?"

" 'Tis not funny, Saxon," she said in annoyance. "I love my brother dearly, as he well knows, but I like having my hall run smoothly, which it never does when he is about. Mayhap if you would take him out and break his nose, as I have suggested more than once—"

Royce cut in with a hoot. "You never did."

"I should have."

"I suppose I could go with him," Royce said to placate her, "to stand as the second interpreter."

"With the way you hate Danes? You would go there with one hand on your sword and the other gripping a dagger. Better I go than you, and there would be no need for a second translator, since I speak both languages."

The narrowing of his green eyes proved Royce did not take well to *that* suggestion. Send his beautiful Kristen into a host of Danes who had just spent years pillaging and ravishing and taking for themselves whatever struck their fancy? He would put her back in chains first, even though the last time he had done so, she had made his life miserable.

All he said was, "Nay, you will not." But his look dared her to argue about it.

Selig intervened before she thought to. "Father would skin me alive did I let you journey to East Anglia without a full army at your back, Kris, and well you know it. Nor would you care to be parted from your children and husband that long. Both of you have better things to do, but I do not. And besides, Royce has a number of men who speak Celtic, any one of whom could stand as the second interpreter."

"Elfmar could do that well enough, I suppose," Royce allowed, only to point out, "But the bishop may not like things so complicated, having his words pass through two others before they reach Guthrum."

"As to that," Selig replied, " 'tis more than likely that Guthrum will have his own interpreter on hand who can be used, while Elfmar and I merely stand present to assure that Saxon interests are protected. Either way, the deed would get accomplished."

"Aye, well, 'tis a moot point, and the bishop's decision to make." And Royce grinned to show that what he was about to add didn't reflect his own feelings. "He may prefer to return to Alfred rather than trust a Norwegian Viking to represent Saxons against a Danish Viking. You would be amazed how many Saxons do not differentiate 'tween the two."

Selig laughed at those last words. "I recall clearly there was a time when you did not."

"That was before I came to know this particular Viking." And Royce hauled Kristen across the bench and onto his lap—without protest, Selig noted, and no easy task, for his sister was a giant compared with Saxon women. "She has a way of making a man think of other than war."

"And what are you thinking of now, husband?" Kristen asked, wrapping her arms around his neck.

"That the hour grows late."

Selig grinned, watching their play. It was a fact that he and his family had had to accept, that she loved this Saxon dearly.

"Aye," he said. "I needs must find my own bed if I am to be off to East Anglia come the morn."

"*If* you are," Kristen retorted. "And make your choice quickly if you mean to share that bed. I do not care to hear them fighting over you as happened the last time, not when I have guests to be wakened by it."

Selig rolled his eyes in protest. "That was not my fault, Kris. Edith had not understood yet that I will not—cannot—tolerate jealousy."

"Aye, you would drive a jealous woman to murder right quickly."

"Leave go, vixen," Royce interjected, just managing to keep from laughing. "You have teased him enough this eventide. He begins to blush."

"Him?" she scoffed, feigning disbelief. "He stopped blushing over his women when he was ten and five. My brother has no shame—"

"Since she will not heed her husband," Royce cut in, lifting Kristen in his arms as he stood up, "I will see if I cannot occupy her mind with other things."

Selig heard no complaint to that suggestion. Kristen said merely, "You will break your back trying to carry me up those stairs again, milord."

"God's mercy, I *hate* it when you throw out challenges like that."

Royce did carry her all the way to their chamber upstairs, and if it was difficult for him—her extreme height guaranteed she was no lightweight— he would no doubt see that his wife made up for it with those "other things" he had mentioned.

Kristen was right, however, about her brother. There were too many women here to choose from, too many willing and eager to be that choice. And if Selig hadn't spread himself around to all those who were available, he wouldn't have such problems. Truly, he ought to be more discriminating . . . nay, he couldn't be that selfish.

He grinned and crooked a finger at Edith. He should have picked another. She had fought over him—and won—but he had punished her enough by consoling the loser of that fight. Yet Edith's jealousy and possessiveness were a unique experience for him. He had never had such feelings himself, and his women knew better than to succumb to them as well. If they wanted faithfulness, they would have to look to another for it.

"You want more ale, milord?" Edith asked as she reached him, a degree of sulkiness in her tone.

He gave her the smile that had won him the hearts of more women than he could count. "Just you, sweetling."

She nearly knocked him off his bench, no easy task when he topped her by more than a foot and outweighed her by a hundred pounds. Yet she threw herself at him with such force, he was unprepared for her, her mouth voracious on his, her hands already slipping beneath his tunic. He had to laugh. Mayhap jealousy was not such a bad thing after all.

Chapter 3

SELIG DEPARTED FOR East Anglia the next morn. As it happened, the old bishop was delighted to accept his services, and in fact knew a smattering of Celtic himself. Elfmar still joined their party, however, for the sake of clarity. Only the bishop, though, was looking forward to entering the land now ruled by the Danes. The others had all fought against them too many times to feel comfortable going amongst them, peace or no peace—except Selig, who had known Danes long before he knew Saxons, and bore them no grudges.

But it would be several days before they left the borders of Wessex behind, for, due to the bishop's advanced years, their journey was slow, with many stops for rest at manors they came to, or along the roadside when there were none.

The slow progress didn't bother Selig. His was a very easy nature, slow to temper, quick to laughter. And he hadn't seen much of this land that he had decided to live in, other than when he had searched for Kristen and the others after he had recovered from the wound Royce's cousin had given him, and when he had joined the war. So he was enjoying the trip.

His sister had been there to send him off with a promise. "I will see that Ivarr and your men do not wreck your new home if they return before you. But you had better hope there are no women at Guthrum's court, or they will not let you leave."

He had merely laughed. She did love to tease him, though half of what she said was perfectly true and only meant to annoy, though it rarely did. His men did likewise enjoy teasing, calling him Selig Angel's-face rather than Selig the Blessed, as he had been dubbed at his birth, a name which came not from a face that mesmerized women, but because the midwife had pronounced him dead at birth, yet his father had breathed life into him.

14

The second day of the journey dawned with a cloudless sky and a hot sun that had them riding even slower for the bishop's sake. But the company was pleasant, the land lovely, with all the colors of fertility in full bloom.

As they passed through a small woods with welcome shade cast over the narrow way, Elfmar was amusing Selig with tales, and was now telling of a pagan goddess who had come down to earth in search of a mortal lover. But all the great and mighty warriors were off to war, and the only person she could find to bestow her favors on was a lowly swineherd. Yet this was no ordinary swineherd, was in truth a god in disguise, one who was so smitten by the goddess that he would do anything to spend one night in her bed, even wallow in earthy muck. But the goddess had guessed the god's trickery and—

The ambush took the party completely unawares.

Out of the trees they dropped, and from the bushes they leapt, with clubs and daggers swinging. There was no time to draw a sword or offer a last prayer, so swiftly did the blows fall. Out of a dozen faces, Selig saw only one, no one he recognized—a thief, he supposed, though the man did seem too finely dressed, the sword that cut the bishop down too finely wrought. And then pain exploded in the back of his head and he was falling.

A young man led a fine destrier out of the woods to his lord. The lord mounted to survey the carnage his men had left behind.

"Take their horses," he ordered his captain. "And what coin they have so it will appear they were robbed."

"And what if Alfred sends others?"

"Then they will meet the same fate."

Chapter 4

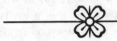

LADY ERIKA PUT the large ladle to her lips to taste the green pea pottage and sighed, for once again the cook needed instruction. "More saffron, Herbert, and do not be so stingy with the salt either. The merchant is due back again, and I will replenish all the supplies that have gone missing, including your spices."

She should not have had to say so. Seven years was long enough for these people to learn that their new lord, though a Dane, was not the miser their old lord had been. But they were a timid lot, these serfs, and no wonder, with as brutish and cruel as she had found the houseguards to be.

Erika had put an end to the indiscriminate beatings when she had come to live here four years ago—her brother Ragnar giving her a free hand. Not that she was soft. She could order a whipping when called for—a hanging, too, for that matter. She couldn't rule her brother's holdings in his absence without doing what was necessary when the situation warranted it, and she had no difficulty with that. She merely believed in being fair and having the punishment fit the crime.

She had taken her brother to task for what he had let continue for the three years before she came. Yet it wasn't actually his fault that he had done naught, since he had been away with the army for most of those three years, and therefore unaware of the situation.

It was a fine holding he had, and he had obtained it without bloodshed. The old Anglian lord who had lived here had been terrified he would lose all he possessed to the invading army, and so had offered Ragnar Haraldsson his only daughter in marriage. And Ragnar had been delighted to have her and all she brought with her, which included the loyalty of her people.

The old father died of natural causes soon after, and the transition of lordship had gone smoothly because Ragnar was wed to the daughter of the

16

house. And because there had been a lawful marriage, the people's loyalty easily survived the sad death of their lady in childbirth nine months after she was wedded. They were Ragnar's people now—and Erika's.

When she had come here, not only the beatings had ended, but also the near starvation, the rapes, the deaths for minor crimes. However, these people had lived too long under such a brutal yoke, just about every one of them bearing the marks of the lash. It would take more than a handful of years for them to forget the drudgery of the past.

Which was why she had spoken so softly to the cook, and now tempered the reprimand with a smile. "Mayhap a bit thicker, too, Herbert, as I know you like to make it. I do so prefer your recipe to mine."

The praise had the cook beaming as Erika left the kitchen. But then, that was her usual effect on the servants, whether she offered praise or not—at least on the male servants. Because she was uncommonly pretty, just a smile would do it.

Her beauty was not something she had always appreciated, since it had caused her female siblings to pick on her for many years. Yet she was comfortable with her looks now, even glad of them finally. She had high cheekbones, a short, straight nose, lips rosy and full. Her eyes were powder blue, with thick lashes and gently arched brows. But her glory was her hair, long and golden with a subtle shading of red.

She was a tall woman compared with the people she lived among. But she was small-boned, which gave her a willowy, delicate appearance. Not to say she was skinny. Her curves were well rounded and dented in all the right places, her breasts larger than most but well proportioned to her size, her long legs lean and firm.

Eyes would follow her as she crossed a room, and did now as she left the kitchen. Rarely noticed anymore was the shadow that moved away from the wall to follow her out into the bailey.

Torches lit the way to the hall. She hadn't realized the hour had grown so late, or that everyone would be waiting to eat. The last meal of the day had been delayed because of the latest thefts, and taking a tally of exactly what was missing this time had occupied her and the kitchen staff for several hours. So she hurried to the hall because Herbert wouldn't begin sending the food in until she had taken her seat. But her mind was still on the thefts.

"Seven loaves of bread and half the spices," she said to her shadow. "The spices will be sold, no doubt, but the bread? . . . Have you noticed anyone getting fat?"

The grunt she received in reply meant No.

"Has Wulnoth no clues who our thief is?" she asked next.

The same grunt. Erika sighed. They had been plagued for a fortnight now with the pilfering of their food supplies, weapons, even several of the livestock. Either there was a very clever stranger sneaking in and out of the manor, or one of their own was selling the goods in Bedford for a tidy profit. It was a wonder Wulnoth, the captain of the guard, hadn't caught him yet, for the crime warranted a lashing at least, and he did so love using his whip.

She despised the beefy Saxon captain, and had since the first day she met him. The man was arrogant, just short of insolent, and with an inherent cruel streak that could make any wrongdoer tremble in unholy terror. She would have dismissed him long ago except he had bowed to her edicts once made, giving her no cause, and the other men obeyed him, fearing him more than they did her, she had no doubt. He still suggested harsher punishments than she thought necessary, but he always acceded to her judgments, albeit with ill grace.

She reached the hall, finding it well lit, the manor folk milling about in small groups, but avoiding the tables that had been set up. She could imagine that half of them were anxious that the days of little or no food were returning. They should all know better, yet old fears were hard to let go of. New fears were easier to set aside, and she was pleased to note that conversations no longer ceased when she walked into a room, as they had for most of her first year here. Of course, it had never been she who had caused this phenomenon, but her shadow, which was perfectly understandable.

Turgeis Ten Feet was his name, the "Ten Feet" an exaggeration, as were most Viking names, but not by much in Turgeis's case. Seven feet tall he was, and barrel-chested, a great bear of a man with a shaggy mane and beard of bright red, and gentle brown eyes—at least she thought them gentle eyes. No one else did, not even her brother, for Turgeis, with his great ax three times the size of a normal one, could inspire fear in the stoutest heart. And he was never far from Erika's side, never beyond the sound of her voice.

It had been so since her tenth year, when she had found him near her secret pond, where she went to escape the bickering and unpleasantness of her home. He had been half dead, lying in a pool of his own blood, with an ax embedded in his back and a half-dozen gaping slashes on other parts of his body. He was Norwegian and had been sold into slavery by his own brother, who had been jealous of him, and feared him, and been promised by the unscrupulous slave traders that Turgeis would be lost in the slave markets of the Far East. The crew had taunted him that he would fetch a great price as a harem guard, but would have to lose his manhood first. Little wonder he tried to escape when the ship put in for supplies at her family's dock. The entire crew had given chase, and their bodies littered the woods from the docks to her secret pool.

Erika had learned all of this later, but it was his body that concerned her. To bring help to him would give away her private spot, but to let him die and rot there would ruin it just the same. So she had taken her needle to him and applied what herbs she knew for healing, and miraculously he had lived. And while he was recovering, her father had confiscated the crewless ship and its human cargo, which he sold at Birka. Because of that, he had asked few questions about the bodies that were discovered eventually, and even less of Turgeis the day Erika brought him home and said simply, "He is my friend." He had been her shadow ever since.

It was not such a bad thing to have a shadow like Turgeis. He was a man of few words, and she had come to understand the grunting sounds he made in response as a language of his own. He was indeed her dearest friend. Also, he had kept her father's heavy hand from falling on her, as it so often did on her many brothers and sisters.

Her father had had two lawful wives and three bedslaves, all of whom had given him numerous children. The count had been twenty at his death, and Erika had been close to none of them except her true brother, Ragnar. Their mother had been the second wife. The first wife had given the old man four daughters and three sons, all much older than the rest.

In fact, the oldest son, who took their father's place in their Danish lands, had three daughters himself for whom he would be concerned with finding husbands before he would think to arrange marriages for Erika and his one other sister still unwed. And with most of the young men in the area having left to seek their fortunes in new lands, it was little wonder she had supposed she would never have a husband or a home of her own.

But her brother had been one of those to leave home to find a place for himself elsewhere, with great success. And it had been one of the happiest days of Erika's life when he had sent for her to live with him in his newly conquered East Anglian holdings. She had had few expectations, was merely pleased to leave a home overcrowded and rife with petty jealousies, where she had never felt truly welcome or even needed.

But Ragnar had shared his new wealth with her, had given her the highest authority in his home, that of the lady of the manor, and complete command in his absence. No longer was there no hope of a marriage. She had had five offers already from Ragnar's men, stalwart Vikings, all, which he had turned down himself. He had higher aspirations for her, a wealthy lord at least, with many men at his command. This was their new home. It was time to strengthen their position with alliances. And now Ragnar had gone with his men to seek marriage contracts for them both.

Erika should be ecstatic. He had promised her she would be well pleased with the man he brought home for her, and she had little doubt she would be, for Ragnar wanted her to be happy. The trouble was, a husband of her own was no longer such a hoped-for circumstance. Her brother had given her so much—spoiled her, actually—that she was perfectly happy to remain where she was. Even her desire for children was answered in Ragnar's son, Thurston, whose upbringing she had taken over.

In truth, she did still want a husband, and did still hope for love to come her way, and she prayed often that the man Ragnar found for her would be that love. But she was so content as she was, that she feared a change, feared she wouldn't be as happy as she was now.

She supposed her fears were normal, the same shared by most women when faced with imminent marriage to an unknown man. Her life would change again, when she was not long used to the one she had.

Yet she knew her lot would change anyway when Ragnar married again. That was inevitable. And although she would be welcome in Ragnar's home for the rest of her life if she chose to stay here, she didn't care to feel useless and unneeded again.

So she hadn't mentioned her preference when the subject first came up, nor did she ask for a year or two of grace before she must wed. Ragnar thought he was giving her her fondest wish. She let him think so. But she wasn't all that happy about it. She simply wished that things could remain just as they were now. But then, she had no idea that things were about to change drastically, and much sooner than she expected.

Chapter 5

THE OXCART TRUDGED slowly down the wooded lane, an old woman, hands gnarled, gray hair straggly, sitting behind the reins. A young woman limped beside the cart, though without pain, the limp caused by one leg being shorter than the other, a phenomenon she was born with. The stench of death met them long before they came upon the bodies in the road. It was a smell old Valda welcomed. It was a smell her young niece, Blythe, abhorred, but had grown used to.

Seeing the corpses finally, Valda guided the cart to the side of the road and eagerly jumped down. She was spry for an old woman, and swift to move through the dead, searching through a pocket here, turning a body over there.

It wasn't long before Blythe heard her grumble. "Faugh, scavengers have beat us to them."

She should have said *other* scavengers, for Valda supported herself and her niece on the leavings of the dead. The wars that had ravaged the land for so many years were a boon to her and her kind, and she would follow in the wake of the Danish armies. With the excuse that she was looking for her son, no one would bother her as she picked through the bodies of the fallen, pocketing whatever coin or jewelry came easily to hand.

But what Valda had said was true. Other scavengers had already found these dead men and picked them clean. All the boots save one hole-ridden pair were missing; all the cloaks, the leather, the weapons, the wool. Only two tunics remained, these rent so badly by the inflicted wounds as to make them unwanted even by a scavenger. Most of the men still had their braies on, bloodied and stinking of death, though their chausses were gone. Two were completely naked, even their underwear fine enough to warrant taking. Lords, likely, those two.

Blythe stood upwind of the carnage, patiently waiting for her aunt to finish. Valda was angry that naught had been left behind for her, and was yanking off one of the remaining tunics. Blythe knew that she would wash the garment, stitch it, and sell it at market for a hot meal.

Blythe was loath to touch the dead bodies herself, and her aunt never insisted she help, which she was grateful for. She did the selling of whatever they found, and the selling of herself when times were lean. Valda had raised her, and it was the only life she knew. But Valda was getting on in years and yearned for a roof over her head instead of an oxcart and the cold ground for her bed.

It was not a vain hope, at least now it wasn't, for Valda had heard that her cousin's wife had died, and she and Blythe were on their way to visit him in Bedford. It was Aldrich's wife who wouldn't take them in before when they had asked, but his wife was dead now, and it was Valda's hope that he would marry Blythe and give them the home she so desperately wanted. Blythe was also hopeful that it would be as Valda predicted. Aldrich was much older than she, but not a mean or ugly man, so she wouldn't mind marrying him. Also, he had always looked kindly on her, despite her deformity. And a home and food every day would be nice, very nice.

Her eyes wandered as she waited for her aunt to finish. She hated death, had seen so much of it, yet her eyes were drawn to it still in morbid fascination. And her gaze came back to one man repeatedly, until she finally approached him.

He was one of the two men who had been picked clean, and Valda had turned him over—grunting and swearing the while, he was so big—looking for rings on his hands. He must not have worn any, for none of his fingers were missing, which was the quickest way for a scavenger to remove a ring that bloated joints would not release.

His was a fine young body, without a wound that Blythe could see, though with enough scars to claim him as a fighting man. His was also the longest, largest body she had ever seen. But it was his face she couldn't take her eyes from, the face of an angel, so beautiful it brought pain to her chest. And for the first time in all the years that she had seen men dead like this, tears gathered in her eyes.

It was typical of his effect on women that Blythe, who didn't know him and had never seen him before, could cry over the death of a man who looked like him. This she was doing, unbeknownst to her aunt, and she even dropped to her knees beside him, her hand drawn to his cheek. The skin was warm and supple, which brought a gasp of surprise from her. But she jerked her hand back with a shriek when she felt his breath on it.

"Aunt Valda, this man is not dead!"

Valda looked up from folding the tunic she had claimed and said with no concern, "So? He will be soon."

"But he has no wound on him either!"

Valda came to her side to look down at the man. She had wrestled long enough with his back to get it turned that she knew it bore no wound now hidden. She bent down to lift his head with both hands to feel there, and found the lump that had struck him down, the size of her small fist.

She let his head drop back to the hard ground without a care for the pain it might cause him. He made not a sound.

"His skull has been cracked," she said offhandedly. "They rarely waken from that."

"But he could?"

"Aye, he could, with constant care, which he will not be getting out here. Now, come along. I am finished—"

"I could care for him."

Valda's expression turned vexed. "Nay, how could you? We have not enough food to make camp here. And it would be a waste of time if we did. He is more like to die than not."

Staring again at the man, Blythe became stubborn. "If there is a chance to save him, I will take it."

"I tell you, we cannot linger here. We needs reach the next village to replenish—"

"Then we take him with us."

Valda threw up her hands in disgust. "Are you daft, girl? Why would we do a stupid thing like that?"

"To save him," Blythe said simply.

"But he is naught to us."

At which point Blythe mentioned the one thing guaranteed to make Valda agreeable. "He will reward us for saving him, and not just a few pennies, but a hundred at least. He is a lord. Why else would his every stitch have been taken? Would you not like to arrive at Aldrich's this time with coin in your pocket so we do not appear so needy?"

Valda was caught by the notion, but still frowned. " 'Tis no easy task to force gruel down the throat of a man who is half dead and cannot swallow. He will weaken by the day and perish in a sennight."

"Mayhap two hundred—"

"So help me get him into the cart. But I warn you, girl, if he has not wakened by the time we reach Bedford, I will dump him in the bushes myself. We cannot come to Aldrich with this man, or he would not let us in the door. My cousin does not like to draw the attention of nobles, even grateful ones. Naught good ever comes of it. So your promise, or he does not budge from this spot. There will be no argument from you when the time comes to be rid of him."

Blythe nodded eagerly, her confidence strong that they could heal the man in a fortnight, the time it would likely take to reach Bedford with their old ox. He did not fit in the cart, of course. The back had to be left down so his feet could hang over the end, and even then because his legs were so long, every bump in the road had his feet striking the ground. None of which woke him.

The days passed, with Valda grumbling continuously, though she did show Blythe how to rub the man's throat to get liquid to trickle down it. Not much liquid went down in that way, however, though she couldn't tell if he was weakening, he had been so healthy and muscular to begin with.

But she gave him the tenderest care, already far gone in love with him. She even sold herself to buy meat for his broth, when she and Valda rarely ever had meat for themselves. She did it gladly, determined that he would live despite the fact that he never made a sound, never moved a limb on his own, never opened his eyes, and was running a fever that came and went.

In truth, Blythe did the best she could, though neither she nor Valda knew aught of healing. Still, they reached Bedford with the man's condition unchanged. With the promise she had made hanging over her head, Blythe managed to cajole and coerce her aunt into making camp for two extra days, but she could ask for no more than that. Her own future was at stake, a better life to be gained. Valda made sure she realized that their future couldn't be risked for a man they did not know.

But, God help her, it was the hardest thing Blythe had ever done, leaving the man behind. She cried all the while she dressed him from Valda's store of stolen garments, fighting with her aunt to do so, for Valda could not see the waste, whereas Blythe refused to leave the man as naked as they had found him. That was the least she could do, now that she was deserting him. But her feelings also overwhelmed her at the end, and she slapped him again and again, screaming at him to wake up, raging at the unfairness of it, after all she had done, to have her aunt be right. He was not going to wake up, ever.

Finally Valda dragged her away, complaining about her puffy eyes, complaining that Aldrich wouldn't like a weeping woman. Blythe didn't care at the moment. She would get Aldrich to wed her, puffy eyes or not. And although she would never see the man again, whoever he was, she was going to remember him for the rest of her life.

Chapter 6

IT WAS THE rain that woke Selig, steady drops that gathered on the clump of leaves over his head and struck the dead center of his forehead. But the pain at the back of his head that greeted him was so excruciating, it sent him straight into blackness for another day.

The sun was shining when he woke again, and the very brightness of it hurt him, even though he could see, through the narrow slit of his eyes, that it didn't touch him directly, that he was shielded by the bushes he lay under. That other pain was there again also, and it wasn't so merciful this time, did not render him into oblivion again and did not go away either. He was afraid to move because of it, and for long, disoriented minutes he did not, adjusting to the throb of it, gritting his teeth to keep from groaning.

When he finally lifted a hand to locate the source of the pain, his fingers shook, and his arm wouldn't remain lifted, but fell back to the ground. Weakness, he realized. His blood loss must have been great to account for it, and he began to worry that he was in serious trouble. He could be close to death, for all he knew, and he still had no idea of what kind of wound he had sustained.

He waited a while before he tried once more to find the wound, and this time he succeeded. He felt over his face first, for the pain seemed to be everywhere, yet all he found was a slight stubble of beard there. That assured him he hadn't been unconscious for long, mayhap a day, but then, he had no way of knowing that a tender hand had been shaving him for the past ten. He found the lump on the back of his head at last, bringing a gasp from him as he pressed the tender spot. It was nowhere near as swollen as it had been, of a size now to relieve his mind that it wasn't so serious as he had feared. But there was no stickiness of blood either, so what, then, accounted for the weakness of his limbs?

25

He suspected first that he must be wounded elsewhere as well, just had yet to feel it. So he took stock of the rest of his body, shaking each limb slightly to see if pain would accompany the movement. None did, other than a general discomfort and stiffness all over, a hollow ache in his belly, which didn't surprise him if he had gone a day without food, and a strange soreness on the soles of his feet, as if someone had taken a stick to them. And since that made no sense to him, any more than his weakness did, he didn't dwell on it, for thinking only increased the pain in his head.

He did wonder, however, how he was going to return to Wyndhurst, which was no more than a day away, possibly two on foot, when just the thought of sitting up filled him with dread. He lay there for another hour, loath to try it, but finally he did, lifting himself to his elbows first, then pushing upward until he was sitting straight. He had been right to dread it, for immediately he was assailed by dizziness, but worse was the nausea that quickly followed. He bent to the side, ready to spill his guts, but nothing came out. That didn't stop the gagging, however, which he did again and again, each time jerking his whole body and sending extra knives into his skull, until the pain was once more too much for him to bear.

It was still daylight the next time he awoke, but he couldn't say if it was the same day. The pain was still there, too, still just as bad, and memory of his attempt to rise kept him from trying again for a long while. It was the ache in his belly, and the strange weakness that would not go away, that finally prompted him to move. He needed food—Odin help him, he felt as if he were starving—and a soft bed, and his sister to fuss over him, none of which he would get remaining where he was. So he finally gritted his teeth, determined to make it to his feet this time and be on his way, but he did so in *very* slow degrees.

The dizziness came again when he was sitting upright, but he fought it with what strength he had, and managed to keep the accompanying nausea at bay. Only now he noticed a blurriness of vision, which, fortunately, was not constant, but came and went.

However, sitting there, in no hurry to make the final plunge to his feet, he had time to note his surroundings as well as the clothes he was wearing, which were not his own. The mud-colored braies fit him so tightly they didn't need to be cross-gartered, and they stopped just short of his knees. The gray tunic was wide but short, no doubt made for a man who liked his food overmuch. It was so loose he didn't note his weight loss, which would have explained the weakness, but not the why of it. The cloth shoes had holes on their soles, which might account for his sore feet if he had done some walking—which was possible, he supposed.

He was reminded of the time he had wandered the south coast of Wessex when he searched for his sister in the guise of a fisherman from Devon of Celtic origin, and a poor one at that, dressed in threadbare clothes. But before that, there had been the feverish delirium he had suffered before he found help for his wound. He had had powerful dreams then, whilst he recovered, and he felt a moment's fear that this was still that time, that all that had happened since was no more than dreams. He shook the notion off quickly, though, for he couldn't have dreamed someone like his brother-in-law before he had even met the man. Royce was too unique— and the pain in his head was too real and unrelated to that other time.

The clothes were not, however. They were just as ragged as those others had been, and it made no sense that he should be wearing them. For that matter, his party had been on the road when they were attacked, so why had he been moved to the side of it? Actually, he could see the road through the foliage, and there were no corpses lying about on it. Had they been discovered already and he himself overlooked because he had crawled into these bushes? And if he had got there on his own, how had he come by the clothes?

To concentrate on those questions still hurt his head, so he didn't dwell on them long. And the time of day became urgent now. With the sun dipped low, he knew not if it was morn or late in the day, but he needed to find aid before nightfall, and he couldn't do that unless he got to his feet.

It was not easy. The first few tries landed him back on his hands and knees until the dizziness passed, and the first few steps he finally managed were laughable, his legs giving out beneath him, they were so weak. But it became a matter of determination and stubbornness now, not just survival, and at last he was plodding his way through the woods, pushing himself from tree to tree, which he used for support, stumbling when there were none, falling another half-dozen times before he finally got somewhere.

He stayed to the woods because the road wasn't safe to travel alone, especially without weapons, and none had been left to him. His long ax was gone, his Frisian sword, the jeweled dagger he wore in his belt, and his belt for that matter, with the silver-buckle talisman engraved with Thor's hammer. If he ever found those thieves again . . .

He smelled the food before he saw the hut, and the luck that was associated with his name returned, for only the goodwife was there, and she took one look at him and set him down at her table. Loaves of freshly baked bread she put before him, along with creamy butter and whatever had been left from her morning meal, while she cooked him more, including the grouse she had set out for her husband's supper.

A round cherub of a woman, in her middle years, she pampered him as he was used to being pampered by women, though he couldn't understand a word she said. Saxon, he supposed she was speaking, but with an accent unfamiliar to him. And although he tried a number of languages on her, she could understand him no better than he did her. But he ate everything she set before him until he couldn't stuff another bite down his throat—and yet he felt as if he could eat more.

He was tempted to pass the night there. Some of his strength had returned, but nowise all of it, and the constant ache in his head hadn't lessened with the nourishment he had taken. However, what he needed now was a healer, not just rest, and he doubted the goodwife could help him in that, even if he could manage to make her understand what was wrong.

He was afraid, too, that he was getting feverish, for his thinking wouldn't stay clear, was off and on becoming muddled, so that in one moment he knew where he was, but in the next he wasn't sure. All he was sure of was that he had to get to someone who could understand him and have word sent to his sister. She would then come and fetch him home, because he was no longer certain that he could make it there on his own.

So he trudged on, moving south. The sun was definitely on its descent, giving him the right direction to take. And he now had a sack of victuals in his possession that would last him a day or two, thanks to the goodwife. It was, in fact, almost too heavy for him to carry, since he needed all his strength just to put one foot in front of the other. His unexplained weakness was still perplexing him, and his head still hurt too much for him to concentrate on that or the other puzzles plaguing him.

Hours passed, the sun set, the sky slowly darkened, and Selig's strength was nearly gone—but his luck was holding. There was just enough light left to make out the manor he had come to at last, a large hall well fortified by thick wooden walls surrounding it. He wasn't sure if they had passed it on the way to East Anglia, but a place this large had to have at least one person who could speak Celtic.

He followed the high wall around to the gate, anticipating a soft bed, anticipating women fussing over him and seeing to his comfort. But he didn't quite make it to the gate. Dizziness assailed him again, and he slumped down against the wall, unable to go on until it passed.

He thought he heard voices on the other side of the wall, but they were too low for him to distinguish any of the words, and he wasn't sure he had enough strength left to call out loudly enough to be heard. It wasn't necessary. Four riders approached the gate, likely a returning patrol, and two veered off in his direction. Selig sighed in relief, which was unfortunately a bit premature, for it was not help he found in this place, but the agonies of hell.

Chapter 7

ERIKA HAD VAGUELY noticed the returning patrol on her way to the hall. She was late for the evening meal again, a recurring habit of late, thanks to their wily thief. The culprit had struck once more that afternoon, this time stealing a piece of jewelry, hers. So her mind was preoccupied with that and her frustration at being unable to catch the thief after so many weeks of trying.

But she had no sooner reached the high table and greeted her nephew with a great hug than one of the guards appeared at her side to tell her that Wulnoth had captured a spy and requested permission to hang him. Typical of Wulnoth, to ask for judgment before she had time to even think about it—or hear all the facts.

"Bring the prisoner here anon, when the hall is less crowded," she told the guard.

He hesitated uneasily before replying. " 'Twould be a kindness, milady, did you come to him instead. It took six men to drag him to the pit. He refuses to walk."

"Why is that?"

"He would not say—actually, he speaks a tongue we know not."

She scoffed at that. "Come, now, if the man is a spy, he must be able to understand us, or he could learn naught except what he or anyone else can plainly see. Why does Wulnoth accuse him?"

"He did not say."

Erika sighed. "Very well, I will come after I have eaten. Surely this matter will wait until then?"

He blushed at her dry tone, nodded, and hurried away. But as she partook of the fare set before her, she did so absently, puzzling over the guard's words. Six men to get one into the pit? That made no sense whatsoever,

29

unless this supposed spy was someone like Turgeis; and to her knowledge, Turgeis was one of a kind.

But her curiosity had been aroused, which had her leaving the hall before her hunger had been completely appeased. Her shadow, of course, followed, looking back longingly at his own unfinished meal, for his appetite was perforce much greater than hers.

The pit was no longer the deep hole in the earth that it had once been, that prisoners had been tossed into. It was now a sturdy shed of modest size, without windows, and with chains attached to each wall. The name it was called was the only thing that was the same about it.

Erika had been there only once before, not because there had been so few prisoners, but because she preferred to deal with them in the hall, and before they were incarcerated, in case they need not be incarcerated at all. She hated the pit herself, with the brutality of it, the chains, the whips hanging on the walls, and the stink of the place, not just of foul odors, but of fear.

Fortunately, prisoners were judged quickly, so they didn't have to spend much time in the pit. And if men or women could not meet the fines of their crimes, then Erika preferred the local custom of enslaving them for a period of time, usually no more than a year, rather than Wulnoth's custom of whipping them half to death.

But spying was a different matter altogether, without a fine attached to it, since it dealt with war and defenses, and strategies gleaned that could wipe out whole armies. Hanging would be a merciful death for a spy caught in the midst of war, and since Erika had to deal with this one, she could be glad the wars were over and the charge not so serious in her mind. Ragnar, who had fought in those wars, would be of a different opinion. But he wasn't here.

Wulnoth was still there when the guard let her into the shed. One torch was burning, not enough to light the whole area, but enough to put a blanket of smoke over their heads and burn the eyes. She indicated that the door should be left open, making it easier to breathe. The pit was Wulnoth's domain, but did he never have it cleaned?

Turgeis settled inconspicuously against the wall that the door was set in, where the light barely reached. The prisoner was chained to the far wall, his arms stretched high above his head. But that was all that was seen of him, since the stocky Wulnoth stood directly in front of him, blocking him from her view. Wulnoth had, in fact, been gripping the man's hair to hold his head up when she came in, but he let go now and stepped aside. The man's head had already slumped to his chest, as if he were unconscious.

Erika stiffened, her temper rising, but all she did was lift a questioning brow at Wulnoth, whose expression mirrored not guilt, but a definite degree of frustration.

"He gives us naught but pretense, milady," Wulnoth said in the local dialect.

Erika had been teaching these people Danish, the language she wanted them eventually to use, but it was a slow process, and when she was not around, she knew they reverted to Anglo-Saxon. Wulnoth, in particular, clung to his own language even when she was present, and although she could understand it well enough, she refused to answer in kind, forcing him to switch to Danish or get no further conversation from her.

It was typical of the man's character to play this little game of dominance with her every time they had words together. She supposed he hoped to catch her up at least once, to hear her answer him in Anglo-Saxon. He would feel he had won some sort of victory over her if she did. It was a source of satisfaction to her that she never made that mistake.

"He pretends ignorance of our language," Wulnoth continued, "and he pretends to be so weak he cannot even stand, when you have only to look at him to see his strength."

Erika was looking at him, and Wulnoth was correct. The strength was there, couldn't help but be there, in a very wide and muscular chest, and in the arms that stretched so tautly above his head that every thick cord in them stood out. And unnoticed before, because Wulnoth had stood in front of him, was that his feet did not dangle just above the floor, as the position of the chains was supposed to ensure. The man's feet were planted firmly on the ground and his knees were actually bent, suggesting that he would tower over the captain if he were standing erect.

So much for the puzzle of needing six men to get him here, Erika mused. A man this large and tall would weigh a very great amount, and these local men who now paid allegiance to her brother could not compare in size. But he was indeed pretending weakness. That, or mayhap he was just so exhausted he couldn't remain awake. Less likely things were known to happen. Or mayhap Wulnoth had already tortured him vilely, though she was sure he would not dare.

His clothes were those of a serf, but that could be a disguise. His long hair hadn't been altered, though. Raven-black it was, clearly suggesting Celtic origins.

She replied to Wulnoth in Danish, once again spoiling his hope that she might forget and speak his tongue. "The man could as like be tired as weak. And a Celt may not know your language, but a spy would of necessity know mine. Did you try mine?"

His reddened face told her he had not. And a new voice told her she had guessed correctly.

"You speak Danish?"

The prisoner had lifted his head to ask that, and Erika could do no more than stare and continue staring, until she realized what she was doing and color crept hotly into her cheeks. But she excused her bemusement immediately. Her eyes were not deceiving her. The man had a face so handsome it defied description. *Beautiful* was all she could think to call him, and even that didn't do him justice.

Oh, he could learn secrets easily enough—from women. But women rarely knew the secrets of war . . . Erika was appalled at how quickly she was ready to dismiss the charges against him because she found him handsome, incredibly handsome—unbelievably handsome. She would have to guard against that, judge him only on the facts.

She finally answered him. "What else would I speak? But you speak Danish well yourself, for a Celt. Of course, you would have had to learn it in order to spy here."

It was as if he hadn't heard her, for his next question was unrelated. "What is a Dane doing in Wessex?"

"Ah, so now we know for whom you spy."

"Answer me, wench."

Erika stiffened in something close to outrage, though she curbed it well, adding, "And that you are used to command. But we will ask the questions here. I am Lady Erika, sister of Ragnar Haraldsson, who holds Gronwood and these lands hereabouts. In his absence, I am the authority you must answer to, and you may begin with your name."

"You sound as bossy as my sister."

The grin he gave her had Erika blushing again and even forgetting the demeaning name he had called her. It also caused a warmth to uncurl deep in her belly. She couldn't say why she felt his words to be a compliment, or why that should please her. And then she groaned inwardly. She was reacting to his handsomeness again, like some silly maid who had naught better to do than sigh and simper over his flattery. She could have none of that if she wished to maintain her authority.

"Your name?" she snapped again.

He sighed, and seemed to slump a bit farther down the wall. Why he would stretch his arms so torturously when he had only to stand up to relieve the pressure . . . ?

"I am Selig the Blessed, of the Haardrad clan of Norway."

Erika heard Turgeis stir behind her. He would be sympathetic to another Norwegian. She hoped he didn't credit such an obvious lie, and it annoyed her that the man couldn't have come up with a better one than that.

"Your looks betray you," she scoffed, then heard herself offer, "I have heard the Cornish Celts are giants, and 'tis more like you are one of them.

Why would you lie? We are not enemies with them. They have even helped our men against the Saxons."

"How do you come to be in Wessex?"

His evasion infuriated her, as did the confusion he portrayed so convincingly. She had given him an identity that would have benefited him, could have allowed her to let him go, yet he hadn't accepted it, had in fact ignored it. Loki take him, then, for she would be damned if she would attempt to aid him again.

"You are in East Anglia, as if you did not know, near Bedford."

" 'Tis not possible."

Now he called *her* a liar? Tight-lipped, she turned to Wulnoth. "Why is he accused of spying?" Her very expression warned him not to answer in anything but Danish, and so he did, and fluently.

"The returning patrol found him lying outside the wall, trying to escape their notice in the dark, and 'twas just opposite the wall where the changing of the guard was being discussed."

The prisoner addressed that before she could. "I was sitting, not lying, and I wanted their notice because I doubt I could have moved another step on my own."

"His sack was full of newly cooked food," Wulnoth quickly added, "that could have come from our kitchen. Mayhap he hurt himself climbing over the wall to escape, since the gate had been locked."

Erika's brow tilted. "So now you would have him as our thief, too?"

"One or the other," Wulnoth insisted. "Or mayhap even an escaped slave."

She could see Wulnoth was determined to have a victim, but the last was a moot point. If he was an escaped slave, she doubted he had always been so, and he was welcome to his freedom. Others had sought sanctuary with the Danes and found it more often than not, just as Danish slaves escaped to Wessex and West Mercia. As for him being their thief . . .

"The food came from a goodwife north of here," the prisoner said, sounding almost drunk with weariness. "It would be a simple matter to find her and question her."

Erika was inclined to believe that just because she could *not* believe this beautiful giant had been able to come into the manor without being noticed. But a spy he could definitely be, and her brother would deal harshly with him. There were too many years of war and surprise campaigns, in which thousands of lives were at risk if plans were not kept secret, for Ragnar not to have him killed outright. That they were supposedly at peace now would make no difference.

But his fate was in her hands, not Ragnar's.

She couldn't simply dismiss the charge out of hand. Sneaking and hiding both warranted suspicion, as did a Celt's fluent grasp of the Danish tongue. But they were at peace, which did make a difference. And the changing of the guard, what he was supposed to have been overhearing, was no great secret, could be figured out by anyone keeping watch on the manor. She could be generous.

"As to thievery, your story will indeed be looked into," she told him. "But what excuse have you for being found where and how you were found?"

She thought he was refusing to answer when he shook his head, but he replied, slowly, "I was seeking aid. My head . . . I was injured—clubbed, I believe—when my party was attacked by thieves."

Immediate concern assailed Erika, so that she snapped at the captain, "Check his head for injury, Wulnoth!" and stood there anxiously waiting while he did so. It would explain much—the man's weakness, his confusion—but not what he was doing in East Anglia.

"I find no abnormality," Wulnoth stated.

Anger came again, that she could be so gullible, and so quick to pardon the man. His bright gray eyes had closed, and she heard him sigh.

"Your man lies," he said to her. "The knot was there this morn. It could not have gone so quickly. Feel for yourself, wench."

Erika gritted her teeth. If he called her *wench* one more time, she would leave him to Wulnoth's tender care. As for touching him herself, it showed churlish arrogance on his part even to suggest it.

"Whether you are injured or not does not say why you are in East Anglia," she told him, then pointed out the obvious. "Who better to spy for a Saxon than a Celt, who would be less suspect if found."

"I do not even speak their tongue."

"So you say."

"But I do come from Wessex."

"The truth at last."

Selig tried to focus on her again, but his vision had gone blurry when that Wulnoth had pressed his fingers against the lump on his head. The pain was nigh unbearable now, but he had to bear it. He sensed it was important that he appease the woman—eyes the color of a midday sky, brows gently arched. He wondered why she sounded so sarcastic. Or was it just disbelief he was hearing?

He had trouble believing what he had been told as well. Someone had brought him north? For that to be so, days must have passed that he had no memory of—honey-gold hair sprinkled with cinnamon—the hollow ache in his belly was turning him fanciful, but, this wench was truly lovely, and he didn't need to see her clearly now, as she stood in front of him, to still picture her in his mind. She wasn't as tall as Kristen, mayhap a few inches shorter, and much slimmer, though no thin wisp. There were ample breasts there for his hands—spying? Odin help him, that was a grand jest.

He was a man blessed, smiled on by the Norse gods, tolerated by the Christian god, healthy, strong, and pleasing to the eye, with a wonderful family, a fine home he had helped build with his own hands, his own ship to aid in making his fortune—and all the women a man could ask for. He could not possibly be in this predicament. And with a woman accusing him, no less. She should have had him released immediately, should be fussing over him, should drown him in tender care. His head should be resting comfortably between her breasts. Nay, not hers.

He shook his head again, though the pain stabbed at him. He couldn't keep it straight that she was the lady here, was accusing him, was apparently his judge, when all he wanted to do was entice her, she was so fetching.

Her voice reached his ears through the haze. "If you are a spy, there was naught for you to learn here other than we prosper, are well settled and well defended, a good thing for your King Alfred to know."

The blurring cleared, but now he saw two of her pacing before him. "I doubt he would care," he managed to say. "He defends, he does not invade."

She ignored that to add, "My brother would simply have you killed, but he is not here and I am more practical. If you have ken or a lord who would pay Danegeld for your release, name him now, and I will send word to him."

"I can pay for my own release."

"Show me your coin, or do you think me stupid enough to have you taken to it?"

He would not involve Kristen in this absurd dilemma. It was a woman he had to deal with—lush, inviting lips, a stubborn chin, a contradiction—how hard could it be to charm her into letting him go?

He smiled at her, the smile that had won him so many hearts. "You want the truth, sweetling? I was indeed on King Alfred's business. There were five others with me, including a bishop who held contracts to set before your king, offering three Saxon damsels, fair of face and richly dowered, to be given to whichever high-ranking Danes Guthrum chose to favor. But we were attacked by Saxon thieves before we even left Wessex, the others all killed as far as I know, and myself . . . I cannot say how I came to be here. My last memory was of the attack, yet I woke this morn just north of here."

She didn't look appeased. She stood still now, those azure eyes glaring at him. "And I am to believe that? And you would also have me believe you are a Norse Viking? A Viking doing a *Saxon* king's bidding? By Odin—!"

"By Odin, I swear 'tis so," he cut in before she worked herself into a lather. "That I associate with Saxons is due to circumstance, in that my sister has wed one, no small feat, since she had been his captive slave first, and my father had already rescued her."

Erika was ready to scream with frustration. His other tales were bad enough, utter nonsense, but this last? Slaves marrying their captors? Did he think her a complete idiot?

She refrained from commenting on what he had just told her, too vexed to do so without losing her temper completely, strained as it was. "If you will not give me a name, mayhap I will send word to your King Alfred."

"Nay, you will not, for *your* king, newly made Christian that he is, would not like it when Alfred lodges his complaint, that one of his emissaries has been falsely accused and treated so."

"*Falsely* accused?" she repeated dryly. "When all you have to tell us are lies? If there is no one to ransom you, merely say so."

Selig had no more strength for this. The dizziness was coming on again, and he was not even moving to cause it this time. He feared the fever he had sensed earlier was returning also. Nor was he sure who his antagonist was from one moment to the next, just that she was so lovely—and he hadn't tried her yet.

He could barely concentrate to say, "You and I are not enemies, could never be enemies. Release me, wench. I am in need of a bed, yours if you like."

Erika's temper exploded this time, for him to be so crudely insulting, and in front of her men. "You dare! Mayhap a lashing will give you a civil tongue by the time I question you again, *if* I question you again. I am more of a mind to let you rot in here!"

He didn't notice the shadow that followed her out of his prison. All he saw was the malicious smile of the captain of the guard before he gave in to the pain and let the blessed blackness claim him once more.

Chapter 8

ERIKA HAD MARCHED no more than twenty paces when the horror of what she had just done broke through her fury and she stopped abruptly. Turgeis would have run into her if he didn't know her so well. But he had hung back, expecting her to reverse her decision.

She was not cruel. Had the insult been dealt another of her station, she would have let the decision stand—it was warranted. But for herself she would turn the other cheek, just as she would take the blame unto herself. He wished she wouldn't do that also, but she would.

He was correct. She was appalled by her actions. She had lost control.

The prisoner had made her lose it, but still, she was ultimately at fault for letting him. Yet no one had ever offended her like that Celt had done, and done so repeatedly. He deserved a lashing for that, truly he did, but she would swallow her gall and reverse her order. Nor would she hand him or anyone else over to Wulnoth for punishment. Even when a lashing was necessary, she ordered that another administer it. Wulnoth simply took too much pleasure in inflicting pain.

She turned to have Turgeis see to the matter, for she didn't trust herself to deal with the Celt again. Her emotions turned to mush in his presence, her reactions beyond the norm, and that was unacceptable for someone in her position. But a shout from the hall drew her attention there first.

"Milady, come quick! 'Tis Thurston. He took a fall and I fear broke his arm."

All else was instantly forgotten. Her nephew had been hers to care for since he was a babe of only two winters. Her motherly instincts took over, had her running toward the hall and through the doors, her heart slamming against her ribs, her complexion gone white, and whiter still when she heard the boy's screams as she neared the bedchamber that was his.

He was on the bed. Two of the servants were trying to still his thrashing about. Their healer was already at his side, trying to soothe him. But this was Thurston's first experience with serious pain. He continued to scream, holding the arm that was bent oddly, and Erika wished fervently that she could take the pain unto herself for him, but she couldn't. All she could do was ease his fear of it, and she went immediately to his side to do that.

"Hush, now, my lad," she said softly, cupping his dear face, a miniature of her brother's, in her hands. "It hurts now, but in a few days you will be showing it off to your friends and telling them how brave you were."

"But—but I am not!" Thurston wailed.

"But you will be now that you know Elfwina will fix it good as new." She turned to the healer. "Is that not so?" Her tone and expression positively dared the old woman to deny it.

"I will splint it—" Elfwina began.

"You will straighten it first," Erika snapped at the woman. " 'Tis his sword arm—will be his sword arm. He must have full use of it, and I have seen it done. Do it."

The healer shook her head fearfully. "But I have never. I have not the strength—"

"Turgeis!"

Erika didn't look to see if he was there. He was always there. And he came to the opposite side of the bed and, without being told, took hold of Thurston's wrist.

"Hold him," was all he said to her.

She did, gathering the boy up gently into her arms and whispering against his cheek, "This may hurt a bit more, dear heart, before it gets better. 'Tis all right for you to scream once more."

He did, right in her ear, before he slumped in her arms, unconscious. She carefully laid him back down, wiping the tears from his cheeks, ignoring her own, glad he had fainted for the while. She caught Turgeis's eye, was about to thank him, but remembered instead. The prisoner. And again the color drained from her face.

"Go!" she gasped out, praying she wasn't too late. "Stop Wulnoth from hurting the Celt, and mayhap *you* can get a name out of him so we can be rid of him."

Turgeis had only waited for her permission. He ran now, and the rafters shook down dust motes in his wake, the servants amazed to see a man his size moving so fast. But Turgeis was also afraid too much time had passed, and when he arrived at the pit, he wasn't pleased to be proved right.

Wulnoth didn't hear him enter, too intent on what he was doing. Turgeis caught his upraised arm before it could descend again, and used it to hurl the man across the room, where he slammed into the wall.

"She did not tell you to kill him," Turgeis growled.

There wasn't a man alive, Wulnoth was sure, who wouldn't be terrified of this Viking if that man earned his fury. "I had barely begun," he protested, though he said no more. Turgeis imagined that was so, that Wulnoth would have continued for several hours if he had had his way. Turgeis ignored him for the moment to see what damage had been done, and was relieved to see it was not serious.

The prisoner had been twisted around so he faced the wall, his tunic cut from his body and now lying at his feet. More than two dozen vivid welts were raised across the man's back and tender sides, where the lash had curled around him. A goodly number dripped blood. But at least Wulnoth had not deviated from what he had been told. Erika had said a lashing, and he had used the short, multi-stripped lash rather than his skin-mutilating whip. The cuts didn't look deep enough to scar, as long as they didn't fester, but the whole would cause considerable pain for a while.

Yet it was plain to see the man was unconscious. That, of course, wouldn't have stopped Wulnoth. But it shouldn't be so, not after so few strokes, and Turgeis could not credit that a man this size had so little tolerance for pain, when he knew what he himself was capable of withstanding.

Something was not right. He had thought so earlier, watching the prisoner wax repeatedly between seeming drunkenness that slowed his words and sharp clarity, between bemused confusion and perfect understanding wherein he had ready answers for each charge. And he had to be crazy to insult Erika as he had done, when his fate rested in her hands. That, or he had a death wish.

If Turgeis had thought those insults had been intentional, he would have challenged the man himself. But he didn't think so. They seemed more a slip of the tongue, or a natural response to a woman. Either way, the prisoner hadn't seemed surprised by the slips, hadn't asked pardon for them, and hadn't even realized he was giving offense.

Turgeis had also wondered why, with the kind of muscle that was capable of it, the man hadn't yanked the hooked spike that his chains were attached to right out of the wall. Even if he had been biding his time for the best advantage, surely he would have prevented the lashing if he were able. Only Wulnoth had remained to administer it. The man calling himself Selig the Blessed could have easily escaped. Yet he hung there against the wall, unconscious, his back crisscrossed with blistering stripes that would make movement extremely painful now.

Turgeis suddenly cast a suspicious look at Wulnoth, who hadn't moved from where he had been hurled. "Was he even awake when you began this?"

"I did not notice," Wulnoth replied belligerently, beginning to resent the Viking's interference, since nothing more had come of it.

Turgeis grunted, a sound Erika would have recognized clearly to mean "You lie." And in fact, he doubted the prisoner had felt any of the lashing yet. He also suspected Wulnoth had not bothered to rouse him because he had known full well his lady would recant her decision, and he did not want to lose a moment of wielding that lash while he had the opportunity. Wulnoth might prefer his victims to experience their torture fully, but in this case, he would settle for the pain that would be felt afterward.

Turgeis proved now what a simple matter it was to yank that spike from the wall if you had the strength for it, which he certainly did. He caught the man before he fell, surprised, even though he had expected it, that he was so heavy, despite a marked leanness across his torso that made the muscles stand out even more.

Turgeis carefully lowered him to the floor, laying him on his stomach, positioning his head on a bent arm. Holding him, he had felt the heat of fever, and now, the lump on the back of his head.

Again the Viking's eyes pinned Wulnoth, with enough accusation in them that the captain of the guard started backing toward the door. "You lied to her," Turgeis said low. "He has the injury he claimed to have."

Wulnoth still lied, though his lack of color proclaimed it loudly. "I felt naught."

"What you *will* feel—!"

Turgeis didn't finish, unaccustomed to being this angry and showing it. He had learned at a tender age to control all emotion. His size demanded it. His one lapse had nearly killed his own brother, which was never forgotten, and why his brother had plotted to be rid of him.

He turned his back on Wulnoth, adding only, "Come near him again and I will kill you."

A simple statement. He was a simple man of few words. In fact, he had said more this eventide than he had in the past month. And he had no idea what to do now. Illness and injuries were beyond his ken. But he couldn't send for the healer yet. She would be busy still with Thurston. Erika knew the ways of healing also, but she would not leave the boy now either, and besides, he wasn't going to tell her of this if he could avoid it. Which still did not tell him what to do for Selig the Blessed now.

He thought to move him to a cleaner place, but he didn't think the man would notice much of his surroundings when he woke—if he woke. So he went out to summon one of the guards to him.

"Find a servant to fetch a pallet, blankets, candles, water—and food. Lots of food. Bring them to the pit, then wait outside the young lord's chamber. The moment the healer leaves him, bring her to me." The guard knew Turgeis well, sat near him at table each day, and was amazed to hear so much out of him. And he was not done. "Lady Erika is to know naught of this, especially that I need the healer."

Turgeis returned to the pit, in time to hear the prisoner's groan and a hissed "Thor's teeth cannot be this sharp."

He moved to squat beside him. The man hadn't stirred other than to utter those words. He had spoken in Turgeis's native Norse, and it had been sweet indeed to hear. As unlikely as it seemed, he was afraid everything the man had claimed was true. Wulnoth, that miserable slime, had accused him simply because he was a stranger to them, when they should have given him the aid he had been seeking.

The man's eyes were squeezed shut, his fists clenched. Another groan escaped him. Turgeis could only guess at the headache that lump was causing.

Turgeis spoke Norwegian himself for the first time in many years. "I would suggest you do not move."

A half moan, half chuckle. "I do not think I care to try. What ails me, that my back is afire?"

He had no memory of the lashing? That was good, yet shame stirred in Turgeis that made him distinctly uncomfortable. He could have prevented it. Erika should not have ordered it, and wouldn't have if she hadn't lost her temper. He decided not to answer that question.

"Give me the name of someone who will aid you."

It seemed to Selig that he had waited forever to hear those words. It was what he had been seeking. Aid. Word sent to his sister so she would come for him. And he had found a fellow Norseman, someone he could trust.

"My sister, Kristen, wed to Royce of Wyndhurst, near Winchester. He will—"

He had moved slightly, unaware that it would send the nerves screaming across his back. That he instinctively tensed against the pain only made it worse. Air hissed out of him. Coherent thought fled.

"Be easy," Turgeis said. "The healer will attend you shortly."

Selig didn't hear, for it had come to him why he was in so much agony. "She . . . beat . . . me. She actually . . ."

He could not retain the thought. It floated away with all the others, leaving nothing to explain what plagued him—until much later, when the laughter came, and with it, she.

Honey-gold hair topped with flame, lush lips that sneered at him, promising sweetness, but never for him. Just out of reach she stayed, while the tortures were inflicted, the fire and ice, the hammers and whips, the white-hot brand that sealed his wounds before more were opened, the poison they forced down his throat, which made him vomit again and again so that he would never get his strength back.

He knew he screamed repeatedly, he must have, though he heard not the sound of it, just her laughter, louder and louder, until it echoed through his mind and became the worst agony of all, for he felt shamed by it, humiliated beyond reason. Her laughter, her amusement at his expense, her contempt for his weakness. He could not escape them, or the pain. She was always there, watching, laughing, sometimes wielding the whip herself, which was a puny effort, but the worst blow to his lacerated pride.

Such treatment from a woman, a young one, no more than a score of years, too young to be so cruel. He had wanted her comfort so badly, it was yet another ache he had to deal with, but all she wanted was to torment him. And the laughter continued. He was going to die hearing it.

Turgeis stayed with Selig the Blessed until Elfwina arrived to tend him. He left him with the healer while he went to check on Erika. But she was still with Thurston, and was not likely to leave him that night.

Turgeis had already sent a man to Wessex, so he caught a few hours' sleep while he had the chance. It was near dawn when he returned to the pit. Hearing the healer's laughter as he entered led him to believe Selig's condition must have improved, and he voiced his assumption.

"He is better?"

Elfwina didn't even try to hide her humor, still chuckling to herself. "Nay, his fever is worse. 'Tis so high he is like to die from it."

Turgeis stiffened. "Then why do you laugh?"

She was not intimidated by the scowl he was giving her. "Because it pleases me to see a Celt suffering so. 'Twas one like him killed my husband, you know."

He didn't know and didn't care. "If you have not aided him due to malice—"

"Nay, be easy, Viking. I am bound to give him what aid I can, despite my dislike of him. Healing is my life, which gives me no choice. But I am pleased to say that all I have done for him is not like to help, and there is naught else to do." She dared to laugh again, an unpleasant sound that grated. "Even the purging has not worked. His fever still rises, taking him deep into nightmares. I have been as gentle as I can with him, but he thinks he is being tortured. Through no fault of mine, he suffers dreams of the damned, and you wonder why I laugh? 'Tis out of my hands."

"Begone, then, if you can do no more," Turgeis growled. "Your humor is not meet."

"So *you* say, but I beg to differ. I never thought I would have vengeance for my man, but here I am given it, and without lifting a hand in harm. That is justice, Viking."

"He is not even a Celt, you fool."

The old witch made a scoffing sound to that. "I have eyes. He can be no other thing."

He didn't tell her again to leave. He yanked her up and shoved her out the door. Behind him, Selig groaned, still deep in the agony of delirium.

It was dawn before Erika left her nephew's chamber for her own. She hadn't slept. She had sat by Thurston's side all night, holding his little hand, aching each time he stirred and whimpered. Turgeis had straightened the bone, Elfwina had bound it tightly and left potions for the pain and swelling, but it would be many weeks before the pain became tolerable, and many months before they knew if his arm would mend properly. And she would worry each hour of that time, and pray she had done the right thing.

She had told Elfwina that she had seen bones straightened before, but in truth she had seen it done only once before, for her brother when he broke his leg. Ragnar had begged her to have Turgeis try to straighten the bone before it was splinted, something she had never heard of and neither had he, yet he was desperate, nigh full grown, with plans made for his life that he was not willing to give up because an accident had crippled him. One of their half brothers had had a like injury and would bear a limp and pain the rest of his life because of it. And he was not kindly treated, by his own father, by his other siblings, and certainly not by strangers.

Ragnar had been willing to try anything to avoid the same fate for himself. And it had worked, was such a logical thing to do really, if you took the time to think about it. Yet who was to say it would work every time, or work on an arm as well as a leg, or on a boy instead of a man? Erika knew something of herbs and she could sew skin together with a neat stitch, but she knew nothing about things that went wrong beneath the skin. So few healers did.

She was exhausted both physically and mentally from the strain of worrying. And for several hours she had sat there brooding not about Thurston, but about that prisoner in the pit, and his unreasonable attitude—and her unreasonable reaction to him.

She didn't care what his excuse might be. *She* had none.

She was accustomed to arrogant men. Danish men—Vikings, as the rest of the world called them—were as arrogant as they come. She was accustomed to handsome men. Ragnar was one himself, and he had several others who followed him who could make a girl sigh sweetly. She was *not* used to being insulted, but was that enough reason to make a fool of herself? To cause another harm?

She wasn't surprised to find Turgeis awaiting her outside Thurston's chamber. She didn't want to speak of the Celt, didn't want to know if Wulnoth had done him much damage. Her guilt wouldn't be able to bear it.

Yet she had to ask, "Will the man be all right?"

Turgeis had slept little himself. And he couldn't give her the answer she wanted without lying. But he knew very well what the truth would do to her. The man had asked her to feel his head for herself. She couldn't be expected to, but she would castigate herself because she had not. The whipping he could easily survive, but that other injury and the resulting fever? Elfwina, their only healer, hadn't offered much hope, and he could not enlist her aid further, vindictive witch that she was.

So he lied. "He will be fine."

Her tired smile justified his falsehood. If the Norwegian died, he would simply get rid of the body and tell her he had escaped, killing Wulnoth in the process. It would be a pleasure to make that a truth.

Chapter 9

KRISTEN WAS IN the stable, readying her white destrier, when the messenger was brought to her. The two men didn't come near, with the huge animal unrestrained.

Hers was a horse Royce had found for her when she had laughed so hard at the palfrey he had first given her. But he had to agree she was too big for the small lady's mount when he saw her on it, so he had brought home the white war-horse, still a young colt and not trained yet for war. Kristen had been able to train him herself, and he made a fine, if overly large, riding horse for her.

She didn't want to be bothered with the messenger right now, not recognizing him, so knowing him not to be from Royce, and thereby of no interest to her. It was Royce she was bent on following, and having made up her mind to do so, against his express wishes, she didn't want to be delayed by something that might demand her time.

Ivarr and Thorolf were both waiting for her at the gate, already mounted. They had returned just that morning, and having been told of the rumor that had reached Wyndhurst only yesterday, they were of the same mind as she. She simply could not sit at home and wait while her husband verified if her brother was dead or not.

That was the rumor that had come to them, and so damned long in the coming that the bishop and his party might have been set upon by thieves no more than a day's ride northeast of Wyndhurst, and it was possible they were all dead.

Kristen would not believe it. It was merely a rumor, and not even a sure rumor. *Might* have been attacked didn't mean they had been. And although there was usually some small truth to be ferreted out of every rumor, the worst of the rumor was rarely that truth. Selig's party could have been attacked, aye, but they also could have beat off their attackers and gone on to East Anglia.

Royce had left immediately at her insistence, to discover what truth there was to find. But in return he demanded she remain behind.

It had been unreasonable of him to insist on that, just because of that mention of thieves in the area of the "alleged" attack. He knew how she felt about her brother. Once before she had thought him dead, had seen him fall in battle, yet he had survived. She would not think so again without seeing his body. Nor could she just sit here and wait for Royce to return and tell her, especially with the women of her hall all weeping, all mourning Selig already, and infuriating her with their lack of faith.

Less than a day's ride on a swift horse, Royce had said. He would be back by this morn, he had said, if he had to ride through the night. But he wasn't back yet, the morn was long gone, the sun was high overhead, and she was waiting no longer.

But one of the men had brought this messenger to her. She tried to ignore them. She even began walking her mount out of the stable, putting the large animal between her and them. Her man was persistent.

"He asks to speak to either you or Lord Royce, milady."

She sighed, but didn't stop when she said, "You told him Royce is not here?"

"Aye."

"Well, neither am I."

" 'Tis about your brother."

It was the messenger who had spoken this time. Kristen came immediately around the horse to confront him. "From where do you come?"

"Gronwood, south of Bedford."

She slashed a hand dismissively at names she didn't recognize. "Where is that?"

"In East Anglia."

She laughed then, as the meaning of that sank in and relief washed over her. She had told herself that Selig was not dead, but still she had feared. "So he has reached King Guthrum?"

"I know naught of that. Lady Erika of Gronwood holds him prisoner—"

Kristen grabbed hold of the front of his tunic, jerking his face close to hers. She was several inches taller than he was, and likely as strong. He certainly didn't try to find out by resisting her.

"Prisoner for what reason?" she demanded.

"He was caught spying."

She let him go, confusion pushing aside her anger for the moment. "Spying? That is absurd. He went there as interpreter for a Saxon bishop. Spying?"

"I know not the why of it," the messenger admitted. " 'Twas Turgeis Ten Feet, my lady's man, who sent me, telling me only to make haste, which I have done."

"Is it ransom they want?"

"Turgeis did not say. But I am to lead you there, if 'tis your wish."

"*If?*" Kristen snorted, then asked, "How long will it take to reach this Gronwood if we ride hard?"

"I came here in two days."

"We will make it sooner than that. Be ready to ride again within the hour."

"But my horse will not—"

"Choose another," was all she said as she left the stable to shout for Ivarr and Thorolf to join her in the hall. She was already telling Eda what extra clothes to pack for her when they came up behind her.

" 'Tis just like a woman to create delays—" Ivarr began to complain.

Kristen whirled on him with a warning. "Do not missay me, Ivarr, if you have a care for your ears." That she was known to box them had him stepping back with a grin to placate her, but she had no time to waste on teasing. "Selig is found and we must ride to fetch him, but not where we thought. He is in East Anglia."

"But that is where he is supposed to be," Thorolf pointed out.

"As their guest, aye. But one of their women, a Lady Erika, has imprisoned him instead."

Ivarr exploded. "Thor's teeth, he smiled at the wrong damn wench, and now she will not let him go!"

Kristen smiled tightly. "My own first thought, but not so. He is accused of spying, and do not ask why, for the messenger did not say, merely that I should come for him."

"With a hefty sack of Danegeld, no doubt," Ivarr said, truly angry himself now.

"That was not mentioned either, though I will raid Royce's coffer just in case. But it can no longer be just we three who go. Royce will be furious enough that I will go among his hated enemy, but he would have the skin from my back if I am not prepared for any eventuality, including a fight. So go quickly and see how many of Selig's men wish to join us."

"They will all come."

She hadn't doubted that. "Then tell them we travel light to travel fast, so bring only enough food to last for a day or two, for we will stop only to rest the horses until I have my brother free. I will gather a like number of Royce's men to leave within the hour."

"The Danes' own tactics, for their many surprise attacks." Thorolf grinned approvingly.

She shook her head at them, knowing them so well. "We are not *looking* for a fight."

It was Ivarr who shrugged. "Then we will merely hope one finds us."

Chapter 10

THE GATES WERE slammed shut against them as they approached Gronwood, but that was to be expected with a party as large as theirs, unidentified yet as friend or foe. The same would have been done at Wyndhurst. The same had been done at holdings they had merely come near on the way here. But then, they had twenty-five Vikings in their party, all large, impressive men, and another twenty well-armed Saxon warriors.

It was an odd sight to see the two riding together after so many years of war. But having an equal number of Saxons along had kept people on the Wessex lands Kristen's party passed through from thinking they were being invaded again, and likewise, so many Vikings kept the Danes from taking up arms to ride out to meet them.

They halted a far distance from the walls, the men spreading out along the tree line fronting Gronwood. There was a short argument when Thorolf tried to hold Kristen back with the men, which he lost. She rode forward, with only Thorolf and Ivarr on either side of her, and the Gronwood messenger in the lead to explain their business.

They had to wait a while for someone in authority to be summoned. Kristen did not expect they would be invited inside, nor would they have accepted if they were. But neither did she expect the gates to be opened and a veritable giant to step forth, followed by a woman and four other men.

The smaller guards nervously kept their hands near their swords. Ivarr and Thorolf paid them no mind, but eyed the giant Viking warily, and the monstrous battle-ax strung across his back. Kristen made a low sound of disgust, having no patience for the male practice of taking each other's measure, particularly in this case when there were doubtless dozens more up on the walls with arrows at the ready.

The woman was likely Lady Erika, though Kristen couldn't even see her yet, with the Viking standing protectively in front of her. She nudged her horse forward, stopping midway of the half-dozen yards that still separated the two groups. She dismounted there, wanting the matter done with, wanting her brother freed immediately, annoyed that she must parlay first. That she came forward alone almost dared the other woman to do likewise. She did, putting a restraining hand on the giant's arm to keep him from following.

She is too young to have imprisoned Selig, Kristen thought, seeing Erika clearly now.

She is a Valkyrie war maiden, Erika thought as she came near enough to experience Kristen's full height of nearly six feet.

The messenger had announced who Kristen was. The rich embroidery and fine blue linen of Erika's outer gown proclaimed her own status, as did her jewel-encrusted girdle and the silk ribbons entwined through her long double braids. She was without weapon, other than her eating dagger. She appeared perfectly at ease.

Kristen's surprise at her young age was reflected in her first question. "Is yours the only authority here?"

"Whilst my brother is away, aye," Erika replied, and looking beyond at the army in wait, she added, "You come prepared for war."

It was an accusation, though mildly made, and it was certainly true. Even Kristen was prepared, having cast off her long-sleeved, narrow-skirted under chainse for convenience in riding and movement, and in deference to the warm weather of these southern lands, which she doubted she would ever grow accustomed to. That left only her sleeveless outer gown, which was shorter in length, falling above her ankles, and split up the sides. And under this she wore trousers tightly cross-gartered, which she had borrowed from one of the men close to her size, and her own fur-trimmed boots.

With her long golden hair in a single braid down her back, she could have been mistaken for a man from a distance, especially with the sword hooked to her saddle within easy reach and plain sight, and her most prized possession, her father's long-bladed dagger secured at her hip.

This was clearly no eating dagger, as Erika's was, but a splendid weapon, ivory-handled with a snarling dragon's head at its base, and runes etched onto the blade giving it Odin's blessing. Garrick had given it to her after hearing Royce recount the tale of how she had wounded his cousin Alden just after Alden's blade had cut down Selig.

Kristen and her mother had both sunk low in their chairs during the telling, waiting for Garrick's explosion, for he would never have given his permission for Kristen to learn the use of weapons, and didn't know that

Brenna had taught her in secret. His feeling had always been that it was his right to protect his only daughter. But Brenna believed it was Kristen's right first, and her father could help after as he would. And he hadn't been furious. He had handed her his own dagger instead, and she had sensed his pride in her, which made it all the more special to her.

"I come for my brother, at whatever the cost," Kristen said, the warning unmistakable. "You hold him prisoner. I want him now."

"You come quickly if you come from Wessex as he claimed to."

The skepticism in her tone had Kristen snapping in annoyance, "You were a fool not to believe him. My brother is no spy. He came here on business your king would have found to his liking."

"So he said, but there were enough circumstances to doubt him. However, you may have him back."

"Without Danegeld?" Kristen sneered.

Erika shrugged. "You have verified his claims, so I will demand no ransom." She turned to call back to one of her men, "Wulnoth, fetch—"

The giant interrupted. "I will get him."

Erika was surprised by his offer, and a bit distressed that he would leave her with this horde at the gate. But then, it was only the Celt's sister and two Norsemen who were near, the rest of their army far back, and she had four others with her—Celt? Nay, he couldn't be that either, or not just that, not if this very obvious Norsewoman was his sister. Or mayhap he was not this woman's ken. Possibly his lies had gone so deep as to bring someone else's sister here to collect him.

Suspicious now that this had occurred to her, Erika suggested, "Mayhap I should verify first if 'tis actually your brother I hold prisoner, and not some man merely claiming to be him."

"Selig is the most handsome man you will ever chance to see." At Erika's blush, Kristen added, "Aye, you have the right man."

"But he does not look a Viking," Erika pointed out. "He has the look of—"

"Our mother is a Welsh Celt," Kristen said, not really paying attention now, watching the open gate instead, where that giant the messenger had named Turgeis Ten Feet would soon appear with Selig. " 'Tis her he favors, except in his size, which we both have from our father."

"I see," Erika said, though she did not, nor did she particularly care. She hadn't expected an army to come for the prisoner, but since one had, she wanted them gone the soonest. It made her uncomfortable just to stand near the other woman, whose larger, more thickly muscled and boned frame made her feel puny, even though she was not so many inches shorter in her own height.

None of which showed in her demeanor. She was secure in her own status, with her own army nearer to hand. She hadn't as many men, what with Ragnar having taken so many with him, but these Norse Vikings and Saxons didn't know that, which made all the difference. And once they had the prisoner, they would have no reason to tarry.

Inside Gronwood, in the pit where Selig had suffered the agonies of hell these past days, Turgeis nudged him awake to tell him, "The fever has been purged from you, and your sister has come. Do you walk, or do I carry you to her?"

Selig squinted at him, recognizing one of the faces from his nightmares. "You again? And you cannot carry me." He stated what he thought was obvious, thinking no man could. "But you can give me a hand up."

He was jerked upright too quickly. Turgeis had to catch him before he fell over.

"Give me a minute," Selig requested, cursing the weakness that was still with him and much worse than before.

"I do not have a minute," Turgeis replied. "I do not like leaving my lady alone with your people."

The mention of the lady, *her*, brought back the worst of the nightmare Selig had just lived through, and with it, the helpless rage he had experienced. "They will not harm her," he said. They would not dare. That right he reserved for himself.

Kristen was pacing in her impatience. Though it did not seem so, she was exhausted, having slept little the night the rumor first came to them, and not at all last eventide, having ridden straight through the night to get here. That had not been the wisest thing to do, she supposed. Her men were not so long without rest as she, though they wouldn't be at their best either. But she couldn't have done differently, not with Selig's freedom at stake.

Erika stood near, arms crossed, composed, yet beginning to worry over what was taking Turgeis so long. Did the damned prisoner not want to leave? Were, in fact, his lies about to be revealed? Other men could be as handsome. It wasn't impossible. That one description didn't truly describe the man, or the allowance that he looked Celtic.

Neither woman was expecting the baggage wain that plodded slowly through the gate, dividing Erika's four men, who had been standing before it. Kristen was forced to move back as well when the long wagon passed near her, leaving her horse and sword on the other side of it. She didn't even notice that. She was frowning, her suspicions aroused at the sight of the driver, the giant Viking, but no sight of her brother.

Behind her, Erika was also frowning, and demanded of her man, "What means this, Turgeis?"

Kristen didn't wait for his reply. The end of the baggage wain had reached her and she leapt up onto it, pushing back the rough hide that covered the top half of the bed, her heart in her throat, fearing she was going to find her brother's lifeless body. What she saw was nearly as bad.

She barely recognized Selig, he had lost so much weight. The hand she picked up gave back no reassuring squeeze. He had the beginnings of a beard, which he never sported. His hair was matted to his skull; his skin was loose, pale; his eyes were sunken. They were open, and she read the relief in them, but also the pain—and the anger.

He spoke, but it was such a whisper, she had to bend down for him to repeat it. "Take her—for me."

"The Danish lady?"

There was the barest nod. "I owe her for this."

Kristen didn't need to hear any more. She could see for herself that they had starved him, broken him. And she hadn't felt such mindless rage since she had thought him dead, killed before her eyes. That rage didn't take into account her precarious position, so close to the walls of Gronwood, or the other alarming consequences that could result from what he asked her to do. None of that mattered next to the words *I owe her for this.*

She lifted her head, swinging around to see that the giant Viking had tied off the reins and was about to jump down to join his lady. Kristen jumped first, her movement so swift and unexpected that no one had time to react, least of all Erika, who found that long-bladed Viking dagger pressed to the tender cords of her throat, and a steely arm around her waist that she didn't dare attempt to remove.

Chapter 11

KRISTEN HELD THE Danish woman pressed tight to the front of her, but that left her back exposed to Gronwood's right wall and however many men manned it. Yet it was those just in front of her whom she was most concerned with at the moment, in particular the giant Turgeis, who topped her by more than a foot and was too close for her peace of mind.

"Get back," she told him, nodding in the direction of the gate.

He didn't move. "I cannot let you harm her, lady." His voice was calmness itself, though a deep rumble.

Kristen's was filled with fury. "I will kill her if you force my hand!"

Erika tensed as the blade pressed closer and she felt the blood trickle to the base of her neck, but it was the rage she sensed in Kristen that put the alarm in her voice. "Do as she says, Turgeis!" Erika beseeched him.

He did, but not quickly enough to suit Kristen. It terrified her that Selig was completely exposed to those arrows on the walls, and the giant was closer to him than she was, could turn the tables on her in the blink of an eye by threatening his life.

"Away from the wagon!" she shouted at him.

"What goes here, Kristen?"

It was Thorolf who asked, with Ivarr beside him. They had come up to the front of the baggage wain, but she didn't glance their way. "Selig is nigh dead from what they have done to him," she told them.

They both moved their horses to the end of the wagon to see for themselves. Thorolf sucked in his breath. Ivarr started swearing.

Turgeis cut in to that, answering Kristen's charge. "Nay, lady, he was injured before he came here."

"He says she owes him for his condition," Kristen snapped, "And 'tis my brother I will believe, not you."

Turgeis did not give up so easily. "But he has not been in his right mind, has been consumed with fever. The injury was to his head. My lady did not know."

Kristen heard Erika's gasp, if no one else did, and hissed in her ear, "He lies well to protect you, or do you also claim innocence? That my brother came to you with an injury, likely seeking help, and you imprisoned him instead?"

Put that way, Erika was damned no matter which she claimed. The circumstances and Wulnoth's disclaimer of the man's previous injury wouldn't dismiss her responsibility, or lessen her guilt in the sister's mind. And no answer was all the answer Kristen needed.

The hiss came again in Erika's ear. "Tell them not to ride after you, or your fate will be settled by me, rather than by my brother once he is recovered, and I tell you truly, lady. If he dies, you die."

Erika closed her eyes briefly. She did not doubt those words, but she couldn't believe the man would die either; she *had* to believe this would be straightened out and she would be released. But something was not right. She wanted to ask Turgeis how badly the man had been whipped, but she did not dare, for he must have been whipped severely for his condition to be so dire the sister thought he might yet die.

Was Turgeis lying for her? He must be, for she couldn't believe that head injury, real or not, had felled the man, since he had appeared no more than exhausted when she had questioned him just four nights ago. She wished Turgeis hadn't kept it from her. It would have been better to know, despite how terrible she would have felt over it. She could have at least attended the man's hurt herself, to make amends. But Turgeis had tried to spare her, and now, with a dagger at her throat, she would have to cooperate for the time being.

Loudly, so there would be no mistake, Erika told her men, "I will go with them for the nonce. Await my brother's return and tell him what has occurred." But to Kristen, softly, she felt it fair to warn, "This could lead to war."

"If that is so, you will not live to see it. But you flatter yourself, Dane. When your king hears of the outrage you have committed, he will be eager to make amends, and you will be the least of his concessions."

It was Turgeis Kristen looked at as she said this, but whether he heard her or not, she didn't trust him to abide his lady's orders. The others would, but he would not.

So Kristen told him plainly, "You follow at her peril. For every second that I see you, she will get ten lashes—if I do not kill her outright."

"Then you will not see me, lady."

Kristen glared at him for that response, for they understood each other perfectly. He was Norwegian like her, and loyalty was involved. She wouldn't see him, but he would be near, and there was nothing more she could say to make it otherwise. So be it.

Kristen looked to her horse, but quickly discarded the notion of riding with Erika. She would be too exposed while getting her into the saddle. So she dragged her to the end of the wagon and dropped the back flap, intending to haul her in without taking the dagger from her throat. Ivarr even moved his mount to partially shield her while she managed it. But Selig had heard most of what had transpired, and he was turned enough that he could see her and her hostage.

His whisper came to her, stopping her cold. "Keep her away from me, Kris, until I can defend myself."

Erika paled, hearing those words. For the next moment she was sure she would be killed right there, so much fury did she sense in the woman holding her. Held facing Gronwood's walls, Erika had yet to see Selig's true condition. But his words were clear. He feared her, and the notion appalled her as much as it did his sister.

But Kristen controlled whatever impulses she had and looked to Ivarr in front of her. "Take her up with you."

He hadn't heard Selig's words. "Nay, I would strangle her," he said with so much disgust Kristen was surprised he didn't spit on the woman.

She turned to Thorolf then, but he said, "Let her walk," before she could even ask him the same.

"And slow us?"

Kristen made a low growl of frustration. Damned stubborn Vikings. They were affronted because a woman had done this to Selig. Had it been a man, they would simply have killed him. Had it been a man, *she* would simply have killed him, and to hell with fighting their way out of there. But she wouldn't argue with them in front of the woman.

"Take my horse, then," she said angrily, "And, Ivarr, lead this wagon until we reach the others." She then pulled Erika behind her into the wagon, and without looking back at her brother yet, said sharply, "Not another word, Selig. She will not harm you whilst I am here."

Kristen didn't stop until they reached the front of the wagon bed, no easy feat, since Selig had been placed on a pallet that took up more than half the floor space. Cramped, she pulled the hide cover over them, so it could not be readily seen that her dagger was no longer at Erika's throat. But before she moved to sit, lifting Selig's head carefully onto her lap, she yanked the neck of Erika's gown back to stab her dagger through the cloth, pinning

Erika to the bed of the wagon and leaving her lying prone next to him, the dagger still within her own reach.

It was not the most comfortable position for Erika. The neck of her gown choked her now, but to relieve the tightness of it had her shoulder touching the sharp edge of the dagger. Still, it was better than having the blade at her throat, she reasoned—until she chanced to turn her head and caught Selig's eyes on her.

She shivered at the loathing she saw there in those bright gray eyes. With that reaction came the urge to grasp the dagger holding her in place, pull it out, and run. But she doubted she could work it loose quickly enough, her prone position giving her no leverage, and she didn't care to find out yet what would happen if she tried and failed. She was away from immediate help now. These people had no reason to keep her alive, least of all the fierce Norsewoman, whose hand was tender only on her brother's cheek.

Through the end of the wagon, still lowered, Kristen could see the gate and the men standing there as the party rolled away from it. So she was witness to one of those men getting his neck broken with the Viking's assistance.

Seeing it happen, and so easily, caused a shiver of her own, though Kristen quickly shook it off. She had already known a man as large as Turgeis Ten Feet would have incredible strength. A demonstration of it hadn't been necessary. And she had no reason to fear him. He could be held at bay as long as they held his lady. She wasn't foolish enough to dismiss him as a worry, but neither would she let the promise of his dogging them plague her.

What was left was a mild curiosity that Kristen saw no reason not to appease. "Why would the giant kill one of your own men?"

Erika closed her eyes, groaning inwardly at the question. It had to be Wulnoth the woman referred to. Turgeis did not kill for no reason.

"If he has killed him, 'tis for what he thinks I will suffer before he has me back. He would blame that one for what has occurred this day."

"And who do you blame?" she was asked with scathing contempt.

"Myself," Erika admitted regrettably.

"We are agreed," Kristen said.

"Very much agreed."

That came in a whisper from the man beside her, and although Erika refused to look at him again, she could imagine the loathing was even brighter in his eyes. Turgeis was correct if he thought she was going to suffer. Selig the Blessed was going to demand it.

Chapter 12

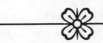

THE WAGON HALTED when it reached the rest of the men, but only long enough for Kristen to explain what had happened, and to assign a driver for it. They wouldn't be leaving East Anglia as soon as anticipated now, not with the baggage wain slowing their progress. But at least a sturdy horse had been hitched to the conveyance, rather than a lumbering ox, which would have slowed them even more.

Kristen stayed with Selig, so she was forced to keep the Dane with her also, unwilling to let the woman out of her sight while still so close to Gronwood. Lady Erika was all she had to bargain with if her threats were ignored and an army was gathered to pursue them. Until they were safely in Wessex, she wanted her close at hand.

Selig might not like the Dane's close proximity, but he had said no more about it, had in fact fallen asleep with the steady sway of the wagon. Kristen would have preferred he wait until she had learned what exactly was wrong with him, but she didn't wake him to find out. Sleep was as beneficial as anything else she knew for healing, which, unfortunately, was not much.

She had sent two men ahead to a village they had passed near dawn, to arrange for food in plenty and to inquire of a healer. The rest of them should reach there by nightfall, and would make camp nearby.

It was as far ahead as Kristen could plan. As it was, she was afraid she was not thinking clearly, she was so groggy herself. Already she was beginning to dread her husband's reaction, not just of her coming for Selig, but in taking the Dane prisoner.

Royce hated all Danes, but he did not make war on women. Neither did Selig, for that matter. So what in God's mercy had the woman done to him to make him want revenge on her?

58

She was too tired to reason it out, and Selig would tell her soon enough. And the sway of the wagon was working on her, too. She could barely keep her eyes open any longer. But she was still clearheaded enough to realize she needed to secure her prisoner better before she succumbed to exhaustion.

Unlike the other two occupants of the wagon, Erika was wide awake with her anxieties and self-recriminations. So she could not miss the sudden removal of the dagger at her shoulder, nor did she mistake the sound of cloth being ripped behind her. And the curt demand for her to sit up and pass her hands back for binding was also expected.

She still had to protest. "This is not necessary, Lady Kristen. You have an army surrounding me."

"Be quiet," she was told in a low hiss. "Until I can turn you over to Selig to deal with as he will, you are my responsibility. So you can forget about escaping, Erika. You will find no opportunity for it."

To have her title of respect and station dispensed with was telling. But then, Erika had already supposed that she wouldn't be given the courtesies due her. She had not been found merely by accident and taken for ransom. She had been taken to exact revenge, and now she knew for a certainty who would do the exacting.

"Swing about to give me your feet, and be careful not to disturb my brother."

Erika did so, but what she was careful of was not to even look at the brother. She didn't sense his eyes on her any longer, but she didn't want to chance seeing him gloat, now that their positions were reversed.

Her shoes were yanked off and cast aside, her ankles fastened tight together. Kristen had cut off the hem of her own gown to use for the binding. At least it was not coarse rope or chain—yet.

Erika remained sitting, since she had not been told she could not, and scooted back until she could lean against the side of the wagon. She continued to watch the Norsewoman, who ignored her now as she settled back into the corner, returning her brother's head to her lap.

She was beautiful, Erika realized, very beautiful. But that was to be expected, she supposed, with a brother beyond handsome. Kristen's hands just now were wrapped tenderly around his face. Obviously, she loved her brother dearly. Erika loved hers as well, and had to wonder how she would have reacted in the same circumstances. She hoped never to find out.

Despite her resolve not to, her eyes eventually focused on Selig's face. When she had been snared by his eyes earlier, she had seen nothing but those eyes and the hate blazing in them. Now she noted the ravages to his face that hadn't been there when she had seen him last. Had the fever Turgeis mentioned done that?

Her eyes drifted lower, caught first by his lack of tunic, unexpected, then by the sunken cavity between his ribs and hipbones, both protruding. If there had been a fever, a consuming one as Turgeis claimed, Elfwina would have purged it—he would not have eaten in the three days he had been imprisoned, and in fact, he did look as if he had been starved. Erika did not agree with that remedy. Logic told her a body needed nourishment despite what evil humors had taken root inside it—but she hadn't been there to use logic.

His arm moved suddenly, lifting away from his side to drop over his sister's legs. She looked quickly back to his face, but he had not awakened. Neither had his sister, who was now also sleeping. But his brow was creased briefly with pain from his unconscious movement. How much pain was he in from that head injury? It could not be a recent wound, if he had received it in Wessex as he said. At least she couldn't be blamed for that, too.

But as she continued her visual examination, she found the thin cuts at the base of his hands, scabbed over now, and the chafed skin just under the cuts. She winced, knowing the iron shackles that had held him to the wall in the pit had made those marks, with the pressure of his full weight pulling on them. And she had let him hang there, thinking him only exhausted, while he had been in pain . . .

She saw it then, what his arm had covered before. Lines of dark blue streaked up his sides—bruises, she realized, and knew exactly the cause of them. Heat stole over her. Her hands even began to sweat. She had so been hoping that Turgeis had been in time to stop Wulnoth, that her only mistake had been holding the man prisoner and not seeing he got better care for his head injury. But no, *she* was the cause of those bruises. She had called for a lashing in anger, and it had been given—to an injured man, a man already in pain, a man beset with fever and Odin knew what else.

He had said to her, "You and I are not enemies, could never be enemies."

But Erika knew that would not be true now. He had come to Gronwood for help and had been chained in the pit instead. He had spoken only the truth, but had not been believed. And she had treated his injury with a beating.

Her guilt was so great it nigh choked her. If she were not so afraid, she could almost welcome his revenge in atonement. But she was afraid, and so could only make amends in some other way if she was given a chance to. Yet she could think of no way to atone for her cruel actions.

The rest of the day passed without Erika's awareness, so deep did she sink into her misery and guilt. But the abrupt halt of the wagon brought her out of it, and also woke Kristen as well.

"God's mercy." The sound Kristen made was a definite moan as she looked down at her brother. "I had hoped 'twas only a dream."

Erika could have wished the same, but didn't say so, said instead, "He needs food. If he did have a fever whilst at Gronwood, it would have been purged by our healer, so 'tis likely he has not eaten for several days."

Kristen looked toward her, her tawny brows sharply narrowed. "Do not tell me what my brother needs. And if you knew him, you could see plainly 'tis more like he has gone with little or no food for the last fortnight. He is nigh wasted away to naught."

Worse and worse. He had already been starved when he came to Gronwood, and Erika hadn't been there to see that Elfwina not purge him.

"I doubt me you will believe this, but I am sorry," was all Erika could think to say at the moment.

"I am sure you are—now. But where was your sympathy when he needed it?"

Drowned by her temper. Buried by her confusion over her reaction to him. Yet she *had* felt it, briefly, when he had first mentioned his injury, that and more concern than was warranted for a man she did not know. An angel-faced man. Then Wulnoth had made his disclaimer, making her believe Selig had lied—again.

But she said none of that, and lost her chance to speak as the hide cover was suddenly thrown back and several men appeared at the end of the wagon. One she recognized from earlier, the sandy-haired, blue-eyed man who had wanted her walking all the way to Wessex.

"Ivarr is bringing food, Kris," Thorolf told her, though his eyes were on Selig, on his sunken belly in particular. "Thor's teeth, it will take buckets to fill up that hole."

"More than that, I fear," Kristen answered.

Their voices had stirred Selig, and his waking groan had them each wincing. But it also disturbed Kristen that Erika had heard it, too. Selig wouldn't like it that the woman he despised should see him like this, and knowing that, Kristen liked it even less.

So she said, a bit more irritably than intended, "Take her out of here, Thorolf. See to her needs or whatever, but keep her away from here. And you may untie her, but do not let her out of your sight for a second if you do. I will fetch her back after I have tended Selig."

Erika gasped as Thorolf's long arm simply reached in and yanked her out of the wagon. He did indeed untie her, so he would not have to carry her, telling her plainly, "I would as soon not touch you, so do not give me a reason to."

But he would not leave her side either, not for a second, so she declined his surly offer to escort her into the bushes, even though she had need to go there. For the moment, her mortification was worse than her need, because she knew he would give her no privacy. But she had no idea what she would do when her need became the greater.

And that was her only need he was willing to see to. She realized that when he shoved her down next to him in front of a fire that had been lit for their camp and began to partake of the food that had been obtained from the village nearby, without offering her a single morsel.

She was not surprised. The hostility radiating from him was so powerful she could feel it even when she was not looking at him. And the same came from every other man she happened to notice, Saxon and Viking alike.

But she had seen Thorolf's expression when he had stared at Selig's sunken belly. The blame for his deterioration was being given to her personally, rather than to the fever he had had, so she was going to be dealt with in kind. To be denied food was actually the least of her fears, for she had the sinking suspicion that Lady Kristen had not even noticed the condition of her brother's back yet, and there was a sick feeling in the pit of her stomach as she imagined what was going to happen when she did.

Chapter 13

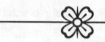

KRISTEN WAS SHOVELING the thick stew down Selig's throat with such speed, she was not giving him a chance to chew it, much less swallow it. When he had trouble breathing as well, he finally had to turn his head aside to say around a mouthful, "Blast it, Kris, I swear to you, how fast you feed me will have no effect on how quickly I recover."

He was surprised he would say that, as ravenous as he was, with his urge to wolf the food down the same as hers, to get it into him the soonest. Yet *he* would rather be doing it, had tried doing it, but his arm had grown tired and trembling after only a few attempts.

The weakness was making him testy, of course. It absolutely infuriated him that he could not do for himself. And he could only hope that it *was* from lack of nourishment, rather than from some strange malady related to his head injury that might not go away, just as the pain refused to go away. The thought that he might never be the same again was not so terrifying as it was simply unacceptable. And that he was even weaker than before was not encouraging.

He could not believe how much that earlier short trip from his prison to the wagon, even with the giant Turgeis's support, had drained what little strength he had gained from his one night of undisturbed sleep. But the sleep he had just wakened from had restored him somewhat, at least enough so that when he spoke, he did not sound like he was dying.

Kristen was waiting patiently for his mouth to open again, no apology forthcoming for her overeagerness, none expected. But he asked, before he accepted the next bite, "Where is Royce?"

"Still in Wessex, I would imagine."

Selig stopped chewing in his surprise. He had assumed his brother-in-law was merely busy somewhere in the camp, not that he was not in the camp at all.

"He actually let you come for me without him?"

She didn't meet his eyes. "He was not there for me to tell him my intentions."

Selig digested that for a moment, then said simply, "He will be angry."

She tried to appear unconcerned, shrugging. "I suppose he will."

"*Very* angry."

She glared at him now. "I *know*, brother, so belabor the point no further. 'Tis my worry, not yours. Now tell me all that ails you so I can apprise the healer—"

"Nay—if you love me, no more healers," he cut in and actually shuddered. "The one just done with me called herself such, but all she did was force poison on me that let no food reach my belly."

"Then you *were* given food?"

"Aye, but none that would stay down me long enough to do any good, thanks to that old witch."

Kristen nodded thoughtfully. "The Dane said you were purged to rid you of the fever, and it must have worked, for you are cool to the touch now."

"My fever was not so great—" He paused, those long hours of confusion and pain such a muddle in his mind. The delirium, the poison, the laughter. "At least not the last I recall of it," he amended.

"You had it the whole three days you were at Gronwood?" she asked.

"*Three?*"

He choked on the spoonful she had managed to get by him while asking her questions. His movements were so slow that, if he did not know her so well to anticipate her reactions, he would not have had the time to put up a hand to stop her when she thoughtlessly leaned forward to pound on him. Now he simply scowled at her for the pain she would have inflicted by trying to help.

Defensively, Kristen scowled right back and said huffily, "I have never pretended a great skill in tending the ill or wounded, Brother."

"Or even a small skill," he agreed. "You are more apt at inflicting wounds than fixing them."

She ignored that, continuing. "But you are stuck with me for the nonce, so you will just have to bear with me."

He was grinning at her after that, and willing to accept another mouthful of food, saying around it, "Somehow I will manage—to survive your tender—nay, you cannot box my ears just now."

She sat back, smiling. "A shame. They need it."

He was no longer grinning, but was eyeing her with chagrin. "I suppose the very day I am recovered—?"

"Aye."

"Verily do I wish your memory were not so long." He sighed. "Actually, I could wish mine were not so lacking now. Explain to me that 'three' days."

" 'Tis how long you were imprisoned."

"I do not remember it being so long."

"What do you remember?"

His expression altered drastically, became fraught with deep anger. "The pain . . . and her laughter. Always her laughter. I never knew a woman could find pleasure in another's suffering."

Kristen gritted her teeth upon hearing that. "I was not going to tax you, but mayhap you had better tell me all of it."

That brought a sigh from him, draining some of the anger. "It will not tax me, Kris, there is so little to tell. We were attacked whilst still in Wessex; thieves, I suppose. They fell from the trees, and so many of them."

"Aye, the rumor finally reached us that you might all be dead. 'Twas where Royce went, to investigate. And you took a blow to your head?"

"From behind. Clubbed, likely, since there was no blood that I could find. It felled me instantly. When I woke, I was alone, in clothes not mine, and with such pain in my head I could barely move. Also, I was puking for no reason, and seeing two of single things, and as weak as a babe. Thor! I have never felt so wretched."

She cringed, feeling wretched for him. "The blow had to have been severe," she speculated. "I have felt the small lump you still bear. Likely 'twas thrice that size or more, if received so long ago."

"Likely," he agreed. "But when I woke, I thought myself still in Wessex, that only a day or so had passed, since I had no beard to account for longer. Yet I was in East Anglia, as I learned that very day to my regret, and have no memory of how I came to be there."

"Nigh a fortnight with no memory?"

"Aye."

"And no beard?"

"Aye."

She was thoughtful for only a moment. " 'Tis obvious someone took you with them to East Anglia and cared for you the while, though you slept through the whole of it. I wonder why they then abandoned you."

"I merely wonder who they were and why they bothered with me at all. I cannot imagine Saxon thieves hiding out in East Anglia."

"Nay, so mayhap they were East Anglian thieves come down to Wessex."

"And decided I was worth ransoming?"

She nodded. "But they gave up waiting for you to wake up and tell them who to send their demands to."

"Possibly," he allowed.

Kristen sighed. "Most like we will never know. But if you never woke during that time, 'tis doubtful they got much food into you, if they even bothered to try. That at least explains the lack of flesh on your bones. And I take it your head still pains you?"

"Aye, but not as constant, and not as severe. If I am completely still, it even goes away for a short time. But now I have that other ache to contend with."

"Where?"

"My back."

She had not seen his back. He was without a tunic, but he had been placed on his back in the wagon and hadn't stirred from that position. Even now, to feed him, she had merely called for her sack of extra clothes to place under his head so he was lifted enough to swallow more easily.

"Another wound?"

Again his expression altered to a mask of pure rage. "Ask that Danish bitch."

Kristen didn't wait that long. She pushed his shoulder until he slowly turned for her onto his stomach. She heard his hiss of pain and saw why. What scabs had formed had stuck to the pallet and just been ripped off. And that solid mass of blue and blister-puffed skin, now oozing blood . . .

It was too much for Kristen to grasp. Falsely accused of spying and then tortured for a confession? And a woman had ordered it? A *woman*?

Selig couldn't see the wound, could only feel it, so she made light of it, though she was seething. " 'Tis not as bad as it looks."

"It feels worse."

"Most like because you are so weak." She tried to make him forget it, though she could not. "Have you had any sustenance at all in all this time?"

"The day I awoke, before I reached Gronwood."

Briskly now, she said, "Well, you are going to finish this stew—and more, I hope. I want you eating constantly, as often as you can, as much as you can." She set the bowl down on the pallet, next to his face. "You can manage the rest of this yourself, I think, with not so far to reach it. I am going to go and fetch that healer now, and not a word against it. She will have salves to apply, and something to ease your pain, and no purges, I swear it."

She gave him no opportunity to argue, not that it would have done him any good. She left the wagon, careful not to jar it and so jar him. But it was not the healer she was seeking—not yet. She looked for and found the Dane, sitting with Thorolf not so many feet away.

Erika had been watching the wagon for Kristen's appearance. She jumped to her feet, causing Thorolf to scramble hastily to his, thinking she was bolting, until he, too, saw Kristen approaching.

Erika didn't run, stood her ground, though she was trembling. *She has seen his back, seen what I did in anger, no excuse, no excuse, no matter the provocation . . .*

"I asked you before," Kristen said, reaching them, her voice calm, surprising Erika with that calmness. "I will have an answer this time. If Selig came to Gronwood injured, as Turgeis Ten Feet claimed, then he was seeking help. How did you aid him?"

"I had him lashed."

It was the worst time for Erika's guilt to make such a vocal appearance, but then, she had been wallowing in it all day. Kristen heard not the guilt, though, merely the words confirming the conclusions she had reached, and she released her rage with a backhanded fist.

It was a powerful blow, coming from a woman her size, a woman no longer holding her anger in check. It knocked Erika to the ground, where she sprawled at Thorolf's feet, her golden hair puddled in the dirt. He didn't try to stop her fall. He could have, but he merely moved aside.

Erika's cheek felt afire. It had been smashed against the edges of her teeth, slicing the inside open. Blood pooled in the bottom of her mouth, so much that some trickled out of the corners, and she was forced to spit it out or choke on it.

Kristen stood over her, both fists clenched, arms rigid, shouting at her to get up, that she was not done with her. She was going to beat her senseless, Erika was sure of it, and there wasn't a single man there who would stop her—Turgeis. Ah, sweet Freya, nay. If he was near, if he was somehow watching, he would abandon all caution and come forward to help her. Nothing would stop him from trying, and he would die in the attempt. And Kristen was still shouting at her to get up.

"Lady, please, not where he can see."

If pleas had been anticipated, that was not one of them. Kristen scoffed. "Do you delude yourself into thinking someone here cares what happens to you?"

"Turgeis does." The blue eyes were deep with meaning.

The mere mention of the name caused a half-dozen swords to be drawn by those near enough to have heard her. But Kristen was not daunted by the prospect of that hulking giant's possible appearance. She was too angry.

"Then let him come. I doubt me you and I will even notice. Now get up—"

She was cut off, and by a voice that was least expected. "Nay, Kris. Feed her. Keep her well. What she suffers is to come from me."

Kristen made a furious sound of frustration and marched back to the wagon. Selig had actually pulled himself to a sitting position and now clung to the side of the wagon to remain that way.

"Let me—" she began.

"Nay. She owes me, not you."

His voice was not as strong now, but no less stubborn. It had cost him to make the effort to stop her, and he would argue further if she insisted. She could see that plainly, which was why she conceded, though with ill grace.

"Very well, but I like it not. And you lie back. Rest is as important for you as food just now. Do not let me see you ignoring either one again."

Selig took one more look at his slender, slim-hipped tormentor, huddled in the dirt, and smiled, or tried to. Even that was too much of an effort for him, and he dropped back onto the pallet with a groan.

Kristen gnashed her teeth together. Her rage was on his behalf, yet he was the one denying her an outlet for it, and it was so strong, she really did need to do something. Yet she could see his point. Had she been abused thusly, she wouldn't want her family taking revenge for it if she were capable of taking her own. And Selig would be capable of it once he was recovered— he had *better* recover.

She glanced once more toward the Dane, staring hard at her for a long moment before she approached again. Erika was still on the ground, though sitting up now, and she didn't rise. Kristen's expression was no less wrathful than it had been. Erika's was wary.

But it was to Thorolf whom Kristen looked when she reached them, to ask, "Has she eaten?"

"She does not deserve it," was his curt opinion.

Much as she agreed with him, she grudgingly admitted, "Though it seemed otherwise, Selig was not denied food by her or her people. And you heard him," she added with disgust. "She is to be kept hale and hearty for the time he can deal with her himself."

"*You* mean to restrain yourself?"

It was said to calm her ire somewhat, and to a degree it did just that. His sister Tyra had been her closest friend during her growing years, and Thorolf had taken his sister's place for Kristen in her new home. In fact, he could tease her as her brothers did and get away with it, whereas others could not.

That he teased her now made her look at herself critically and brought a sigh. "I will content myself with imagining what Selig will eventually do to her."

"Boiling in oil?"

"At the very least."

Neither noticed that Erika had gone chalk-white, unaware that they were both teasing. Panic rose, and bile that she had to swallow down. And if they had not gone on to talk of camp and sentries and plans for the morrow, she would never have been able to compose herself before those light aqua eyes of the Norsewoman fell on her again.

"Feed her, Thorolf," Kristen ordered, her tone sharp once more. "Then bring her to me to secure for the night. I will need rope. If we have none, send someone to the village for it."

She turned to leave. Erika stopped her. She had just been treated like an object, talked about, not spoken to. It was enough to make her lose her temper entirely, though she merely noted it, was too dejected and frightened still to have room for anger. Which was a good thing, for it would be stupid indeed to further antagonize these people.

"You may as well secure me now, for I cannot eat."

"You will—"

"I cannot chew, Lady Kristen."

It was no lie. The inside of Erika's cheek had gone numb and would as like be eaten as any food. Nor did she add that the very thought of food made her nauseous.

She said instead, "Mayhap in the morn."

Kristen said nothing for a moment, debating whether to force the issue, but finally conceded with a nod and a final word to Thorolf. "Fetch the rope now." Then she yanked Erika to her feet and dragged her back to the wagon.

Erika was not returned to the wagon bed as she had half expected. She was shoved back to sitting on the ground, with one of the wagon wheels at her back. Kristen stood beside her, tapping her foot impatiently while she waited for the rope. Still, no word had been said to Erika directly, and none seemed forthcoming.

As the minutes passed, Erika began to squirm. She knew she was going to be bound and ignored for the rest of the night, and the thought recalled to her that she had not . . .

Her face was already heating, but she had to ask, "Could you?—I need to—that is—"

A frown came with the blunt interruption. "Was Thorolf so lax that he did not take you to the bushes?"

Erika's face was now flaming, but she got out, "Nay, but I could not— with him. You told him not to let me out of his sight."

"Nor would he have, but a prisoner cannot afford to be missish."

"Please. I am asking you, woman to woman. If you would but put yourself in my place—"

"I *have* been in your place, Dane. I was a prisoner, with most of these Vikings you see here in chains alongside me, and most of these very Saxons guarding us. Think you I had any privacy?"

So that had been true also, what Selig had said about his sister marrying her captor. And those previous prisoners and previous guards now rode together as comrades-in-arms? Erika still could not fathom how that could come about; she wanted to ask, but did not dare.

She said only, "Please!"

But it was said with enough desperation that Kristen growled, "Bah," and jerked her to her feet. "If I did not feel the need myself . . ."

Erika felt only relief, not even caring how Kristen's fingers, nigh as strong as a man's, bit into her arm as she was pulled behind her long stride. Yet Kristen halted just short of the concealing shrubbery, her eyes scanning the shadows beyond, and Erika groaned inwardly, thinking the woman had changed her mind.

So it came as a surprise to merely hear, "The giant, is he your husband?"

Erika didn't think to lie. "He is my shadow, has been since the day I saved his life when I was yet a child. I am as a daughter to him."

"And you believe he is out there?"

Now she did think to lie, but couldn't see much point in it after what she had said earlier. "I would be surprised if he is not," she admitted. " 'Tis rarely that I am ever beyond his hearing or sight."

"Hearing and sight will do him no good," Kristen replied. "What you are is beyond his reach, even should he follow all the way to Wessex."

So saying, she called to one of the men who was near and told him to gather five others and spread out beyond the area she intended to enter. She was taking no chances with her prisoner, and her prisoner's cheeks were flaming again.

Kristen, seeing that, mumbled contemptuously, "Too missish by half."

Erika heard her and stiffened in reflex. "I cannot help it."

"Then you would be wise to get over it," Kristen shot back. "When my brother is done with you, embarrassment will be the least of your woes."

It sounded like a promise to Erika's ears. The Norsewoman might content herself, imagining what her brother was going to do, but Erika was going to drive herself mad with those same imaginings. She had to escape. She *had* to. But how, when one or more pairs of eyes would always be on her?

Chapter 14

ERIKA COULDN'T SAY what had roused her from her sleep, but when she opened her eyes the next morn, it was to see a pair of legs standing near her right shoulder. They were long legs, thickly male in mesh chausses and calf-length boots of finely worked leather. Trying to see what else went with them was a mistake, however, that brought a wince and a sharp gasp of pain.

She had forgotten her position, tied tight to the large wagon wheel at her back, with thick rope wrapped round and round her waist, chest, and throat to make sure she would still be sitting there come morn, and so she was. She remembered trying to keep her head straight, but it must have rolled to the side once she slept, and now her neck muscles were screaming in complaint.

For that matter, she detected no feeling in her hands and lower arms, which were secured at her back. But that was mayhap a blessing, for she also recalled trying to work her hands loose of the thinner rope that bound them. It had been a much coarser rope, to discourage just such an attempt, yet she had still tried to pull loose of it, and had scraped her skin raw in the attempt. Her feet were also numb, the thin hose on one ankle torn by the rope where she had tried the same loosening effort on her feet, without success.

The man was forgotten for the moment while she took stock of all her discomforts. She kept her tongue away from the raw meat on the inside of her cheek, fearing what pain that would bring with the numbness worn off there. And she twisted her head around slowly, working out the kinks until she could turn it without wincing. That, at least, she could manage, and finally tilted her head back far enough to look up at the silent man next to her.

He hadn't moved once from his wide-legged stance. She saw the sword still in its scabbard, the short, single-edged knife called the *scramasax* that Saxons used to finish off a felled opponent. It was tucked into a wide, metal-studded belt with a single garnet at the center of its buckle. A green tunic ended at his wrists, but was covered by a short-sleeved mail shirt with thicker chain links than the chausses. The shoulders were very wide for the narrowness shown by the tightly cinched belt at his waist.

Powerful arms were crossed over his chest. Dark brown hair fell a ways over his shoulders. Deepest green eyes were looking down at her, and not without expression. She was not sure what emotion rode his features, but whatever it was, it was close to violence.

That alone did not bring her second gasp when her gaze rose far enough to see it. Some of her surprise came from how very handsome he was—and so tall. She would have taken him for a Saxon if not for his height, which surely topped her own brother's by a half foot. And she didn't recognize him, for she had made a point of looking over all the men in the camp yesterday, in the hopes of finding at least one with a kindly face. She had had no luck there, but she would have remembered this man had she seen him.

Though he looked down on her, he was not facing her, he was facing the wagon. And although she knew he could not see inside it with the hide cover pulled over it, he could see partially under it, to where the Norsewoman slept on, blissfully unaware of him.

Erika remembered how annoyed she had been that the other woman was going to sleep so near to her, just on the other side of the wheel, so she would hear Erika's slightest stirring. Even with men set to sentry duty and told to keep their eyes on Erika the while they also watched for the giant, Kristen had still remained close with her dagger in hand.

Just now the warrior sister was twisted about, with her unbound hair spread out on the ground beyond the edge of the wagon, making her impossible to miss. And, in fact, one of the man's boots was planted firmly on that tawny length of hair, by accident or . . . Not by accident. He was patiently waiting for the Norsewoman to move, thereby pulling her own hair, which would be certain to wake her.

Erika's eyes widened when she saw that, and brought her third gasp with the conclusion she drew. Sweet Freya, the man was an enemy of these people, could be no other thing with the rage so clearly writ across his handsome face, not just for her, not even for her, but definitely for the sister. And if he could have come into the camp without being stopped, why hadn't Turgeis tried it?

The camp? She looked out to see if all were dead, but none were. In fact, the men were all stirring, some eating, some seeing to the horses, a great many looking toward the wagon. The man was no enemy, then, was one of them, but whence came the anger? And why didn't it disturb the others to see it directed at their lady?

"Ouch!"

Kristen had finally moved enough that she pulled her hair. Her head turned to see what she was caught on, saw the foot, and followed it up to see who would dare. Aqua eyes flared wide, but in the next instant, her dagger flashed out to swipe at the leg within reach.

The man jumped back, almost as if he were expecting just such an attack. With her hair free now, Kristen immediately rolled out from beneath the wagon, but on the other side of it, where Erika could no longer see her. The man still could, both of them tall enough to see easily over the bed, and both were now glaring at each other.

"I knew I would rue the day your father gave you that," he said.

He spoke of the dagger, Erika realized, though she had not understood every word. Anglo-Saxon was his tongue, and although she had learned it by necessity when she first came to this land, she had not learned it in depth, preferring to teach Ragnar's people Danish instead.

But the Norsewoman spoke it fluently and with the same unfamiliar accent the man used. "Give me a moment and I will fetch the sword *you* gave me, Saxon."

His brows came together, his frown had grown so dark. "I am going to beat you till you cannot walk, Viking. I can do no other thing," he shouted.

"Who is going to help you manage that?" Kristen shouted right back.

Erika was amazed at that provoking response on top of the other one. And it hit the mark. The Saxon bellowed and started to climb over the wagon to get to her. He was certainly big enough to do it.

But Kristen cried out, "Nay, you will shake Selig. I will come around."

Come around and put herself within his reach again? Erika wouldn't have dared, would be running in the opposite direction right quickly. And Kristen did appear on Erika's left, not even noticing her except to step over her outstretched legs to get to the man. Reaching him, she actually punched him squarely in the chest. He didn't budge, but didn't raise a hand to strike her back either. His expression hadn't changed, though, was still furious. So was hers.

"You could at least keep your voice down, you great lout," Kristen hissed at him. "They are laughing their blasted heads off."

Quite a few of the men were doing just that, Erika noted. It went a ways toward easing her own anxiety, with the two furious people right next to her.

"They will laugh even more when I put you across my knee," was his gritted reply.

Kristen took a step back at that. Another and she would have tripped over Erika's legs, but she only needed the one to separate her from the man. Possibility of a spanking had intimidated her, whereas a beating had not. Erika found that fascinating.

With considerably less heat, Kristen told him, "I can explain, Royce."

Obviously, he was not interested. "You can explain after I beat you."

"Oh, unfair!"

"You ride off with my men—!"

"And Selig's," she cut in to point out. "Combined, naught but a great army could cause us harm, and all the great armies are disbanded."

That didn't pacify him either. "You willfully disobeyed me, woman. Never would I have allowed you to come here, and well you know it."

That had the Norsewoman's back stiffening again. "Had you returned when you *said* you would return, you would have been there to hear the messenger claiming Selig was being held prisoner. Think you I could have remained home knowing that? And 'tis well I did not wait for you. He is nigh dead from what was done to him. Another day at Gronwood could well have killed him."

Erika winced at that prejudiced opinion. The man's anger drained, however, and in fact, he pulled Kristen into his arms. It was comfort he was intent on giving, and comfort the Norsewoman gladly took. Watching them brought Erika's dejection a mite lower.

"Where is he?" Royce asked after a few moments of mutual squeezing.

"In the wagon, and likely awake from all the noise you were making. 'Tis a good thing he cannot understand us, or he would be crawling out here to protect me, and doing himself more damage."

Royce grunted. "He knows better than to try to protect you from me, wife. And you *will* be getting that beating for the fright you gave me, but I will wait until we are home to see to it."

"You are *so* kind," she retorted with a grimace and pushed away from him.

The movement brought Erika to his notice again, and this time his frown was just for her, though his remark was for his wife. "I believe you have more explaining to do."

Kristen followed his look and her own frown was back, as well as the contempt in her voice that Erika was now quite familiar with. "Lady Erika of Gronwood—now Selig's prisoner."

"Nigh dead and *he* captured her?" Royce asked, one brow lifted doubtfully.

"So I did it for him. He would have if he were able, but thanks to her, he can barely feed himself just now, let alone exact his revenge."

After a moment, the Saxon's frown turned implacable. "You will send her back."

Erika's heart leapt at those words, but her hopes were as quickly dashed by Kristen's reply. "I will not. Selig cannot fight you on this now, so I will have to for him. She stays."

He was not expecting an argument. "A *Danish* prisoner?" he exploded. "We are at peace!"

Kristen yelled back at him. "She did not consider that when she falsely accused him, imprisoned him, and had him lashed! He had a severe head injury, was already starved and burning with fever. He came to Gronwood for help, and she had him chained and whipped instead. Look at him and tell me he does not warrant revenge!"

So that he could do that very thing, Kristen tossed back the hide cover. Royce stepped closer to the wagon to look over the edge. Erika could not bear to see his expression of horror. His whispered "God's mercy" was bad enough.

She closed her eyes. If she could have sunk into the ground, she would have. Selig said something in a light, teasing tone, possibly to put his brother-in-law at ease, but she had no understanding of the Celtic tongue he used. And whatever he had said had no effect on the tall Saxon.

Royce pulled his wife away from the wagon to say reasonably, "There is a mistake here, Kristen. There must be. Women do not treat *your* brother so."

"Normal women would not, but this is a heartless bitch who takes pleasure in others' pain. It came from her own lips, what she did to him, and his men know it. If you order her released, *they* will kill her, doubt it not."

His expression was rife with frustration. "Alfred will have my hide if he learns I am party to this."

"Not if he also learns what *she* did," Kristen countered. "But if it bothers you, take your men and go. What I do for my kin has no bearing on you."

"Does it not?" he growled, taking a step toward her that had her backing up. "I believe I will change my mind about the time and place of your beating."

The dagger was at Kristen's hip, but she didn't draw it. Her chin came up, though, and she warned him, "If you want to end up with as many bruises, go ahead. I do not come meekly when I am in the right."

"When do you ever come meekly?" he replied, but his expression now said the urge for immediate violence had passed. "And you were not in the right in coming here without me, when it would have cost you no more than an hour to ride northeast to find me. 'Tis because you knew I would have sent you home that you did not bother, and that is why you will still get that beating."

At which point Kristen laughed and wrapped her arms around his neck. "I can make you forget the scare I gave you," she said confidently.

" 'Tis doubtful, but I will give you the opportunity to try."

Erika watched them move off to speak with others where she could no longer hear what was said. She was forgotten for the moment, and just as well, with bitterness starting to rise in her.

How close freedom had just come! Only to be snatched away by a stronger will. Or was it only that? Nay, she could have wished the Saxon had been more insistent, but knew why he had given in. The sight of Selig had done it, a sight clearly recalled to her own mind, and her bitterness was gone that quickly.

"Could you understand them?"

She had heard the wagon move, felt it even, but had not guessed Selig was moving to the end of it. She quickly glanced up to the left to see him sitting at the end, tall enough to lean over the side to look down at her, his arms holding to the wood to keep him steady.

Even with his face ravaged from fever and pain, he was still too handsome for words, the perfectly molded cheekbones perhaps more prominent than normal due to his weight loss, the longest lashes she had ever seen on a man, lips so sensual they promised—Erika shook such disturbing thoughts from her mind, though she still stared at him, amazed that he was not scowling at her this time, amazed that he had spoken to her at all, so amazed it was a while before she thought to answer him.

"Mostly," she said in the same casual tone he had used, though with a degree of caution. "Could you not?"

"Nay," he said. "With Royce and a goodly number of his people knowing Celtic, I never bothered to learn. Do you know Celtic?"

"Nay."

"Then 'tis well you and I know the northern tongues. What were they arguing about?"

Erika could not believe she was having this conversation. *What she suffers will come from me.* She had heard those words clearly, did not doubt them. Yet he spoke to her now as if they did not have that between them.

Should she apologize while he was in this strange, almost amiable mood? Should she beg his forgiveness? Explain about Wulnoth?

With those bright gray eyes so directly on her, all she could manage was to answer his question. "They are in disagreement about my presence."

He considered that for a moment before saying, "Aye, Royce hates Danes with a passion. He would not want to be near one—for whatever the reason."

Allusions to her predicament, no matter how mildly stated. The bitterness came back. She couldn't help it.

"Have no fear, your sister won."

He nodded, as if he expected no other answer. "Should you be released without my leave, or escape, I will come after you. There is nowhere in this land or any other that you can hide from me."

His expression had not changed, was no more than it had been, which was no expression at all. She began to tremble, though he couldn't see it. How easily he could catch her off guard. How easily he could move in for the kill whilst she was least suspecting. How did he do it? *Why* had he done it?

"You mean to toy with me," she accused, no other reason coming to mind.

"Certainly—until I am able to do more than that." And he smiled, an absolutely beautiful smile that made her catch her breath. "The ropes becomes you, lady," he added in a pleasant tone, staring at her throat. "I particularly like the one around your neck."

Erika blanched. He meant to hang her. He was letting her know so she could think about it, dread it, so the fear would eat away at her sanity. *What she suffers will come from me.* She closed her eyes, fighting tears.

Selig watched her, pleased by her reaction. She was so damned beautiful, so damned desirable—even now, hating her, he acknowledged her ability to stir his senses—yet so damned cruel. He had never known a woman to be like that. Was it the power her brother gave her that made it so? His mother and sister held such power, yet they did not abuse it as this Dane did. She'd had him lashed, and for what? Because he had offered to share her bed. When any other woman would have leapt at the chance.

Lashed . . . and she had stood there and laughed the while, a coldhearted, malicious—beautiful—witch. But she was going to pay for what she'd done. He was going to enjoy seeing to it. Before he was through with her, she would beg for mercy, and he would be the one to laugh and deny it.

"I like that rope around your neck so well," he continued, "I think I will have an iron collar made for you, with a ring attached. I am sure I can think of many things to do with that ring."

Erika looked up to see that he was still smiling, but the hate was in his eyes again, deeply smoldering. No hanging, then, but the fear remained, as he had intended. Toy with her? He meant to drive her mad.

"You did not find that amusing?" he asked.

Words failed her at that point. She could only shake her head.

"Good," he said, his tone positively chilling now. "Because I mean to see you never laugh again."

That sounded significant, as if there were more to those words than threat or promise. But Erika was too shaken to question him, and he moved away from the side of the wagon until she could no longer see him. Sweet Freya, if only she might never see him again.

Chapter 15

THE DAY PROGRESSED as Erika might have expected. Kristen mounted and rode beside her husband, which meant the terrible Dane could not be left alone in the wagon with the defenseless Selig. Defenseless? The man might still be weak as a babe, but he had weapons aplenty in his words.

Erika was grateful she would *not* be forced to endure his close company, even though what was left to her was to walk. The walking she wouldn't have minded at all, except her shoes had not been returned to her.

She wasn't even sure if it was a deliberate oversight, for Kristen hadn't been the one to tie her wrists before her with a long length of rope attached to the wagon. Thorolf had done that, and she doubted he had noticed she was without shoes, her under chainse was so long. The Norsewoman could merely have forgotten that she had removed the shoes the day before, or, as was more likely the case and a common enough practice, it was hoped her feet would suffer enough damage that she would be in no condition to escape by foot if the opportunity should present itself.

Erika had noticed the oversight immediately, but for some ridiculous reason, probably because Selig had been watching whilst she was being tied to the back of the wagon, her pride had reared its head and she refused to ask for her shoes. The wagon didn't move so swiftly that she couldn't keep up with it, but her hose were no protection from the rough ground.

She had begun by walking beside the wagon, where she couldn't see inside it, nor could the man inside it see her. But as the hours passed, she fell behind. She didn't once fall, but the exertion, coupled with the rising heat of the day, had the sweat pouring from her.

The sun was high when the Saxon lord drew his horse next to her and offered her a skin of water. He hated Danes, according to his brother-in-law, but she saw no hate in his eyes. Curiosity, disturbance, but no animosity like she experienced from everyone else.

She handed back the skin, expecting him to leave, but he spoke instead. "Who hit you?"

The swelling on her cheek was, of course, quite noticeable. Besides the tightness of the swelling, she could actually see it when she looked down. She wondered if it had bruised as well. She wasn't going to ask anyone.

"Your wife," she said in answer.

His expression didn't change. "She sees to her own quite fiercely."

Fiercely indeed. Erika doubted she would ever forget the dagger at her throat. "I was expecting it."

"Were you? Why?"

She glanced up at him, wondering if he was merely curious, or if there was another reason for these questions. Hesitantly, she gave him the truth. "I suspected she had not seen her brother's back yet."

"Ah, the lashing. Why did you do it?"

She was surprised that he would ask that. Had his wife told him nothing?

"He was an accused spy. His answers did not ring true when he was put to questioning." That wasn't the whole of it, wasn't even the why of it, he had insulted her, asked for her bed, but she wanted to know, "Why does everyone here find that lashing so unusual? I doubt me you would have done differently."

"Possibly, but then, I am a man and his angel's face would have no effect on me."

"I do not see what difference—" she said defensively.

"Do you not? Women dote on him. They adore him. They do not abuse him."

Nor would she have, Erika realized, if circumstances hadn't interfered. It began to annoy her considerably, that Selig the Blessed could likely get away with just about anything—if a woman was to judge him. These people thought so. His sister thought so. And remembering his insult to her, she knew *he* undoubtedly thought so.

"So you wanted a confession?"

"What?" She glanced at him again, bemused, until she recalled he had asked of the lashing. "Nay—I—he insulted me and I lost my temper."

Royce threw back his head and laughed. Erika gritted her teeth. She never should have owned up to that truth.

" 'Tis not funny," she said.

"God's truth, it is just that. Your temper? Now does this absurdity make sense."

He was implying that no less could be expected of a woman, and Erika resented that. Hers had been only a momentary loss, her control returned right quickly. If she hadn't been distracted by Thurston's accident . . .

Selig watched them through narrowed eyes. He didn't like it that Royce was showing an interest in his prisoner, particularly since he couldn't hear what was being said between them. He liked it even less that Royce could, if he chose, release the woman, and there was nothing Selig could do about it in his present condition, short of starting a war between their two groups, which he would not do.

But it would be a close thing, something he did not want to put to the test. She was *not* going to be released, not by him, not until he had exacted a full measure of revenge against her, and that could take years, considering the way he was feeling.

He watched them, and knew to the second when she became angry and thereafter ignored Royce until he rode off. Selig had an uncanny ability for reading women's emotions—even those women he hated. Nay, not those, just this one, for he had never hated a woman before, and was in fact having difficulty adjusting to it. Especially one as shapely as this Dane. As when his sister had come by just a few hours after they had set off that morn, to casually suggest that Erika had been walking long enough.

His first reaction had been concern, and he had been immediately appalled by it. He still could not believe he had felt it. He had had to remind himself that this was no ordinary woman to him, that he was nowise going to treat her as he would any other woman. It would help if he could forget she *was* a woman, but that was not possible.

He had refused Kristen's suggestion, though typically, she had thought to argue with him. "Do you mean her to drop and be dragged? It makes no difference to me, but she may break something—" his sister added.

He had been unwilling to argue about it. "She is stronger than that. Leave her. When she is near exhaustion will be soon enough to let her ride."

He was still annoyed with himself for those few seconds of concern. It might have been a natural reaction for him, but it was one he meant to ignore henceforth. In fact, he now hoped she would fall. He decided he would not have her put into the wagon until she did.

And it shouldn't be much longer. Where before the rope had been lax and she had found it necessary to carry it to keep from tripping on it, it now dragged her. He felt exhausted just watching her. But he didn't stop. Not once had he stopped watching since she had fallen back to where he could see her.

He lay on his pallet, slowly going through the mountainous pile of food Kristen had left for him, enjoying every moment of the Danish woman's difficulty. His own pain was ignored by dent of will, aided by having Erika No Heart to concentrate on. In return, she was ignoring him completely, had not returned his gaze even once, which was no easy feat, considering she was facing him.

When she did trip, her eyes came immediately to him, telling him that she was not so unaware of his perusal as she would have him think. She didn't fall, caught herself in time, but it was a near thing, close enough for Selig.

He beckoned her toward the wagon. Her chin went up, giving him her refusal. He stiffened, which set off a number of twinges and aches throughout his body. It absolutely infuriated him that he couldn't immediately get to her, pick her up, and toss her into the wagon. She knew he couldn't, which was why she had the nerve to defy him. But he had other options available to him, not as satisfying as seeing to the matter himself, but adequate to see his will met.

He sat up to catch Ivarr's attention—Ivarr was riding to the rear of the wagon—and called him forward to say simply, "Bring her."

Ivarr did, without comment, but Erika shrieked at his method. Without dismounting, he picked her up by a fistful of her gown at the back of her neck and literally dropped her into the wagon. She landed on her knees first, but her hands, tied wrist to wrist, were useless to prevent her full collapse forward.

Belly-down, she lay there for a moment, thankful that her face hadn't scraped the wood, but not the least bit thankful to be back in the wagon with her nemesis again. She had endured enough this morning. She would prefer the physical discomforts to the mental ones he could inflict, and determined to have her own choice in at least that.

Fully intent on resuming her walking, she rolled to sit up, but got no farther than that when she heard his curt order. "Stay, or I will have you bound tight again."

Had he read her mind? He did sound angry. Because she had ignored his summons? Too bad for him. She was not here willingly, was not going to obey his every command. And if he wanted to make an issue of it, wanted to get the tortures started sooner because of it, well, he could do that very thing and be damned to him.

But Erika didn't act on her rebellious thoughts except to turn around and give him her back. She was *his* prisoner. That had been well established. To defy him further would only assuage her pride. It wouldn't help her predicament. But that was not the only reason she stayed in the wagon.

Even as weak and incapacitated as he was, she was frightened of him on some deep, primitive level that she didn't begin to understand. It wasn't even the mental tortures he could inflict, it was him, being near him like this, so aware, so close she could touch . . . and wanting to touch. Sweet Freya, what an insane thought.

The sudden yank on her left braid brought her prone again, and the steady tugging that followed forced her to scoot back with elbows and feet. Her heart had picked up its beat by the time the pulling ended, and not from the exertion. She was now lying right next to him, though several inches lower, since the pallet he was on was only wide enough to accommodate him. Because of that, she didn't have to turn her head very far to see that he had wrapped her braid around his fist, and didn't unwrap it now that she was where he wanted her.

He could have just asked, or ordered. Either way, she would probably have complied, knowing he could force the matter—as he had just done. She thought to tell him so, but didn't, caught once more by that face of his that was so mesmerizing. He had sounded angry, but he didn't look it. Satisfied was how he looked.

"Not so pretty now, are you, wench?" he said in his low voice, though it was a lie. Somehow, her bedraggled state gave her an earthy quality that he found incredibly sexy. And a little dirt couldn't detract from her lush beauty, which was becoming more and more difficult for him to ignore. But she wasn't going to know that, so for good measure, he added, "Nor so high and mighty."

For some unaccountable reason, she blushed. It was nothing to her how she looked, shouldn't have been anyway, since it usually wasn't, but she knew she likely had never looked worse. Enough of her hair had come loose from her braids that it was straggled around her face and stuck in places from her sweat. The dust of the road coated her and had been smeared the few times she had tried to wipe her face on her arms. She had smelled her stench long enough that she no longer smelled it, but he undoubtedly did, and that mortified her the most.

Ravaged, with dark circles beneath his eyes, he still looked magnificent. She had wilted to drab and knew it. That *he* wanted her to know it showed what she could expect from this newest exchange between them.

She decided not to play his game this time. "Just kill me and be done with it."

He didn't know any woman of his acquaintance with that kind of spunk— besides his mother and sister. He was surprised, though he didn't show it. He smiled at her instead.

She really wished he wouldn't do that. It made him so much more handsome—and frightening.

"Nay, no death for you," he said. "No ransom either. Just endless torment such as you gave to me."

"Yours was not endless," she dared to point out.

"Three days in your pit *was* endless, lady. 'Tis a shame I have nothing like it to offer you."

Her mouth was suddenly dry, but she found the nerve to ask, "What do you mean to do with me?"

"Besides enslave you?"

The sharply drawn breath escaped her. "You cannot enslave me."

"I already have."

"But my brother will come for me," she said frantically. "He will pay whatever man-price you are worth."

"I am no Saxon, nor do I accept their wergild price for damages. A Viking will have revenge. You should know that—Viking."

But he lived in Wessex. His sister was wed to a Saxon lord. He had to obey their laws. She *had* to believe this could be settled and ended by the paying of fines, or she would have no hope to sustain her.

A slave? He could not do it. She had not been captured in battle, she had been stolen from her own home. Ransom he could demand. Wergild he could demand. Her life he could take, though Ragnar would see he died for it. But enslavement, when her own kin lived not so many leagues away?

Though her emotions were now in turmoil, she tried to sound reasonable. "My brother will never let you keep me. You must consider a price for when he comes."

"Must I?"

He was smiling again, but the sudden pull on her braid proved his anger was back. He had merely clenched his fist around her braid. She doubted he realized it tugged against her scalp.

"Your brother is not at issue," he added. "If he does come, I will have to kill him. And whose fault will that ultimately be?"

She closed her eyes. He was going to make her cry yet. He was likely determined to see it. It was choking her to deny him that.

"Have I found something that matters to you?" His voice was softer yet.

"Aye," she said in a mere whisper.

"How much will you beg me to spare his life?"

She stiffened and met his eyes again. "My brother is no weakling. He can see to himself."

"So you will not beg?"

"Nay."

"Then you have some pride? Good. Crushing it will be one of my priorities. You will make it challenging for me, will you not?"

She wished she knew the strategies of his game. Or were there any besides terrifying her?

"Not if I can help it," she replied cautiously.

"Then you plan to grovel so quickly?"

" 'Tis not what I meant."

"I know. You think to deny me my revenge, but I will have it despite your efforts. By Odin do I swear it."

That his eyes had dropped to her lips as he spoke made her stiffen again. He saw it and laughed. The laughter sounded forced.

"You do not have that to fear—from me," he said. "I am in high enough demand to not have to stoop to the likes of you."

She hoped he meant what she thought, that rape was not in his list of tortures for her. Then again, with his devious mental games, it could be a hope he wanted her to have just so he could crush it.

Chapter 16

BRENNA HAARDRAD LAY back on the grassy bank, letting the sun and warm breeze dry her raven locks and ease the worry from her brow. It was still a smooth brow for a woman of two score and five years. As active as she had always been and still was, her body was as firm as a much younger woman's. Four pregnancies had left only a few marks on it.

A splash drew her attention back to the small lake where her husband still swam. Her warm gray eyes watched Garrick shake his golden head, sending sparkling drops of water in every direction. He had aged well himself, this Viking of hers. He still wielded a sword in practice, though he rarely found the opportunity for its use anymore. The few streaks of gray in his hair that he had attained lately took nothing from his strength or his handsomeness. The man could still make her sigh most pleasantly— and often.

As usual, he was loath to leave the cool water. Brenna sympathized. She had been raised in Wales, not so far north of here, but she had spent more than half her life in Norway, and the heat of southern Wessex took getting used to. But they never stayed long enough to adjust to it, and she knew the heat bothered Garrick much more than it did her. Which was why she never objected when he brought her to the lake so near to Wyndhurst.

Half the time they would find Royce and Kristen there first, or Selig and whichever woman he currently favored, or both, for their children likewise still complained of the hottest part of Wessex summers, though they lived here now. Hell, Brenna still complained of the coldest part of Norway's winters, so she understood perfectly.

She called out to Garrick. "You have been in there so long, you are going to melt."

He looked toward the sun, still high, before he started toward the bank, grumbling. "I do not know why I let you drag me here."

She was aware that he meant Wessex, not the cool lake he so enjoyed. "You were the one so eager to see your grandchildren this summer," she pointed out, as if she hadn't been just as eager.

"And I needs must suffer for it in this god's-cursed heat. I am of a mind to take them back to Norway with us."

"I doubt me Royce will agree to that."

"I was not thinking of asking him."

She laughed. He liked his son-in-law, he truly did, but there was still that part of him that would never admit *any* man was good enough for his only daughter. And it had not really helped that he and Royce began their relationship with a fight to the death. Fortunately, it had not come down to actual killing, and a wedding had quickly followed. But Garrick still, on occasion, gave Royce a hard time. Brenna suspected he did it apurpose, on general principle. She also suspected he enjoyed doing so.

Just now, though, he was seriously annoyed with Royce for allowing Selig to get involved in something that had led to his capture and imprisonment, and allowing Kristen to ride off alone to gain his release. As if the Saxon could have prevented either occurrence.

Brenna had tried to point that out, but Garrick had been too upset to listen. He would have ridden off immediately to go after them if there had been enough horses left at Wyndhurst for him and his men. He was going to go anyway if they did not return by the morrow.

Brenna had kept her own worry to herself. She did not fear so much for Kristen. The girl had a small army with her, a husband fast on her heels, and Brenna had taught her all she knew of weapons, which was considerable. But Selig, imprisoned, helpless among strangers—that caused her a definite mother's dread.

Everyone knew how women reacted to her oldest son, but not everyone noticed how men reacted, men who did not know him, how he frequently stirred sour emotions in them in one form or another. It was a manly thing, she supposed, comprised mainly of jealousy and envy because of his extreme handsomeness, something strangers tried hard not to show. And it rarely amounted to anything, because Selig was, after all, foremost a warrior, with the strength and skill to give most men a healthy caution. But it was something that could turn ugly if Selig was at the mercy of such unrestrained emotions.

If her children did not return by the morrow, she would be riding with her husband to see what was keeping them, whether he liked it or not, and heaven help anyone who got in her way of finding them. But for the moment, with the warm breezes caressing sensually and the man she loved standing beside her in no more than his braies, and those plastered to him, she put her worry aside.

Her eyes ran appreciatively up and down the length of him. Her Viking was all chest, deep, wide; how often she lost herself beneath that chest. He noted her perusal, and the change in her expression, now sultry. The light appeared in his aqua eyes, the one she could always ignite.

"Now that you have cooled off, do you hope to stay that way?" she asked.

It was a provoking question that got her the answer she wanted. He dropped to his knees, and further, stretching out to half cover her body with his. She started to laugh, because he was still wet, his hair dripping on her, but her laughter was cut off by his kiss, and a moan soon followed. It amazed her sometimes that the passion that had started their lives together had never lessened. It could flare just as fiercely as it had in their youth, or smolder to savor, but it was always there, and always shared.

They both heard Garrick's name shouted, and both reacted the same, with worry recalled, passion forgotten for the nonce. Garrick thrust himself instantly to his feet to see over the bank, easily done with his height. Brenna had to scramble up the same bank to see who had disturbed them, in time to hear the news she had prayed for.

"They sent word ahead. They arrive within the hour."

"My son?" Garrick called back.

"With them."

Garrick waved the man off and closed his eyes, his head dropping back on his mighty shoulders to face the clear afternoon sky. Brenna knew he was giving thanks to all the gods known to him, her own god included. She returned to wrap her arms around him, putting her head to his chest, the farthest it would reach. His arms came around her to squeeze. She braced herself to bear it.

Her relief was so great she felt tears gathering. That brought laughter, which they both shared for a time.

Finally, she ventured to ask, "Do you want to ride out to meet them?"

"I believe we have reached an age where it might be more dignified to await them at the hall."

Her brows arched. " 'Twill not take us an hour to return to the hall."

"I know." He grinned.

That quickly did she find herself back on the ground, and her laughter came for a different reason.

Chapter 17

SELIG WAS PUSHING his recovery. Though he was nowise ready to do so, he abandoned the wagon that third morning to ride double with Kristen. Convincing her that he was up to it had taken some doing. Keeping her unaware of his increased pain took even more. But he was determined. He was impatient. And he wanted to be firmly entrenched behind walls before Erika's brother showed up with the demands she had convinced him would be forthcoming.

The walls would be necessary merely to hold the man off until Selig was well enough to face him. He didn't want it coming to a battle of armies—if the brother had one at his disposal. A simple one-on-one confrontation would settle the matter, and he felt no qualms about killing the man, not when he would have been killed for the mere suspicion of spying had Ragnar Haraldsson been at Gronwood instead of only Erika, or so she had claimed.

He remembered her telling him that. Mention of being killed had a way of forging in one's mind. He just wished the fever had not been strong even then and he could recall more of the questioning she had put him through, and the torture that had followed. But killing Ragnar would crush her hopes of rescue, which would suit his purposes just fine.

He had been enraged to see the blood on the wagon bed where her feet had been, that day she had walked behind it. The damned woman would bleed to death before she asked for assistance. As prideful as Kristen, but evil instead of good. He would see her arrogance ended and right quickly—once he was recovered.

In the meantime, he didn't want pain or exhaustion bringing her to her knees. When the time came, he wanted complete, groveling surrender putting her there. Where would be the satisfaction if her body made her succumb but her mind still defied him? So it was *not* consideration for her that kept her from walking again. It was no more than his determination to get home the soonest.

"They came!" Kristen yelled with excitement.

Selig, sitting behind her on her great horse, had just been glad to see Wyndhurst finally before them. But at Kristen's shout, still ringing in his ears, he squinted his eyes to make out their parents up on the outer walls, waving at them.

He groaned inwardly. They had said they might come this year, but under the present circumstances, he had been hoping they would not. And he had wanted coddling? He would get too much from his mother, and he could not gainsay her like he could his sister. She would have him to bed and he would stay there until *she* deemed him able to rise from it. And Kristen had already told him she refused to let him go to his own home until he had his weight back. She didn't trust the women Ivarr had bought to feed him properly.

"Mayhap you could refrain from telling them how little is left of me?" he asked Kristen, his tone teasing, but still hopeful.

"Do not be silly. You can hide that sunken belly with a borrowed tunic, but your loss of flesh is just as noticeable in your face."

He hadn't realized that, but should have. "Not so handsome, then, am I?"

"So ugly I can barely stand it."

She got a pinch, gave him back a giggle, then rode full tilt for Wyndhurst's gate. Just what his throbbing headache needed. But Kristen wasn't thinking of his condition now, and in fact, he had assured her he was fine.

He managed somehow to stay in the saddle without gripping his sister too hard. She was out of it the moment they were through the gate and running toward their parents, who were likewise hurrying toward them.

She reached Brenna first to hug her, lifting her off her feet in her exuberance. Their mother was not a small woman. By Celtic standards, she was actually tall. Yet her daughter topped her by half a foot. Garrick had his turn, and it was Kristen who was now lifted and swung around.

Selig stayed where he was. Actually, he didn't think he could get off the horse by himself without falling flat on his face. He had been eating more food than he ever had in his life these past few days, but his strength was returning only by aggravatingly slow degrees, and the hours they had just ridden had sapped it again.

He took a moment to note where Erika was, and that the rest of their party were coming more slowly through the gate. Royce saw his difficulty and rode toward him, dismounting just before Selig's mother reached him.

Brenna took one look at him and asked, "How bad is the pain?"

Selig sighed. He could lie, but she would see through it. " 'Tis manageable," he said.

"That does not tell me—"

"It does," Garrick cut in, moving in front of Brenna to help Selig to the ground.

He was grateful for his father's strong arm, but he was determined to walk into the hall without assistance, for his mother's sake. He caught the hand she reached toward him and pulled her close for a hug, which was a mistake. He could not squeeze her as he usually did. She noticed.

"Are they dead?" was the first thing she asked in her blunt way.

Selig laughed. Beside them, Garrick and Royce both rolled their eyes over that blood-thirsty question. But Royce shouldn't have been surprised.

He had first met Kristen's mother in the dead of night with her dagger at his throat waking him, and he had little doubt she would have used it had he not given her the correct answers she sought. Soon after, he'd had to fight their Viking champion to the death. It was the eyes that told him who that champion was, the same aqua as Kristen's. Knowing that, he couldn't have killed him even had it been possible, which had never been quite established. But they were a close-knit family. You hurt one and the rest were your mortal enemies. He actually felt sorry for the Dane.

" 'Twas thieves laid me low, Mother," Selig was explaining, "and they are gone, slunk back to their dens. Only one of them would I recognize, so they will be hard to find."

"That was only his first injury," Kristen added. "He went to the Danes for aid and they imprisoned him. He was burning with fever and they lashed him."

Brenna looked to her daughter. "Are *they* dead?"

"Nay, but the one responsible is there." Kristen pointed unerringly in Erika's direction. "And is Selig's to deal with when he is able."

"A *woman*?" Brenna and Garrick said at once.

Selig winced. "Must everyone find that so incredulous? I have not charmed every woman I set out to win. I have failed a few times, to keep my feet on the ground."

A number of disbelieving snorts greeted that statement before Kristen said, with a potent glare for her brother, "He insisted on riding, though I see now 'twas a mistake. I am glad to turn the care of him over to you, Mother. I doubt me he will fool you with his assurances of being *fine* before he actually is."

Sister and brother were both glaring at each other now. Brenna, in full agreement with her daughter, began issuing orders. Selig looked to Royce for help. It might be his home, but Royce wasn't about to argue with his mother-in-law, and his look said so. And then pandemonium broke loose as the women of the hall descended on Selig with a great many noisy tears.

Half were crying because he was alive, half because it was so obvious by the look of him that he had suffered. All of them wanted to assist in his recovery, and he was unable to convince them there was naught to worry over. None would listen to him. Even Kristen had trouble getting them to disperse without specific tasks sending them off, and there weren't enough tasks for all of them.

Royce and Garrick stood back while Selig was carried off to the hall. Royce was amused, until he noted his father-in-law's grim look.

"He will be fine once he has his weight back," Royce said. "The pain in his head may take longer to go away. 'Twas a severe blow, I am told."

"Who starved him?"

"The injury. 'Twas nigh a fortnight he was without consciousness."

"Aye, that would do it," Garrick said with a nod, then added, "I think I will go hunting this summer."

Royce laughed. "Kristen said nearly the same thing, that Wessex has got itself too many thieves and 'tis time we rid ourselves of a few. But Selig wants revenge only against that one. 'Tis surprising how much he hates her."

Garrick followed his look toward the Danish woman, who was being escorted into the hall behind the crowd. She was a bedraggled thing, though shapely, and might possibly be pretty if she were cleaned up.

"What does he mean to do with her?"

"What does any man do with a woman?" Royce countered with a shrug.

"Nay, not if he hates her."

Royce was in a position to disagree. He had hated Vikings, which his wife had been. He had despised her for what she was, and thinking her a whore besides, had despised her even more. But having a woman like Kristen at his mercy had gotten beyond the hate right quickly.

But Kristen had never done him a personal injury, as Lady Erika had done Selig, and therein lay a world of difference.

Chapter 18

ERIKA SAT IN a corner of the bedchamber, unnoticed, on the floor, her wrists and ankles tied again to keep her there. "Until chains can be fashioned for you," she had been told by Ivarr. She was in no hurry to see that done.

The activity in the room had not stopped since she had entered. Water was brought and taken away. More was brought and taken away. Food was brought and taken away before it cooled. More was brought hot to replace it.

The healer, an old woman with scraggly brown hair and a sharp tongue that was not discriminatory in whom it touched, was mixing herbs at a nearby table. Selig had been stripped down, examined, poked at. Several women had been present the while, and not one blush had Erika noted among them. She was to learn later that only the healer had not seen him naked before—aside from herself. And Erika was the only one blushing—and not looking.

The ocean of crying she had witnessed over him was disgusting. You would think all those women were his wives, yet she knew very well Saxons allowed only one wife, and he was living among Saxons. But not one woman there seemed to have the authority of a wife. The only one with authority was the black-haired older woman who tenderly applied a salve to his bruised back.

From what Erika had seen down in the bailey and previously learned from Kristen, she was afraid this was his mother. Another one of his family to despise her. She prayed she wouldn't gain her notice, but wasn't likely to for the while, since the woman's full attention was on her son.

Erika leaned her head back against the wall and closed her eyes, trying to ignore what was happening on the large bed. Her thoughts drifted, as anxious as they had been since her capture. Nothing had occurred to relieve her fears. Arriving at such a well-fortified manor, with strong, high stone walls surrounding it, only increased them.

Turgeis wouldn't be so close now. Gone was the hope that he could steal into camp late of a night and whisk her away to safety. The stone walls here would be amply guarded, the gates locked at night. And Turgeis wasn't a man who could slip through gates unnoticed, day or night.

She could only wait for her brother now, and she knew not how long that might be. She wouldn't tolerate the thought that Selig would kill him, as he had claimed. Ragnar would bring pressure to bear instead and she would be released. She had to cling to that hope.

There had been no more unnerving "talks" with her nemesis, nor had she been forced to ride in the wagon with him again. When they abandoned the conveyance that third morn, she had been made to ride behind Ivarr on his great charger. She wasn't sure which was more unpleasant.

Even worse than Thorolf was Ivarr, in his cold condemnation of her. And riding with him had put a strain on every muscle she possessed, trying to keep from touching him. She had discovered that, as Thorolf was Kristen's closest friend in this land, aside from her family, Ivarr was Selig's. Knowing that, she supposed the hate he bore her was understandable. It just wasn't very palatable for her.

That journey had not been an easy one by any means. Aside from the uncertain future which was so fearful, she had the constant worry that Kristen would abandon her completely to Selig's supervision, especially once her husband joined them. Not so. Erika's plea that first night had worked, and the Norsewoman continued to come and collect her each time she herself had to answer nature's call.

One of those times Erika had even tried to reach through Kristen's dislike of her to what common sense the woman must possess, to remind her of consequences yet to be met that could still be avoided.

"My brother will come for me," she had told her. "Even if he and I were not close, he would come."

"Aye, I suppose he will. But he will not have you back unless *my* brother chooses to release you. You may not want to go back by then."

Erika had been able to think of only one reason she might not want to go home—a tarnished virtue. "You mean he will rape me?"

Kristen had snorted. "Rape a woman he hates? That is one thing you need not fear."

"Then why would I not wish to go home?"

Kristen had shrugged. "Because 'tis likely you will come to love him."

Erika not only had been incredulous, she had very nearly laughed at the absurdity of such a notion. "Love a man who means to harm me? How could you think it?"

"Therein would be a fitting punishment, would it not?"

"It cannot happen."

"Do not say cannot. 'Tis more like you will not be able to help yourself. They never even try."

"They?"

"All the women who love him."

All the women who love him.

An unusual statement, until you considered how unusual the man was in his looks. Erika had no fear that she would come to be included in that "all," but she was surprised to discover firsthand so many who were.

A number of them had been traipsing in and out of this very room. A few almost came to blows over who would fetch what for Selig. And yet this was a man with no warmth in him that Erika could see, no compassion or forgiveness, certainly no mercy. How could so many women be so shallow, to love a man merely for his handsomeness, even as remarkable as his was?

Only the mother and one elderly servant remained in the room when Erika took note of it again. Selig had been covered, was still on his stomach, with his eyes closed, possibly asleep, since the two women were now whispering. They were preparing to leave the room, gathering up the cloths that had been used to clean Selig, the bucket of water, the jar of soft soap, what food remained.

Erika held her breath, still hoping to go unnoticed. It was not to happen. In fact, both women came directly toward her, stopping at her feet. Obviously, they had been aware of her all along.

"I am Brenna Haardrad, Selig's mother."

Her voice was stiff. Her expression, of strong dislike, Erika was quite accustomed to by now. It was mirrored in the servant's face.

"So I guessed," Erika replied.

"He has told me what happened—and your part in it."

"Did he say what his revenge is to be?"

"I would give you a lashing to equal the one you gave him—to begin with. Had I been there to see him when he was released, I would have killed you. But then, that is the way of hot tempers, is it not? Quick to act, with regrets come too late. I must commend my daughter for her restraint."

The color had drained from Erika's face, but it began to return with the word "regrets." "Are you saying you will not kill me now?"

"The decision is not mine to make, but nay, I would not. Death, like tempers, is too quick after all."

That sounded so ominous, Erika was not sure she should be relieved. "But what does *he* mean to do?"

Brenna shrugged. "He did not say, but do not be so eager to find out. You have a reprieve whilst he recovers, which is more than you deserve." Having said all she cared to, she turned to the servant. "Take her down to the bathing chamber, Eda, and she will need new clothes."

"Nay."

The denial came from the bed, clearly stated. Selig had not been sleeping after all, had been listening to every word.

Brenna glanced toward him and answered with the obvious. "She stinks, Selig."

"She can have the bath, but here. She does not leave my presence."

"Why?"

"Ask me about anything else, Mother, but do not question me about her."

His voice was cold, not meant to be argued with. It was the man speaking, not the son. Which would not have stopped Brenna, except she had already decided not to interfere.

All she said was, "I never thought to see the day *you* would hate a woman."

"All things are possible with the right provocation," he replied.

"True." She sighed. "Very well." And to Eda: "Have the bath brought here. He will need it on the morrow anyway."

They were ignoring Erika, had not asked her if she wanted a bath, much less where she would have it. She would certainly not have it here and said so. "I cannot bathe with him watching, Lady Brenna."

Gray eyes just like *his* came back to her. "You do not have a choice."

Erika's chin shifted upward. "I do. I will keep the stink."

"Nay, you will not. My daughter does not abide slovenliness in her hall, nor do I intend to smell it each time I enter this chamber. You may take the bath yourself, or I will summon the women back to give it to you."

At which point Selig made his own wishes known. "Not the women. They will be all over me again. Send Ivarr and two other of my men—"

Erika could not interrupt quickly enough. "I will bathe here!"

"I thought you might."

The smugness in his tone grated on Erika's already distraught nerves, but she refused to say another word. Stating her preference only got her the exact opposite. Obviously, he had decided to toy with her some more.

Brenna returned to the bed long enough to grumble, low-voiced, "I cannot see what you hope to accomplish in your insistence, Selig. 'Tis not as if you are in any condition to—take advantage."

"You mistake the situation, Mother," he said just as low. "She will never know my touch. What I will accomplish is exactly what I mean to, her discomfort."

"I hope not at the expense of your own," she remarked with meaning.

"You worry for naught. The only thing she tempts me to do is strangle her, which would not be nearly as satisfying as what I intend doing."

"Which is?"

He grinned at her. "None of your business, Mother."

At any other time she would have boxed his ears for that answer and he knew it, which was why she laughed and ruffled his hair instead. "Your father and brothers will be up to see you later. After you have finished 'discomfiting' the prisoner, get some rest. I will not be gainsaid on what is needful for your recovery."

"Somehow, I knew that."

Chapter 19

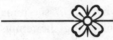

ERIKA STARED AT the large wooden bath with baleful eyes. Steam rose from it. It looked deliciously inviting. But it was set in the center of the room, with the bed not so many feet distant. And Selig might be lying there with his eyes closed, still on his stomach, but she didn't for a moment believe him sleeping this time.

The servant Eda had untied her. Clean clothes, along with washing and drying cloths, waited atop a stool for her use. Beside it were shoes, not hers. Someone had noticed she was lacking.

Erika hadn't moved from her position in the corner, except to rub her limbs when the ropes had come off. She still couldn't bring herself to move. She had said she would bathe here. The alternative was unthinkable. Yet she couldn't garner the nerve required to actually do it, now that the time was at hand.

She could run. She wasn't restrained. No one else was in the room except Selig, and he could never rise quickly enough to stop her. But the stairs led to the hall below, and the only exit she had seen was across that long length of hall. She had nowhere to run to that she wouldn't be brought back from and subjected to worse than this. But this . . .

"Ivarr can still be summoned."

As she thought; not sleeping, waiting. And what he waited for was to experience her humiliation. If she had not hated him before, she did now.

"You are despicable!"

"A matter of opinion, and yours is irrelevant. Do I summon Ivarr?"

He rolled onto his side, facing her, to hear her answer. Those gray eyes rested on her without mercy. It would be pointless to ask for some. This was part of his revenge, a minor part to him, but not so minor to her. Yet he would have it with or without her cooperation, and the indifference in his tone said he really didn't care which way it was to be.

Erika got slowly to her feet. She could have wished for concealing night, for candles, instead of the bright light of late afternoon coming in through the open window. No such luck for her. The most she could do was keep her back to him and pretend he was not there. Enjoy the bath. Deny him her blushes. Think of other things.

All she managed was to keep her back to him as she disrobed.

The tub was large in its roundness, not its depth. It came only to her knees. A short bathing stool had been set in the center of it, just barely covered by the foot of water she had been allowed. She disdained the use of it, preferring to bury herself as deep in the tub as she could. He permitted that for only a few minutes.

"Wash your hair."

She was so rattled by the entire situation, she wouldn't have thought to do that. But she hated being told to. *Ordered* was more like it. What would happen if she refused? Ivarr, of course. Selig was going to hold that damn Viking over her head like a whip.

It took a while to get her braids undone, after so many days and so much dirt matting them. She had to sit up to do it, but once her hair was loose, she dropped down to her back to submerge her head, briskly rubbing her itching scalp under the water before she came up to cover it with the soft soap.

There had been only one bucket of water left for her to rinse with, so she had to save it until she was done. But three times she soaped her hair, until she was satisfied it was clean, so three times she had to dunk her head to rinse it. By the time she finished, a layer of soap scum floated on the water, but she had yet to wash herself.

Ordinarily she would have stood up to finish. Sitting in water turned dirty was distasteful at any time, and this time was no different. The reason for the stool. But she refused to sit or stand, which meant she had to wrap her hair in a towel to keep it out of the dirty water. She had to get up on her knees to do that, and was bright pink again before she was able to duck back down below the rim of the tub.

"You will not get clean in that filthy water."

He was guessing. He couldn't see it. "The water is clear enough," she said, but needn't have bothered. He had decided on further torment for her, and nothing she said would deter him from it.

"Stand up," he commanded. "Should you ever have the opportunity for a private bath, I need to be assured you know how to wash yourself properly. I will not have my mother's nose offended again."

She wondered if giving her these ridiculous excuses was part of his game. Was she supposed to argue with him, remind him that she was not a Saxon, many of whom superstitiously thought bathing an unhealthy practice? His excuses were worth arguing over. Even "offending" his mother with her stench, which he was ultimately responsible for. They had crossed rivers, camped near creeks, but she had not been allowed to wash in them as everyone else had.

His excuses begged for argument. She could at least deny him that.

She stood up, carefully keeping her back to him. The hot color came anyway. She couldn't help that. But she was actually feeling somewhat triumphant. She had thwarted him. She wasn't sure what his true goal had been, probably no more than a further demonstration of his power over her. But she had defeated his purpose.

He laughed softly, which unnerved her, told her he didn't really care about her temporary triumph, that he had other avenues to reach the same goal available to him. She braced herself, expecting the hatchet to fall immediately. It did.

"Turn around, wench. You have a nice ass, but I want to see what else my new slave possesses."

"I am not a slave," Erika whispered fiercely to herself.

"What was that?"

"I am not a slave!"

"As I said, your opinion is irrelevant. You will still do as you are told. Protests on your part will be dealt with, and not to your liking."

Whatever he meant by that, she didn't care to find out. She knew his game now, and his ultimate goal. Humiliation at every opportunity, and utter devastation of her pride. *Crushing it will be one of my priorities.* She should have remembered that promise.

His staring at her nakedness now was done just to shame her, not because he was actually curious about what she looked like. He didn't do it for his pleasure, or even in anticipation of having her. His sister had said that was something she wouldn't have to fear. He had told her nearly the same thing. Normal emotions didn't apply to this. Just her shame, her discomfort, her helplessness.

Erika got angry.

Fear had been controlling her, fear of what the sight of her nakedness could do to a man, and what that man would then want. But she had forgotten that Selig was no ordinary man. He was her enemy, and that particular fear didn't apply to him. He wasn't even capable of coupling just now, if for some reason he should desire it, and even if he was, he wouldn't act on that desire. Coupling would mean he wanted her, and he would never give her something like that to throw up in his face afterward.

The anger came, and with it, an abrupt change in her demeanor as well as her thinking. He wanted to shame her? How could he, when she had wanted this bath more than he wanted her to have it, when his presence presented no actual danger to her, when she had it within her power to make him regret toying with her this time? He wanted to watch? She would give him something to watch. Perhaps she had no power as a lady, but she still had her power as a woman.

Erika had never in her life deliberately tried to entice a man, but some things were instinctive. She turned around to face him. She reached for the soap and spread it on her hands instead of the washcloth. Slowly, with ancient challenge in the sky-blue eyes she locked to his, she rubbed her hands over her breasts, smoothed them over her belly and hips, down the side of her legs to her knees, then, even slower, up the inside of her thighs. He followed those hands with his own bright grey eyes, and she knew the very second that he forgot who she was, and was just watching a woman at her bath.

"Will you wash my back, Viking?"

"Vixen," he hissed.

She wanted to laugh, but didn't. She had never imagined she could salvage her pride this way.

And then, somehow, he turned the tables on her.

It was the way his expression suddenly became sensual. The way his lips softened and curved just so. The way his eyes gleamed more silver than gray as they caressed the intimate parts of her. He was a man who knew how to make love with his eyes, and he was giving her a demonstration of that skill.

Uncertainty returned with a vengeance, making Erika distinctly uncomfortable again. It had been unbelievably stupid of her to provoke this reaction in him. After all, the conclusions she had drawn were not writ in blood. Lust could destroy the strongest resolve.

He still wasn't capable of doing anything about it just now, but that and only that kept her from running, screaming, from the room. She looked away from him instead, and finished her bath with all speed. But she knew he hadn't closed his own eyes.

He watched, and she trembled. She also began to feel something else, something unexpected and not unpleasant that hummed in her core. Was lust contagious? Odin help her if it was, because he could see to his with any one of a dozen women in the hall below, but who would see to hers? Nay, fanciful was what she was. She wouldn't know lust if it bit her. And for him to stir it with just a look? Impossible. Her stomach had merely reacted to such swift changes in emotions, no more than that.

He said no other words to her, and she didn't look his way again. But she had learned a lesson. She was no good at his game.

Chapter 20

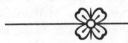

"YOU WILL FIND a comb in the coffer next to you," Selig said.

The offer was so unexpected, and so generous, Erika distrusted it, coming from him. That she had been trying to work the tangles from her hair with her fingers for the past half hour was beside the point. Selig wouldn't give her something she might be grateful for. So why had he?

She opened the coffer warily, expecting some sort of trap to spring, knives to drop from the ceiling, the floor to open and swallow her, rodents to leap out of the trunk itself. Nothing happened. It was an ordinary trunk. And the comb was there, next to an oval looking glass, both set atop a deep pile of male clothes.

The looking glass she simply couldn't resist using, but staring into it brought bemusement. She didn't look as awful as she had expected. In fact, freshly scrubbed, she showed not a sign of hardship on her face. No more than a slight tinge of yellow was on her cheek where she had been struck, telling her she had bruised, but not badly. The swelling was also gone from that area. Her sky-blue eyes were bright, surprise reflected in them. Even the sun had treated her kindly, merely darkening the golden tan she had already begun acquiring since summer had come to the land.

She looked, actually, quite lovely, making her doubt what she was seeing. It had to be the candlelight, glowing throughout the room since a servant had come to light the many tapers at the first signs of approaching dusk. Candlelight could be deceiving . . .

"You thought to see something different?"

The blasted man *could* read minds. "Nay, I—"

"Give me time, wench," he interrupted. There was distinct laughter in his tone. "I will put the suffering there you expect."

"Bastard," she hissed beneath her breath.

She began yanking the comb through her hair. The tears that sprang forth from her stinging scalp forced her to ease up and use the comb properly.

They had both already eaten. The food given her had not been what one might expect for a prisoner, but instead, of surprisingly rich variety and quite tasty. The inside of her mouth was still sore, though had healed enough that she no longer had to be careful in her chewing. But she would have enjoyed the meal better if she didn't have to listen and watch the love-play going on across the room.

The girl, Edith, who had come with the food, did more touching and caressing of Selig than feeding him, and spent a full hour at it. Shameless slut, and he enjoyed every moment of it, exuding more charm and sexual appeal than Erika had ever been witness to. It was obvious they were well "acquainted," and just as obvious they would be again as soon as Selig's strength returned.

The hour was, in fact, grown quite late now, yet no one had come to extinguish the lights or retie her. The water had been emptied from the tub. Lady Brenna had come again, to assure herself that Selig was taking the potions the healer had made for him. Lady Kristen had merely poked her head around the door, to inquire if he needed anything. The most disquieting visit, however, had come from Selig's father and brothers.

The three men dominated the room with their height and brawn, and each had gazed quietly at Erika at different times during their visit, though none addressed her or even asked Selig about her. Kristen had probably told them all there was to know, her version at least. Erika sensed varying degrees of curiosity from them, distaste, perplexity, and anger, but surprisingly, no actual hate. Likely they just hid it better than Selig did.

The younger brothers, Eric and Thorall, were neither one as handsome as Selig, which didn't say they weren't very handsome men. They were each a score in years, Eric mayhap a few years more than that, and they both took after their father as Kristen did, with tawny golden manes, eyes a distinct shade of aqua, and his extreme height.

Erika tried to ignore their presence, but it was next to impossible, especially when what was most interesting was Selig's behavior. To see him with them was to see a different man, one who laughed and teased and bore teasing in return with more laughter. This, on top of the sensual charm he had displayed earlier with the pretty Edith, led her to revise her opinion of him somewhat.

There were certainly more facets to his character than she had thought, though this did not relieve her mind in any way. Rather, it was disconcerting to find that a man who appeared to have such an easy nature could also harbor such a deeply rooted streak of cruelty.

She finished with her hair. Selig had watched her work with it. Most times through the evening, when she had glanced his way, he had been looking elsewhere, deep in his thoughts. Not since she had begun with her hair. And his eyes were still on her, without expression, telling her nothing of what was running through his mind.

His steady gaze was making her edgy. She wanted to sleep. The hour was late enough for it. And a blanket had been left for her earlier, when her own clothes had been taken away. Those she wore now were of the coarsest variety, but no more than she had expected.

She also expected to be retied, and wondered why no one had come to do so. Not for a moment did she think she would be left free for the night. And she wondered why no one had come to put out the lights. Should she offer to do it? Nay, she would offer nothing, would do nothing she wasn't forced to do. She wasn't here to be helpful and wouldn't be, not if she could do otherwise.

The question came from her edginess, her tiredness, anything to break the nerve-racking silence. "The coffer is yours?"

"Aye."

"You live here, then?"

"I have my own hall a short ways west from here. 'Tis newly built, though, and certainly not as comfortable as Wyndhurst. This is my chamber, however, whenever I stay with my sister."

"How long do you intend to stay here?"

His expression turned wry. "I doubt me I will have much say in my leaving. Kristen feels the few slaves I have will not take care of me properly. Unfortunately, my mother is like to agree with her."

The mention of his "slaves" ended the brief conversation for Erika and brought her temper rising. She shook out her blanket, wrapped herself tightly in it, and lay down to face the wall.

But what she had started, he meant to finish. "Mayhap you know how to care for an invalid?"

"You are not an invalid," she gritted out. "There is naught wrong with you that food and rest will not fix right quickly."

"Were that the case, my pain would be gone," he replied. "It is not."

Erika squeezed her eyes shut tight against the guilt those words brought back. She had ordered an injured *and* innocent man lashed. She had added pain to considerable pain. He deserved his full wergild price. He deserved an apology, which she had yet to offer. He deserved her understanding for what he was putting her through— Nay. She had only to recall how much pleasure he got in humiliating her to decide all he would get from her was the wergild.

He said no more. Neither did she. A short while later she had started to doze off, despite the discomfort of her hard bed, when she heard the chains rattle.

She opened her eyes and turned to see Ivarr coming across the room toward her. Alarm struck her first, and she sat up, then realized he must be there to tie her. He had done so on more than one night before. She relaxed, only to hear the chains again.

The alarm was back, worse. Her eyes flew to his hands and widened. He held chains, all right, replete with shackles, a great many of them.

Selig spoke before Ivarr bent to her. "Are they to my specifications?"

"Exactly. The smith got two others to help him and has worked all day. He only just finished."

"Did you test them?"

"Aye," Ivarr replied. "The links held firm, despite their thinness."

"Good. Then bring her here."

Ivarr lifted a brow, since Selig had risen as he said it. "You had better not let Lady Brenna see you sitting up like that. The word is out, she is not letting you out of bed for a fortnight."

Selig ignored the warning completely. "Bring her, Ivarr. I want to put those shackles on myself."

Ivarr shrugged his compliance. Erika drew back as he reached for her, but she had nowhere to cringe to. Without strain, he was able to yank her up and drag her toward the bed, even with her holding back with every ounce of strength she possessed.

She didn't actually fight him, though the urge was powerfully strong to do so. She knew how pointless that would be. They would have her chained anyway, and also be pleased to know how much she loathed the idea. So she didn't fight, and only Ivarr could feel her resistance.

To Selig she showed an indifferent expression. He wasn't going to know how frightened she was. Chains were so permanent, so unbreakable, freedom so completely at the whim of one's captor. Ropes offered a slim chance at escape. Chains offered none.

She knew now why the candles still burned, why Selig had not tried to sleep. He had been waiting for this, likely savoring the thought of it, and now was going to thoroughly enjoy putting the chains on her himself.

Sweet Freya, she didn't want to be chained. Selig the Blessed was not offering a choice.

She was shoved in front of him, practically between his spread knees. It was too close. He was naked sitting there on the bed, with only a corner of his blanket drawn over his lap. But when she tried to step back, it was to encounter Ivarr directly behind her.

The chains were tossed on the bed beside Selig, where Erika was able to get a closer look at them, and in fact jumped at the chance to look elsewhere than at the man. She had understood from Ivarr's words that they were not normal chains, were made special to Selig's specifications, but she was surprised now to see how unusual they were.

The metal links were not just thin, as Ivarr had mentioned, but were also quite small, like none she had ever seen before, at least not for this purpose. Silver and gold chained girdles had links this small. These looked, frankly, useless, too flimsy to hold anything. Hope rose, only to drop in the same instant. Ivarr had tested them. If he couldn't break the links, she certainly couldn't.

The shackles attached to the chains were of a normal size, but again she found the unexpected. The wide iron bands were covered in sleeves of stitched leather, with narrow slits for the attachment rings. Her skin would be protected from the iron. Why Selig should have a care for her skin, she couldn't begin to guess.

"Give me your right hand."

She hesitated for only a second. If she could help it, she wasn't going to show him how much she hated this. Let him think it made no difference to her, what form of restraint he used. But it was difficult to keep from cringing when that first shackle clicked on.

It was a tight fit, with no hope of her being able to slip her hand through it. Not made for a man, then, but still weighty. It dragged her hand back to her side when he let go of her.

She gave him her other hand before he asked. His expression altered at that, wasn't so pleased. Had he hoped to force the chains on her? Too bad.

"Hold to Ivarr and give me your right ankle," she was ordered next.

To hell with Ivarr. She lifted her foot without losing her balance, and maintained her balance as the next shackle went on. Again he got the other foot without having to ask. But when his last command came, her resolve ended.

"On your knees, wench."

She didn't budge. He looked up at her, one brow raised in question. She glared back at him, crossing her arms over her chest. The chain between her hands, a good two feet worth, allowed that.

Selig shook his head when Ivarr put a hand to her shoulder to shove her to the floor. And in the next instant he demonstrated what, besides restraint, the chains could be used for.

He did it slowly, grasping the chain that presently dangled across her waist and tugging it downward. Her arms came uncrossed, then were straightened fully as the chain reached her knees. At that point his own arm was extended, and rather than bend himself, he lifted one leg to hook his foot on the chain, then abruptly brought his foot back to the floor, the chain with it. Erika's arms, perforce, followed, bending her completely over.

To her horror, her chin hit his upper thigh, and her eyes were mere inches above his groin. And with Ivarr still behind her, she couldn't change the position.

"You have a choice, wench. You can remain like this, the rest of the night if necessary, or you can get to your knees as I requested."

He hadn't requested, he had ordered. She knew the difference. A choice? If she bit the thigh her face was fairly pressed against, would she gain her release, or merely punishment and a return to this position? She wanted to swear and rail at him. She did, in fact, want to bite him. On her knees he wanted her. Her only choice?

Erika sat down instead, right between his feet.

Selig and Ivarr both laughed heartily at her temerity, surprising her. She had expected anger for not taking one of the choices given her. She had expected to be set on her knees by force. She didn't expect them to be amused by her outright defiance.

She crossed her arms again, now that she was able to, and stared stonily at Selig's left knee. A hand came to her chin to lift it. She shook it off, but it returned, the grip increased just enough to keep it there.

She disdained meeting his eyes, keeping hers lowered. So she was able to see his other hand reach for what was left on the bed. She stiffened. The last shackle went around her neck anyway.

Her chin was released, for he needed both hands to click it into place beneath her hair. Her own hands came up in a frantic rush to pull the shackle away. But his grip on it was stronger than hers.

She heard the click, felt the snugness around her throat. It wasn't choking, but might as well have been for all the panic she felt. She pulled on it uselessly now. The chain between her hands carefully tugged her fingers away from it.

She looked up at him then. Fully chained, defeated, no longer just a prisoner. The shackle around her throat declared her a slave.

He studied her for a moment before he asked curiously, "Will you beg me to remove it?"

"Go to hell."

He smiled, that smile she hated. "You have had your way. Now I will have mine."

He hooked a finger through the iron ring at the center of the neck shackle. With it, he lifted her, bringing her to her knees after all.

"I knew I would find excellent uses for this," he continued. "Just as I knew chains would become you. Get used to the weight, wench, for they are never coming off."

Color deserted her cheeks. That he had said it gently, softly, made it all the more horrible. And she had not been given all of her chains yet. There was one more, some six feet in length, with larger round links at each end, that he brought to the ring at her neck.

After a few moments of feeling his knuckles brushing against her skin, she heard him chuckle in defeat. "The smith is to be commended. You will have to do this for me, Ivarr, until my strength returns."

He couldn't open the clasping link, which meant she wouldn't be able to either. But she would, somehow. Desperation added strength, and she was not the weakling they seemed to think she was.

Ivarr, of course, did as requested, and within seconds, the last chain was attached to her. "Where do you want the spike?" he asked Selig.

"The corner she favors will do for now."

She hadn't noticed the hooked spike tucked in Ivarr's belt. As he dragged her back across the room by her neck chain, she saw the hammer tucked in his belt at his back. Two strikes embedded the spike in the wall. Two seconds more and she was chained to it.

He left the room immediately thereafter. Erika stood there in the corner, staring at the spike in the wall. It wasn't so high that she couldn't lie down, but she couldn't move more than six feet away from it.

She heard Selig getting comfortable on his soft bed again. He likely watched her for a long while before he finally slept, the candles still burning, savoring her defeat. Erika didn't sleep at all.

Chapter 21

BRENNA SLAMMED A fist into her pillow before she dropped down onto it. She was a cauldron of seething emotions, and had been ever since she realized her son was in pain. She loved all of her children too dearly not to empathize with them completely, and just now she raged over what Selig had gone through.

She looked toward her husband as he stood brooding at the window, which he had been doing for the past hour. He was as bad as she was where their children were concerned. He simply contained his emotions, whereas no one could doubt her mood was on the explosive side.

"She is not going to get what she deserves," she commented, expressing what was on her mind. "He is too softhearted when women are involved."

Garrick didn't need to ask of whom she spoke. "But one has never hurt him before," he reminded her before he drained the wine in his goblet and joined her in the bed. "Just what is it you feel she deserves?"

"I saw his back. It has been nigh a sennight since he was lashed, yet the bruises are still there to attest to the severity of it. And when I think of the pain he was already in from his head injury—"

"You would take a whip to her? A man is strong enough to bear it, but a woman?"

"That is just it," she insisted. "He was *not* strong enough at the time."

He pulled her close to rest against his chest, his hands on her back attempting to soothe her. "He is ours. You are upset because he was hurt at all. I do not like it either. But consider, love, what he was accused of—"

"Falsely—"

"But accused nonetheless, and the Danes have not been at peace long enough to treat spying indifferently. He could have been tortured for a confession and hanged. He could have been whipped instead of lashed, which he might not have survived. Instead of bearing bruises, his back could have been shredded. Be grateful it *was* a woman deciding the matter and she did no more than have him lashed."

"You can be grateful for that," she said. "I can still resent her."

Her tone was less severe, a mere grumble, telling him she had listened and even agreed, though she wouldn't admit it. "It will be interesting to see how Selig perceives the matter once he is hale and hearty again."

Brenna raised her head to look at him. "You think he will just shrug it off and let her go?"

"Not that, but I doubt he will require pain for pain, as he would were she a man."

She shook her head at him. "I know what you are thinking, Garrick, and 'tis just like a man to think it, but you are wrong. He will not force her to his bed. He said as much. His women would tell you *that* would be a reward, and he does not intend to reward her."

Garrick laughed. "I remember how you felt about that first time."

She did as well, with less humor. "Do not remind me of my ignorance and Delia's petty idea of revenge, to make me fear something so wonderful."

He rolled over to grin down at her. "What I remember was that once was not enough for you."

Her fingers came up to trace his beloved face. "Once is never enough for me with you, Viking. But then, I have taught you how to please your wife well."

"Have you indeed?"

"Or mayhap you require more lessons?"

He chuckled, and bent down to kiss her. The noise stopped him, which they both heard. Brenna raised a questioning brow. Garrick had had forewarning from Ivarr, and so guessed accurately.

"You should be pleased," he said. "The dangerous prisoner has just been chained."

The sound made sense to her now. "To a wall?"

He shrugged indifferently. "Merely secured to it, I should imagine."

Brenna snorted. "She is not dangerous."

"Selig must think so."

Garrick had not been present for that bath incident, but she had. "What Selig undoubtedly thinks is that she will hate it. I believe our son has a number of things in store for her that he hopes she will not like."

"So that is the revenge he will take?"

"Or merely part of it. He would not say what he means to do with her. 'Twould seem we must wait to find out the same as she . . .'"

A while later they were awakened by more noise, but this much more obvious, Kristen shouting, Royce growling back, a crash as one of them tackled the other to the floor out in the hall. It was anyone's guess which one.

Brenna started to get up. Garrick pulled her back down with a sigh. "We could have wished he had chosen a less quiet hour to chastise her."

She squirmed to get loose of his hold, but that was one thing she had never been able to accomplish. "She does not appear to agree she needs *chastisement.*"

"Like mother, like daughter."

She ignored that to demand huffily, "You are going to do naught?"

"And what would you have me do when Royce is justified in his grievance? She would not be getting this chastisement if he did not love her. She acted foolhardy. Even she knows it—which is why she is protesting so loudly."

"That makes as little sense as everything else going on around here today," Brenna grumbled.

"Were she not guilty *and* feeling it, she would have just said so. Instead she shouts excuses."

"Valid ones, from what I can hear."

"Not valid enough to ignore the risk she took. Royce could have brought Selig home just as easily, without her help. If she had no husband right now to point that out to her, I would do it."

He grunted from a punch in his side that he got just before she rolled on top of him. "You know better than to account women helpless, Viking. I say Kristen did the right thing, the same thing I would have done."

"Then mayhap she is not the only one who needs chastisement."

"I would advise you not to try it."

Garrick thought about it, he really did. When she challenged him like that, it raised his fighting instinct every time. But he could not see having his wife mad at him over a moot point.

" 'Tis well, then, that you were not here to take her place." And he kissed her before she could take the argument any further.

Chapter 22

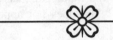

ERIKA AWOKE TO raised voices and the bright light of a new morn pushing at heavy eyelids. The voices she recognized with little difficulty—Selig's and his sister's. She had had more difficulty, though, recognizing the same sort of shouting with the addition of loud thuds when it had awakened her sometime in the middle of the night.

So much racket had occurred, she had wondered aloud, "Are we being invaded?"

She had not expected an answer, but got one, for the noise had awakened Selig, too. "Do not sound so hopeful, wench. 'Tis only Royce chasing my sister. Likely he has recalled that he owes her a beating."

Kristen would blame that on Erika, too. Another reason to hate her. But right now it seemed she was blaming it on Selig—nay, that was not what they were arguing about.

"Chains?" Kristen shouted as she paced back and forth beside the bed. "I cannot believe you would do that! And for what? She is not going anywhere."

"That is a certainty now!" he replied just as loudly in his defense, though he winced in the doing.

Kristen didn't notice the pain so much noise was causing him. She continued to make more. "Damn it, Selig, you know how I feel about them!"

"What I know is that anytime you are angry at Royce, you come to take it out on me," he complained. "Mayhap you could spare me this time, Kris."

"This has naught to do with that great lout," she insisted. "Why could you not wait until you take her to your home, so I would not have to know?"

"I do not intend to lose her because of your prejudice. If you had not been made to wear chains yourself, you would not object so strenuously to them now."

112

"But I did, and I do. If you are so worried about it, lock her up. But get rid—"

"The chains stay."

"Selig!"

"Give it up," he said adamantly. "My mind cannot be changed on this."

She let out an explosive, frustrated breath. "I wish I could hit you!"

Without heat now, seriously, he replied, "I wish you could, too."

Her demeanor changed abruptly, contritely. She bent over him, her hands to his cheeks, her brow to his brow. "I am sorry."

"I know," he said simply. "Now sit down. You have made me dizzy with all that pacing."

"Very funny." She resumed her pacing. "Very funny indeed."

His brows shot up at her sarcastic tone, which led him to make a guess. "So you did not win the argument last night?"

A curt shake of her head and a grimace. He would have laughed if he didn't think she would hit him despite her resolve not to. It was not the first time Royce had taken a hand to Kristen's backside. And she always made him suffer for it for weeks after.

"You should forgive him," he suggested. "Father would have done the same thing to you."

"Oh, shut up." Her voice was rising again. "I rescue you, and even *you* take their side."

"Truth be known, Kris, you were not necessary to my release. I will forever be grateful that you came when I needed you, but Royce could have managed it just as easily."

"Did I know that?" She was back to yelling, and he was back to wincing from it. "But I will tell you what I do know. If you had not got it into your head to go off on a lark, helping a king you are not even sworn to, none of this would have happened."

"Now, that is unfair, damn it. You were in agreement on my going."

"More fool I—"

"Your shouting is causing him pain, Lady Kristen."

They both looked toward Erika with varying degrees of disbelief. Theirs could not equal her own, though. She turned toward the wall to hide a face that must be cherry-red. How had those words escaped her mouth? She had only been thinking them. And besides, it was nothing to her if he was in pain again.

Kristen cleared her throat, glancing guiltily at Selig. "How bad is it?"

He did not answer for a moment. He was still staring in bemusement at Erika's stiff back. Loki take her, how did she dare to speak on his behalf?

"Selig?"

" 'Tis always worse in the morn," he said absently.

"Is it getting no better?"

"It is—nay, I swear it is," he added when he saw her doubting expression. " 'Tis just sudden movements and loud noises make it seem otherwise—sometimes. Not always. But maybe some quiet would be in order."

"Certainly." Kristen was nothing but solicitous now, straightening his pillows, smoothing his brow. "Rest until your meal is prepared. I will have Edith bring—"

"Nay, not her. In fact, if you would do me a service, keep her busy with other tasks. I needs must expend myself too much when she is about."

Kristen chuckled. "Poor Selig. Not feeling up to your usual seductions?"

"Teasing does not come under the heading of quiet," he grumbled.

"I suppose not." She sighed. "Very well, I will keep the wench away until you want her back. Will Eda do?"

"Your Eda will be most welcome."

The door closed a moment later. Erika did not turn around. She hoped he meant to sleep off his present pain. She hoped he would not ask why she had said what she did, because she had no answer for herself, much less for him. Most of all, she hoped he would simply ignore her today. He was good at ignoring her—when he wasn't giving her his undivided attention.

"Are you married, Erika No Heart?"

So much for hoping.

"That is not my name, and nay, I am not—though I will be soon."

Her tone dared him to deny it. For the moment he didn't bother. "Who is your betrothed?"

"I know not. My brother is arranging it. 'Tis where he went."

"You did not want to do the choosing yourself?" he asked with a degree of surprise.

"It mattered not to me. My brother loves me. He will choose well for a strong alliance. I do not expect to be disappointed."

"Yet disappointed you will be, for there will be no marriage now, will there?"

"Because you think I will never have my freedom back?" she asked.

"Even should you have it, who would believe you leave here untouched?"

"I am not known to be a liar," she said stiffly.

There was a shrug in his voice as he answered, "So say most ruined virgins who claim to be otherwise."

She sat up to glare at him. "And I will wager you have ruined your share."

"Actually, wench, virgins do not appeal to me in the least. They are tedious in their fears, clumsy in their lack of experience, and hysterical in their pain. Altogether, quite unsatisfying."

"To know that, you have had your share," she said, her tone indicating her point had just been proved.

"To know that, I have heard the complaints of many a bridegroom."

"So you say."

Who better to spy for a Saxon than a Celt, who would be less suspect if found?

I do not even speak their tongue.

So you say.

Her scoffing remark had caused him to remember those other words, and his helplessness when they had been spoken. She realized it by the sudden change in his expression, from impassive to menacing.

"That is exactly what I say." Each word came out precisely, coated in ice. "Do you dare to call me a liar—again?"

She decided on prudence, saying only, "My nature is skeptical."

He was not appeased in the least. "Your nature had best include subservience. If 'tis not ingrained, it can and will be taught."

Every instinct demanded she argue that. Self-preservation cautioned a retreat—halfway.

"The body can, of course, be forced to bend."

"You think the mind cannot? How long will the mind remain detached when the body can do naught but crawl?"

A very good point, one that had her retreating the rest of the way. Crawl? She shivered with distaste.

Selig smiled to himself when she swung around to give him her back again. She was too easy to defeat. She had pride, but it wasn't stubborn like what the women in his family possessed. He'd been wrong to think she had Kristen's spirit. Too bad. He would have liked to see her on her hands and knees, with that glorious mane of hair falling all around her.

Her hair was utterly magnificent unbound, fire-topped gold, abundantly thick, covering every inch of her back just now, and pooling on the floor at her hips. He had been mesmerized by it yesterday, when she had combed it into such luxuriant waves—just as he had been mesmerized by her body when she had stood naked in that tub.

He stiffened with the memory of that. He had assumed, mistakenly, that his hate would make him indifferent to her charms. Mayhap it would have if she didn't possess so much. Lush, plump breasts thrust high with coral nipples, a narrow, firm waist, slender arms and neck, hips perfect for grasping, and long, long legs.

She was so much taller than the Saxon wenches he had grown accustomed to. He had missed women who weren't so fragile, women with whom a man didn't have to be careful of his every caress. She had not Kristen's large-boned, sturdy strength, yet was there a compact firmness to her body that made the word "delicate" inaccurate.

Even her face, cleaned of its smudges, was more lovely than he had remembered. Gently curved brows, high cheekbones, a short, straight nose, and lips full and inviting. The chin kept her face from being too beautiful, with its strong, arrogant thrust, but the soft azure eyes could make you forget that.

He had been prepared to withstand all temptation. He had not been prepared for sultry eyes, creamy skin glistening with water and soap, and hands moving so sensually over her own curves and hollows.

The vixen. She had stirred his blood apurpose. But even knowing that, he had burned with a need to have her that was stronger than any lust he could remember. Had he been himself, in full strength, he would have acted on that need, and it infuriated him to know that. He had told himself *and* her that he would never touch her in that way, but he had counted on revulsion to see it so. Never would he have expected desire to come along instead.

Chapter 23

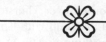

DAYS PASSED, ROLLING one into another without incident. Erika's nervousness and Selig's constant presence made the time pass swiftly, at least for her. A routine quickly developed. Ivarr would come each morn and again each night to see to her chain. He would unlatch it from the wall, but not from her neck. During the day, it had been suggested she drape it around her throat like a necklace. This she did, since it kept her from tripping on it and, surprisingly, weighed no more than a necklace would.

Kristen seemed to hate those chains more than she did. Twice more she came to argue with Selig about getting rid of them, but he could not be budged.

They are never coming off.

He did not tell his sister that, but Erika could not forget those words and how dejected they made her feel. His mother had also made comment on the chains, not with Kristen's passion, merely with curiosity. Selig had told her the same thing.

Erika could not accept his edict, not without making an effort to change it. Her fingertips were constantly sore in her attempt to at least get rid of the chain that locked her to the wall each night. No sooner would the tenderness leave than she would try again, but she never accomplished anything except more soreness.

Even the relief she had felt at being released from the wall during the day did not last long, for as freedom went, she still had none. Eda or Kristen would come by throughout the day to take her to the jakes if needed, but that was the only time she was ever allowed out of Selig's chamber—and away from his presence. That he was given even less freedom than that by his mother was not the same thing. His confinement to his bed would end just as soon as his strength returned. Hers, if Selig had his way, would not.

She didn't ask again what was going to be done with her once he had recovered. On the one hand, she welcomed the delay. On the other, she wanted it over so she would have time to recover from whatever tortures he had planned for her before her brother arrived. That was assuming, of course, that a specified amount of pain given her would be enough to satisfy Selig. There was always the possibility that he had infinite pain in mind instead.

She worried about that. She worried over Thurston and his broken arm, wondering who would coddle and love him with her not there to do it. She worried about Turgeis trying something drastic to rescue her and getting captured himself. And she worried that she could be here for months before Ragnar even learned that she had been taken.

Men would have been sent out to find him, but he had not been going to only one particular place in his search for a wife for himself and a husband for Erika. Guthrum's court would, of course, be visited. But there had also been mention of the Norwegians in the far north, and the Mercians who still retained some power in the east. Ragnar could indeed be away for several more months.

Conversing with Selig was not her idea of fun. She usually ended up angry, or more frightened. So she never started conversations with him. But at times he spoke to her out of sheer boredom, and a few of those times, he showed her that other side of him, the side all those women who adored him knew quite well.

The man could indeed be charming. He could be entertaining. He could make a woman feel special. And he could catch Erika off guard with a certain tone or look that made her heart beat faster. Fantasies are what a man like him inspired, and when she caught herself having one about him, she almost cried, but not before she imagined what it would feel like to have such powerful arms holding her with infinite care, to know the taste of that sensual mouth, to have those silver eyes tender and filled with desire for her and her alone.

Fortunately, he didn't show her enough of that other side of him to make her forget the cruel side he seemed to reserve just for her.

After a full sennight had passed, Selig began leaving his bed without his mother's knowledge. He didn't go so far as to leave the chamber, but he moved about it to work his muscles. And he would pick up Erika's chain and lead her around the room with him, using it like a leash.

"Get used to it," was all he had said to her questioning look the first time he had done it.

"To what?"

He hadn't answered, even when she had asked again. She supposed he had thought she needed the exercise as much as he. Which was in fact true. All she did was sit in her corner, hour after hour, afraid to make free use of his room without his permission, and loath to ask him for anything.

That day was the first she had ever stood next to him, to experience his full six and a half feet. She had seen him standing before, of course, but she had never been near him those times. And knowing he was tall was not the same as finding out just how tall. She was not a short woman herself, at least not in comparison to Saxon women, all of whom she stood well above. Here, only Kristen was taller than she was by a few inches, yet Selig was nearly a foot taller. And now that he was getting his strength back, that height was quite intimidating.

But the day she wasn't going to forget was when he slept, late in the afternoon, with no one there to hear his nightmare begin but her. She had been about to doze herself, the weather was so hot and muggy, with no breeze coming in through the window to relieve it.

The pain-filled moan brought her eyes wide open. She had heard nothing like it since the journey south. Often she knew when Selig's head ached, though he never made a sound. That he did now caused a certain alarm that brought her to the bed before she realized what she was doing. When it did occur to her, she turned on her heel to head back to her corner. Loki could spirit him away for all she cared. She would not lift a single finger to . . .

The low mumble halted her and brought her back to the bed. It took her but a second to see that he was not speaking to her, was sleeping and in the throes of an unpleasant dream that turned his head from side to side in some kind of denial. She started when his fist slammed against the bed. He would be thrashing about next.

She decided to wake him then, before he caused himself an injury. It wasn't that it was the decent thing to do. It wasn't that she didn't like to see anyone suffer, even him. It was that another injury would confine her still longer in this room with him. No other reason bent her over the bed to shake his shoulder.

But closer to him, she could make out the mumbling. "No more . . . no more laughter. Stop it . . . have to."

Erika stiffened with the realization that he was dreaming about her. He had promised she would never laugh again. That was his goal, to cause her such misery that she would never find joy again of any kind. But in his dream, he must not be succeeding, or he wouldn't be so distressed.

Her urge now was to let him dream on. But that wouldn't aid her if he did in fact hurt himself. So, grudgingly, with less care than before, due to the vast amount of vexation she was feeling, she shook him again and got results—of the unexpected kind.

His eyes opened, unfocused. His hand lifted to the back of her head. And before she could even gasp, she was being drawn to him and kissed.

It was like nothing she had ever experienced or ever dreamed of experiencing, the wonder of it felt clear to her toes. Gone was her vexation. There was no room for it with so many new emotions clamoring for attention. His lips brushed back and forth across hers, nudging, pulling, pressing, then opening a pathway for his tongue to enter.

Moist heat, silken-smooth, and a new swirl of sensations. Erika forgot to breathe. She also forgot about bracing herself and caved in against his chest.

That was probably what brought him to full wakefulness, because suddenly he was thrusting her away from him, and rolling back, she rolled right off the bed.

He sat up to glare down at her where she sat stunned on the floor. "By Thor's sacred hammer, what in the name of creation were you doing?"

"*Me?*" She scrambled to her feet, so indignant she could barely speak. "All I did was try to wake you. You were having a bad dream—actually, it was probably a good dream that you just did not like."

He drew the back of his hand across his mouth to add further insult to injury. "I recall no dream."

Erika didn't answer until she had likewise wiped her mouth clean of the taste of him. Then, scathingly: "Too bad."

"I warn you, wench—"

"Do not bother," she snapped. "You are at fault here, not I. And the next time you force a kiss on me, be warned—I will use my teeth."

Hot color flooded his face, he was so angry—and affronted. "You may be assured there will be no next time. I would rather kiss a pig's ass."

That turned Erika's face the same shade as his. "You remark my sentiments exactly."

He threw back his blanket to leave the bed. Erika was too furious to retreat this time. Her hands went to her hips. Her chin jutted forward. That he was wearing his braies, as he had been ever since he had begun his daily exercising earlier in the week, was a blessing, but she would not have backed down had it been otherwise.

"What occurs here?"

Erika was never to learn what might have happened. After she calmed down later, she was to be grateful for that. Just now, she and Selig both turned to find his mother standing in the open doorway. She looked none too pleased.

Selig lay back against his pillows again. "A small difference of opinion, Mother," he said on a sigh.

"Small?" She snorted. "More like loud. But I am glad to see you are able to extend yourself."

He turned onto his elbow. His hopeful look was almost comical. "My confinement is at an end, then?"

"I suppose it must be." She did not sound too pleased about that either. "Though I will allow a good deal of your weight has returned. You even look normal."

Selig grinned. "What has granted me this reprieve that you are less than happy about?"

"Word has come that the king arrives within the hour. Royce feels he will wish to speak with you about the attack on your party that lost him one of his bishops. So if you feel well enough to come down to the hall—"

"I was well enough for that last week."

"It has not been quite a fortnight, Selig. If I had my way—"

"I know, Mother," he interrupted again. He was still grinning. "And I will take an undue amount of time to dress so I do not wear myself out. Mayhap you should leave so I can begin. I am sure it will take the whole of the hour before Alfred arrives."

Her look was skeptical, but she left just the same. And Selig practically flew across the chamber to his coffer.

Erika clucked her tongue. "You should be ashamed of yourself, lying to your mother."

"Why?" he shot back, and he was *still* grinning, their own argument forgotten. "When she knows very well I will be downstairs within ten minutes. Contrary to what you think, 'tis almost impossible to fool that sweet lady."

Chapter 24

Selig had judged correctly the short time it would take for him to adorn himself, yet when he was finished, he looked as if it should have taken him hours. He was, without question, utterly magnificent. Tanned deerskin leggings were cross-gartered with black leather; the white, sleeveless tunic was cinched tight at his waist by a wide leather belt with a Norse, dragon's head buckle.

His black, soft-skinned boots were trimmed with white fur, as was the short black mantle that was pinned to his shoulders with golden clasps. His matching arm rings coiled around thick biceps with, again, dragon's heads on each end, these flashing with small ruby eyes. They fit snugly, proving solid flesh had returned to his thick arms as well as filled out his sunken belly.

Etched on the solid gold disk around his neck were three wolves progressing in size, each with rubies for eyes. The gold chain that held it was much thicker than Erika's chains, and probably twice as heavy.

His black hair, thickened and shining from a recent washing—she had had to endure yet another of his baths just that morn, though she had kept her eyes on the wall as usual—floated over his shoulders with his movements. The contrast with the white tunic was stunning.

Erika could not help staring, and forgot her resolve to avoid conversations not forced on her. "Do the wolves bear some significance to your family?" she asked him.

He didn't even glance at her as he slid a ring on his finger. Another snug fit attesting to his recovery, at least in strength.

"Nay. I merely had two as pets when I was a child," he replied.

She didn't find that so strange. She had brought a wolf cub home herself when she was eight years. Her father had forbidden her to keep it.

"Then why three on the medallion?"

"The third replaced the other two after old age took them."

"The third still lives, then?"

"Aye," he said, and came to stand in front of her. "Now unwrap your chain, wench."

She guessed his intent and objected. "You need not chain me to the wall just because you will not be here. Lock the door instead."

He smiled, that blindingly beautiful smile that warned she wouldn't like his answer. "Since when do you think the choice is yours, wench?"

This was because of the argument they had had, and that damned kiss. She knew it was.

"Nay, you are wrong." He was back to reading minds—or expressions. "You come below with me."

It was the last thing she had expected to hear from him. "To the hall?"

"Aye."

A small bit of freedom, however temporary. It was a reward, so she ought to distrust it. She was too delighted to be suspicious.

She unwrapped her "necklace" and handed the end to him. He didn't take it, reached for the other end at her neck instead. The weight was gone in a second, without any exertion on his part.

"So your strength has returned completely." Her remark came out almost breathlessly.

"Not quite, but enough," he replied, his pleasure so very obvious.

And in the next instant, the chain was attached again to her neck ring. She understood then that he had only been testing his ability to open and close the locking link himself so that Ivarr would no longer have to come each day to do it.

Her disappointment was palpable, making her barely notice that his hand slid down the chain, knocking hers off in the process, until he reached the end, which he wrapped around his fist. He left the room then, pulling her along behind him.

She didn't bother to protest, at least not until they had reached the stairs. When he started down them, still with her chain in his hand, she drew back, stretching it taut between them.

"You can release the chain now. I—"

He turned, lifting a brow at her. "Did I not warn you to get used to this?"

She frowned. "I do not understand."

"You thought you would have the same pain I was given, Erika No Heart?" The smile again—the warning. "Nay, I could not do that to a woman, even you. There are other ways, such as the pain of humiliation and shame." He yanked, and she stumbled down the steps, nearly into him. "Do not lag behind again."

Not torture, but torture nonetheless. So now she knew her fate, what he had intended all along. No normal revenge. Nothing so simple as that for her. Just shame and degradation at every turn, until her pride became a meaningless thing. She would rather have had the physical pain, but the choice was not offered to her. He had made up his mind— Nay, she would not be defeated by this. He could force humiliation on her, but she wasn't going to hand over her pride to him. She would retain it, somehow.

He continued down the stairs. Though she loathed doing it, she stayed so close to him that there could be no question in anyone's mind but that she followed him willingly, making it appear ridiculous, his holding of her "leash."

Color still flooded her cheeks, uncontrollably, as soon as they became visible to the hall. But her head remained high. And she did not avoid eye contact with anyone, including his family, who awaited him at a grouping of tables near a mammoth keg of ale.

Lady Brenna looked on in disapproval. Kristen was even more tight-lipped, actually outraged. Lord Royce was amused. And Selig's father showed no expression at all. He rarely did when he looked at her.

As for the rest of the people in the hall who stopped what they were doing to follow their progress, Erika had to console herself that, being so close to Selig's magnificence, she would be all but invisible herself, especially in the drab servant's clothes she had been given to wear. The dun-gray chainse was inches too short, revealing clearly the shackles at her ankles. It was also much too tight for her ample breasts, though that tightness was hidden by the brown outer gown that was much too loose, and belted with a strip of rope.

He led her directly to that leisure area where his family waited. All were sitting except Garrick, who, with one foot set upon the end of a bench, stood with his elbows braced against his thigh. Selig, as casually as if he had been there earlier and was now returning—alone—sat on the bench opposite them. Given no specific instruction, Erika remained standing stiffly at his back.

Kristen stood up as he sat down, probably because the glare she was giving him was much more effective from a superior height. "This is intolerable, Selig," she began.

"No inquiry after my health, sister?"

She actually seemed to swallow whatever she had been about to add, to say instead, gritting out every word, "Is your pain gone?"

"Mostly."

Her hands slammed against the table as she leaned forward. "Then I repeat, this is intolerable, and do not ask me *what*, you brainless jackdaw, for you know very well. Do you mean to draw her to the king's notice?"

That got her an unconcerned shrug. " 'Tis not unusual to see a slave enchained."

Erika flinched at that and turned aside so she might not hear more. But whatever Selig added was in Celtic, which Kristen also switched to. Since Erika understood none of it, she ignored them for the moment.

"A male slave, mayhap not," Kristen was agreeing. "But the last female chained here was myself. And even should Alfred not notice her, what is to stop her from requesting aid of him? And do not think he would not listen to a Dane. He would *especially* listen to a Dane."

Royce eagerly joined the argument at that point. Because Kristen had not quite forgiven him for the spanking she had received, and because he had been given more cold shoulders than his passionate nature could tolerate comfortably, it behooved him to take her side in this. That her reasoning was valid was less important.

"She is right," he told his brother-in-law. "Alfred could well ask you to release the lady. And 'tis not wise to refuse a king without excellent reason."

"My reason would be sound," Selig insisted.

"As unfair as it might seem, kings do not consider revenge reasonable."

"Particularly when the peace of their realms could be threatened by it," Kristen added.

"And they do not like losing able-bodied men to personal wars," Royce added still more, "when they need those men for their own."

The argument continued apace. Brenna saw no need to join it. Neither did Garrick, so he took the opportunity to move to Erika's side.

"So he has made a pet slave of you?"

The word "pet" was even more galling than "slave" to Erika, for that was exactly what Selig was doing, treating her like an animal, a *pet* for his amusement, a creature not violent or dangerous, but one too dumb to be allowed out without the guidance of a leash.

It was the first time Selig's father had spoken to her, though he had visited Selig in his chamber quite often. She wondered now if he was as bad as the son, to point out her humiliating position. His expression told her nothing, was still unreadable.

"He thinks he has enslaved me."

Her answer caused Garrick to laugh softly. "Those were my wife's sentiments exactly. She would never admit I owned her either."

Erika was incredulous. Both mother *and* daughter at one time enslaved by the men they had married? It was no wonder the idea had come to Selig so readily. He was merely following family tradition.

The thought was a chilling one, but at least she would not end up like his mother and sister, wed to her captor. There was as much chance of that happening as there was of her gaining her freedom within the hour. None.

"But soon it was she who owned me, heart and soul." Garrick was still reminiscing. "Do you know how it was done, wench?"

"I care not—"

"With an indomitable will and pride that would not bend. She was fire in a land of ice, with a warrior's heart—and a warrior's skill. She captured my admiration first, then my heart. Will your pride bend?"

She really wished he had kept his silence where she was concerned. "Nay," she said stiffly. "But for myself, not to impress him."

"Your anger is understandable."

"Anger is but a small part of what I feel toward your son," she informed him.

His gaze turned thoughtful. " 'Tis regrettable, his treatment of you—and unusual."

"You mean he does not enslave every woman who has him lashed?"

"Do not be flip with me, child," he admonished gently. "What I meant was, he has never hurt a woman in his life. He adores them."

"Except me."

"Except you," he agreed.

She thought the conversation had ended. The argument still raged behind her. But Garrick did not step away from her just yet.

After a few moments of uncomfortable silence, he remarked, "My daughter is quite fierce in her championing of your cause."

Erika snorted at that. She couldn't help it. "Your daughter would not lift a finger to help me. She merely detests the sight of these chains."

"Do not be too sure of Kristen's motives. Selig's behavior has her baffled."

"But not you?"

"Not completely."

"You imply that men understand revenge much better than women? I doubt that."

"So now you hunger for revenge as well?"

Erika was surprised, not at the question, but at her answer. "I have not once thought of revenge. Freedom is all I think of. But I suppose eventually I will also think of revenge."

"Then let us hope you have your freedom before then," he said.

More surprise, much stronger. "You do not condone what he does?"

" 'Tis not in his nature to be cruel or abusive. This is what has his sister baffled. What I feel is that he will come to regret what he is doing."

"You could insist he end it."

He smiled at her, not unkindly. "If you have not noticed, Erika of Gronwood, my son is of an age where he no longer must heed his father. I can do no more than advise him."

"Will you?"

"Not about you. My wife and I have decided not to interfere."

Another brief span of hope most thoroughly crushed. Bitterly, Erika turned her back on him to face the rest of the family again. But the rest of the family was no longer there. Only Selig and Royce remained, and Selig had swung around on his bench to watch her—and had likely heard a good deal of what had been said.

Her chin lifted a notch in defiance, only to feel the tug on her neck that pulled her slowly forward. He was winding the chain around his fist. If he continued, he would have her bent over him again. He didn't go quite that far, but she was now so close to him, he had to look up at her. He didn't seem to mind that.

Behind him on the table, she noted that someone had brought him a trencher of food, though it was not near to the dinner hour. The man had had enough food in the past fortnight to feed an army, and the women of this hall were still determined to fatten him more. She began to wonder just how large a man he had been before that head injury.

"You may sit here beside me to eat if you are ready to call me master."

Her eyes came back to him and narrowed. "That is not what I would call you."

He grinned to show he didn't mistake her meaning. "Then you can eat from my hand, at my feet."

She was surprised he did not add, "Like a dog." "I will not eat at all, thank you."

"I think you will. Food is necessary to your continued health, which I mean to maintain. Clothes, on the other hand, are not."

Every last bit of color fled her face. He would do it. He would strip her naked before all these people. How better to humiliate her utterly, and that was what he was striving for, after all.

But her mood was not very tractable at the moment, possibly because she was certain it would come to this eventually, no matter what she did. He would see to that. So now or later, what difference?

"Do as you will," she said with as much nonchalance as she could manage.

"I intend to, wench, exactly what I will."

He laughed, noting her stiffness and that she was braced for the worse. It was more than satisfaction, having this advantage over her. The pleasure he felt was so great, it was almost sexual. He would not lose it due to a disagreement with a king.

"But for today," he continued, "you are reprieved from deciding your own fate. My sister has convinced me it would not be in my best interest to introduce you to the Saxon king. We will have to wait until he departs to find out if you will eat from my hand—or call me master."

Erika hoped the king moved his court to Wyndhurst and stayed indefinitely. What she had to face when he left was intolerable.

Chapter 25

FOR THE NEXT two days, Erika was left alone more than not. She didn't mind that, even though her movements were restricted to her corner of Selig's chamber. He had not only locked the door that day he had returned her abovestairs just before the king's arrival, he had also chained her to the wall. He was taking no chances during his absence. And the same was done each day since.

It amused her that he must think she would try to break her neck crawling out the window. Or mayhap he thought she would try to drown herself in the tub of dirty water that had gone unemptied, the servants were so busy with the royal guests. And those royal guests . . .

Three times, women had come scratching at the door, Saxon ladies by the sound of them, each in search of Selig, who must have momentarily left the hall to make them think he had come up here. Erika wondered how many other times he had entertained court ladies in this chamber, for those three to find it so unerringly. And where was he entertaining them now, with his chamber already occupied, and no doubt every other chamber as well?

Eda came as usual with food, and now with a chamber pot, since she could not release the chain from the wall any more than Erika could, and Selig was rarely there to do it. The old servant no longer looked at her with the disapproval she had first displayed. Her gaze had become more in the way of pitying, which Erika did not exactly appreciate.

She *was* going to be freed from this predicament. It was just a matter of time. And since she had yet to succumb to self-pity, she wanted none from anyone else.

Yesterday, Eda had chatted amiably about the king and his courtiers, expecting no response from Erika and getting none. Apparently Alfred was traveling lightly, not with his full court, and was expected to move on in a few days—which wasn't pleasant news for Erika.

Today, however, Eda didn't just chat to hear herself talk. For the first time she got personal, and surprised Erika with the remark, "You cannot imagine how much you remind me of my Kristen—except she was a fighter."

Erika could not remain silent after that. "Meaning I am not?"

"You make no complaints, lady. You let that rascal have his way."

Erika was incredulous. "I do not see how I am to stop him."

"Do you not? My Lord Royce was a much harder man. He lost half his family in a Viking attack. But Kristen brought him around. And she got him to unchain her simply because he knew she hated those chains. Does Selig know you hate them, or do you let him think you do not care?"

Erika had taken just that approach, but explained herself defensively. "Selig wants revenge on me. It would delight him to know I hate the chains."

Eda snorted. "Revenge is new to that young man. I doubt me he knows what he wants. But 'tis a lady's man you do war with. He lives to please women. Hurting them is alien to him. If he thought he was actually hurting you, I wonder how much longer the hurt would continue."

After Eda left, Erika spent a long while considering what had been said. Hurting women might be alien to Selig, but he was learning quick enough how to go about it—nay, that was unfair. Not once, actually, had Erika been hurt by him. A few raw scrapes that she had caused herself did not count. Nor the few blisters on her feet that had bled and might have been prevented if she could have unbent enough to ask for her shoes. And the blow to her cheek had not been his fault, had in truth been stopped by him.

A great deal of embarrassment was all she had suffered at his hands— and the loss of her freedom, which would in fact hurt quite seriously if she didn't get it back. But what did that say for Selig? Was Eda right? Would his campaign of revenge end if he thought he was doing her serious harm? If she cried, if she whined and complained . . .

Erika's cheeks pinkened merely at the thought. She couldn't do those things—not unless she had no other hope. Her pride simply wouldn't unbend that much.

And she *did* have hope, her brother. She would ride away from this place and never see these people again, never be reminded of the humiliations she had suffered here, never— That was not quite true. How was she going to forget a man like Selig Haardrad when she could picture him so clearly in her mind, he might as well be standing before her? And she was afraid that image was not going to fade for many a year.

The object of nearly all of her thoughts lately joined her early that afternoon, and he was wearing the smile she had learned to dread. The first thing he did was release her from the wall, but he didn't give her the chain as he usually did. He drew her up with it instead.

"You are in luck, wench," Selig said, humor in his tone. "That matter you and I have to settle need not wait until Alfred departs."

Erika groaned inwardly, fully aware of what matter he spoke of. "Why not?"

"Royce has taken the king and his party hunting. They will be away for several hours at the least. Only a few lords remain behind, and most of the ladies."

"Why did you not join the hunt? Or have you overtaxed yourself with the revelries below?"

"How hopeful you sound, yet I fear I must disappoint you," he replied, trying for an apologetic tone, though he couldn't quite manage it. "I simply preferred to spend the time . . . with you."

"The feeling is, of course, not mutual."

He laughed. He was in splendid good cheer and brimming with anticipation. And she knew just what he anticipated. He would not even care which answer she gave him. Either one would suit his purpose.

"You have had ample time to dwell on my ultimatum—"

"I have not thought of it at all," she cut in quickly with the lie.

But procrastination was not going to work. "How unfortunate, yet not really necessary," he took pleasure in telling her. "Little thought is required to decide if you will call me master—or not. Wear no more than your chains—or not. Which do you choose, Erika No Heart?"

"Neither."

"You think to feed from my hand, at my feet? I no longer offer you that choice now. Mayhap some other time, but not right now."

"And I accept none of what you do offer."

"On the contrary. I would say you have made your choice quite clearly."

Erika took a step back from him in denial, but the chain wouldn't let her go very far, and he simply used it to pull her close again.

Her voice rose, measured by her alarm. "I said I do not accept your ridiculous choices."

He replied in a tone one might reserve for slow-witted children. "But you were not given that option. You must abide those you were given, and as you have already decided the matter—"

"I did not!"

"Then I beg your pardon. I could have sworn I did not hear the name 'master' come from your lips. I will allow I was mistaken, if you will but repeat it now."

In answer, her lips compressed so tightly they whitened. He wasn't displeased to see that, though. Quite the contrary. He laughed.

"Nay?" He said it for her. "Then it seems I was correct the first time. You have decided to flaunt what meager charms you have for all to see. I am sure those left in the hall will find the spectacle most amusing. You may remove your clothing now."

If he was trying to make her "supposed" choice sound the worst of two evils, he was succeeding admirably. She detested the way he toyed with her, and that he took such pleasure in it. But Erika was not going to concede graciously or otherwise this time.

"I have no intention of amusing anyone," she said stonily, "least of all you. If you have not noticed, lackwit, I am not cooperating."

He seemed surprised, as if he really hadn't anticipated refusal. Certainly he was not amused. His sudden frown might be feigned, but she doubted it.

"Flagrant defiance?"

She nodded. "This is your idea, not mine. You want my clothes off, you must take them yourself. But do not expect me to stand here meekly the while you do."

The frown only lasted a few moments more, before it was erased with the rumble of a deep chuckle. "I am likely more adept at it than you anyway. But come, you are at a disadvantage, all enchained. Give me your wrists and I will release you."

Fairness? From him? She should have been immediately suspicious, *was* suspicious, but the lure of freedom was too great a temptation to ignore. And he had already produced a key, which he held out toward her. Mayhap he really did want more of a challenge, now that his damned game was to become physical. Either way, it would indeed be to her advantage not to be so encumbered.

She thrust her wrists out. Too late did she realize that her gowns would not come off without being cut off unless at least one of her wrists was freed. But before she jerked her hands back, one shackle was off and dangling from the other. And his expression said exactly what she now surmised. His trick had worked, and it had indeed been a trick.

To show her appreciation, she swung the loose shackle at his head. As a weapon, it was more than adequate. Her skill in using it, however, was not. Selig ducked right handily and caught the wrist that was still chained, bringing it up behind her back.

This, unfortunately, put her within easy reach of him, and while she was trying to push him away with her freed hand, to no avail, he was working the knot on her rope girdle loose with his own free hand. He succeeded where she did not, and before he let go of her, he caught a fistful of her outer gown and yanked upward. As loose as that gown was, the material rose without a hitch—until it encountered Erika's arms, which refused to rise with it.

For a moment she thought she might have defeated him, but he didn't force the matter, content to leave her buried and helpless beneath the outer gown that now hung over her head, while he went after the laces on the tighter chainse beneath. With her arms now trapped, her face covered by material, she shrieked in rage, and tried to twist away from him. An arm around her waist prevented that. So she fought to at least get her arms loose in order to do some damage. But she no sooner got the material back down from her face than the other gown started to rise.

It was infuriating that she was getting nowhere, even with her hands freed of restraint. She tried locking her arms against her sides again, but he merely reached in to grab one wrist, then the other, pulling them both over her head where he could hold them together long enough for the gowns to follow, and follow they did. There was a moment when the loose shackle got caught in the sleeve of her chainse, but one last yank saw to its release.

She had been given no shift to wear with her slave's clothes, no braies or stockings. That easily was she left naked. But embarrassment didn't touch her yet. Her anger was still too high, and since her chained feet made it impossible for her to run, she attacked again instead.

It was, of course, a useless endeavor against a man his size. He didn't feel her punches, merely stood there and raised a brow at her when she tried it twice. She began to wonder how a blow to his head had ever caused him pain. But when she made to swing the shackle at him again, he stopped toying with her and ended her efforts right quickly.

Again her arm was twisted up behind her back, though this time he had no girdle to free. This time she was pressed tight to the front of him. And with her being so close, it was a simple matter for his other hand to follow her free arm down from the shoulder to her wrist, no matter her effort to shake it loose. That arm, too, ended up behind her back.

But when his other hand left her wrist to slide slowly down the chain still attached to it, her eyes widened, for she realized what he meant to do. And he did it, the shackle closing around her free wrist again, the sound of it locking bringing a shudder to her.

He let go of her then, but the length of the chain behind her wouldn't let her arms come forward farther than her sides. She was exposed, completely, helpless even to shield her breasts with her hands. This was how he meant to parade her before a hall filled with women who would take pleasure in seeing a Dane brought so low?

Her pride was momentarily in shock, long enough for him to lead her by her "leash" from the room without any protest from her. Not that protest would have done her any good, and she didn't even consider trying it when the horror of this latest humiliation at his hands subsided somewhat. What was left was anger worse than any she had so far felt.

They had not yet reached the stairs when she acquainted him with it. "Cowardly knave. Swinish oaf. Diseased scum of a trickster!"

He had already swung around, towered over her before the last word was out, and his face was flushed with some anger of his own. "On your knees when you call me names," he ordered in a growl.

Without the least hesitation, she dropped to her knees, leaned forward, and sank her teeth into his right thigh. Selig howled. Bending over her was his first reflex, but before the second took hold, he lost his balance. He grabbed her shoulders to keep from falling, but that only shoved her back and he ended up sprawling on top of her.

The breath was knocked from her for a moment. When she had it back, she made to shove him off her, only to have it recalled that her hands were no longer available for such use, were locked to the floor by her hips. She used what was left to her, her shoulders, her hips. That was a mistake.

She finally noticed that he was making no effort to move, was simply staring down at her. Lying on top of a naked woman might not have stoked his fires, but her own movements to dislodge him had done so. It was there in the intense smoldering of his gray eyes, and in what she could feel hardening near the apex of her thighs.

In a panic, she got out, "Recall that you hate me!" just before his mouth closed on hers.

His hate, apparently, didn't come into this. This was elemental, arousal overruling other emotions. She was made to understand that more clearly when some of that same desire clouded her own thinking.

The man simply surpassed proficiency when it came to kissing. He licked, he nibbled, he sucked, and his tongue plunged. And for a girl who knew next to nothing about it, Erika was overwhelmed by such expertise. Nor did he just kiss her. Mayhap she could have come to her senses otherwise—nay, she was beyond denial, and what else he did merely made it worse.

He had total access to the parts most intimate on her body, and as if they had a will of their own, his hands were drawn to some of them. Both hands slid between their bodies to flatten over her breasts. Both squeezed, both plumped, both found the nipples and plucked them to hardness. The shock was felt clear to her toes. She moaned into his mouth. His own groan was louder.

Neither heard the approaching footsteps, but the dry tone was quite clear. "I suppose you will tell me that the time you have spent in your bed these last weeks has given you an aversion to it."

Selig's new groan was unrelated to passion. "Mother, go . . . away."

Even more dryness. "You mean you did not want an audience? You could have fooled me."

"Mother!"

A sound of disgust greeted that entreaty, then footsteps again, now receding.

Selig sighed and dropped his forehead to Erika's. It took a moment for him to realize that he had relaxed against her; then he stiffened and leaned back. She was already as rigid as the floor beneath her. Ironically, his face was as hot as hers with embarrassment right now. She couldn't quite find any justice or humor in that.

"She did not see you," he offered for some reason she could not fathom.

"What matter if she did?" Erika replied bitterly. "You are the one who would find shame in that. Mine was there before her appearance."

He glowered at her for a moment before he shoved himself to his feet, drawing her up with him by her collar ring. He didn't take the chain that hung down between her breasts, other than to drape it once around her neck so she wouldn't trip on it.

"To bite a man's leg is to invite what you got," he said stiffly.

"Put me to my knees again, and I will see if I can aim for a different part of you."

His face got a little hotter, as did his anger. "You were like a bitch in heat," he reminded her.

"And you desired a woman you profess to hate!" she shot back.

It wasn't the wisest thing to do, to taunt him with his own shame. His finger went back through her collar ring to lift her until their noses almost touched.

In a low, menacing voice he said, "I do despise you, wench, never doubt it. I despise you and the ice that runs through your veins." And then he smiled nastily. "Except it runs hot when a man touches you, does it not?"

She should be grateful he had merely thrown the same taunt back at her. She was still too angry for gratitude—or to retreat.

"At least I do not make excuses, or place the blame elsewhere."

He let go of her with a slight shove, saying in a barely controlled hiss, "Return to my chamber, wench. I will send Eda to assist you. Your excursion below can wait for another day."

"When your mother will not be certain it was I you were rutting with?"

She didn't wait to see if *that* barb drew blood. And in fact, she did leave him there seething—and still so aroused he ached with it. He stayed there for several minutes, trying to gather some calm. It wouldn't come. And it wasn't toward the stairs that he finally headed.

He came to the open doorway—she had been unable to close it herself when she entered—to see her sitting in her corner, her head bent to her upraised knees so that her hair cloaked most of her nakedness. The sight of her dejected pose so affected him, he kicked the doorframe, then swore viciously because he was wearing his soft-skinned boots today. How did she dare make him feel sorry for her at the same time that his passions were aroused?

He had drawn her attention. There weren't tears in the powder-blue eyes that looked toward him, but the fire of her anger was no longer there to sustain his. Misery was what he saw, or thought he saw, and he had never been able to witness it in women without wanting to rid them of it. He left before he did something stupid, like comfort this one.

Chapter 26

IT HAD BEEN too much to hope that his mother would keep to herself what she had seen in the upstairs hall. Not long after the men returned from the hunt, Selig's father was lifting his brow at him and shaking his head, and Royce laughed outright when their eyes met.

At least he was certain they didn't know whom he had lost his head over, which would have made his embarrassment much worse. But he was sure his own body had blocked Erika from his mother's sight.

It was time he moved into his own home, and not because he required more privacy. Wyndhurst was simply too crowded right now, and he had recovered enough that he was definitely in need of a woman. What had happened with the Dane was proof of that. But with the rest of his family visiting, there wasn't an empty room to be found in which a man might dally undisturbed—even his own.

He could, of course, move his captive elsewhere for the time being. There was no specific purpose why she must be kept in his own chamber, except that that was where he wanted her to be—and for some reason, he slept peacefully with her near. Even the return of his carnal appetites didn't take precedence over that.

He could blame that return on what had happened with the Dane, however, and on the fact that he hadn't had a woman since he had left for East Anglia. But what could explain his insistence on stripping her bare, when the last time he had seen her thusly had warned him not to do so again?

He had known it would come to that. He had known her pride wouldn't let her utter the word "master." And he had known what it would do to him to see her like that again. Certainly it would have been a fine revenge—if it wouldn't have affected him personally.

So why had he done it, looked forward to it, enjoyed it more than warranted? For that matter, with so many lovely ladies in the king's party to draw his interest, why had it been so difficult for him to stay away from his own chamber these past days?

Obviously, this revenge business was consuming too much of his energy. He was becoming obsessive about it—and her. But he derived such pleasure from having Erika of Gronwood in his power, having her at hand to bedevil, seeing her eyes flash with impotent fury. What had happened in the hall with her was unrelated to that. What had happened in the hall shouldn't have happened, wouldn't happen again.

He needed to return to his own home, where he had other things to occupy his mind—the new slaves to train, defenses to begin building now that the house was complete. He would make the announcement on the morrow, and withstand all objections from the females in his family—somehow.

Which was what he would have done if Ragnar Haraldsson had not arrived late that afternoon.

Word was brought immediately to Royce of the Danish army amassing before his gates. Unfortunately, the man who brought the information was in something of a panic and simply blurted it out, where those closest could hear. Only Kristen was at Royce's table at the moment—along with the king.

Alfred rose abruptly at the news. Royce had to quickly assure him, "They are not here for you, my lord. This was anticipated. They are here for the lady my wife captured for her brother."

"Her brother?" Alfred looked to where Selig was being entertained across the hall, with a bevy of women vying for his attention. "That handsome wretch who has seduced every woman in my court?"

Royce could not quite keep his grin back. Alfred was only a couple of years older than Selig, which was to say he was young enough to appreciate the ladies—and be a bit envious of the kind of success Selig was accustomed to.

"I doubt me he has gotten to *every* one," Royce commented dryly.

"I would not wager on that," Kristen said beneath her breath, so as not to draw notice. She imagined her husband was not going to be too pleased with her right now for bringing this new dilemma upon them.

Alfred was merely perplexed. "For what conceivable reason would he need a woman captured for him, when anyone with eyes can behold how they fall at his feet in droves? Is she that beautiful?"

Royce could see that Alfred's interest was piqued by that thought, so he quickly disabused him. "She is no more than average in prettiness. She was not taken for what you are thinking, but for revenge."

Royce briefly explained the circumstances as he knew them. Kristen relaxed somewhat, for she didn't come out sounding quite so foolish and irresponsible for her part in it, at least not as much as Royce had made her feel when they had discussed the matter themselves.

He finished the tale with, "If you will excuse me now, my lord, I will see what can be done to send these Danes home again."

"You had better hope you have enough silver on hand," Alfred warned. " 'Tis the first thing those greedy bastards always demand."

Alfred ought to know. He had depleted the royal coffers enough times to meet the exorbitant Danegeld prices demanded of him to get the Danes out of Wessex in the past. But Royce didn't intend to deplete his own store for his brother-in-law. Whatever Danegeld had to be paid, if any did, Selig could pay it.

He had not quite reached the entrance to the hall when he noted that his wife was close on his heels. Without stopping or glancing back at her, he demanded, "And where do you think you go?"

Kristen came up beside him, but also refrained from looking at him. "With you, of course."

"Nay, you will not."

That adamant reply had her tugging on his arm to stop him so she could point out, "You do not speak Danish, Royce. Nor do you wish to speak directly to a Dane, even if you could. You would sooner draw your sword. I will interpret for you. 'Tis the least I can do."

His brow lifted at that last comment. "Do you finally admit you may have made a mistake?"

"If I did not take her when I did, Selig would have gone back for her later. Either way, he would have ended up with her, or died in the trying. Nay, I do not regret my own actions. Better we have her here behind these walls, giving us the upper hand."

His arms crossed his chest in one of his more superior stances. "Upper hand? When we are about to be besieged?"

She grinned at him. "Think you I do not know you have already made allowances for that? And if 'tis necessary, we can always threaten the lady's life to get them to depart. It worked before."

"With mere soldiers, aye. But a bluff may not work on her brother."

"I was not bluffing before."

"Because you were in a rage at the time," he reminded her. "But you would not kill her now any more than I would—any more than Selig would."

Kristen shrugged, acquiescing to that. "Why do we not find out what sort of man we have to deal with before we discuss our own options? Ragnar

Haraldsson could be a complete idiot for all we know, and easily bought off with a few coins or promises. After all, he has ridden into Wessex with an army. If that was not a stupid thing to do—"

"Stupid or in deadly earnest—just as you were when you took an army into East Anglia."

Kristen flushed at *that* pointed reminder. But they continued, through the bailey and up the stairs to the wooden walk built along the length of the stone walls. The captain of the guard already had the parapet fully manned with all weapons at the ready. It was merely a formality, for it was highly unlikely there would be fighting today. Sunset was approaching. Even the initial communications might be put off until the morrow.

The Danes were boldly setting up camp just beyond firing range. From what Kristen could see, they had come prepared for any eventuality, and she estimated that there were some hundred and fifty of them, with as many mounts. Royce could surpass that number, at least in men. But not all would be seasoned fighters as these Danes were guaranteed to be.

Whatever happened, she could not let it come to fighting. If she had to sit on Selig until he agreed to give back the woman, she would. Of course, she would take his side for as long as she was able to. She was not going to give up his prisoner unless it was absolutely necessary.

She scanned the front lines to see if she could figure out which of the large Vikings was Erika's brother. Her eyes fell on Turgeis instead, unmistakable among the others.

"I see her shadow is still around," she remarked, not really surprised to see it so.

"Her what?"

"That is what she calls that giant, Turgeis Ten Feet, who is never far from where she is." She pointed him out in the center of the line. "Look there."

Royce did. "Impressive."

Kristen snorted, remembering how the man looked when you stood on the ground next to him. "You would not think so if you had to fight him."

"So which one is the brother?"

"Mayhap the one arguing with Turgeis. Who else would dare?"

Royce chuckled. Kristen was glad he could find something amusing in this, because she could not.

Chapter 27

THREE RODE FORWARD toward the closed gate. Turgeis Ten Feet was one. The sight of his oversized ax, strung across his back, gave Kristen chills. They would have no need of a battering ram. She imagined that ax alone could shatter their wooden gate if the giant was wielding it.

She decided Ragnar was the one in the middle, though the helmet he wore kept her from seeing his features. Large he was and finely honed by war, but she was pleased to note that her brother was much larger. Selig could take him with ease—if he were fully recovered. Unfortunately, he might be behaving normally again, but that did not mean he was ready for mortal combat.

The horses stopped. Two of the men removed their helmets, tucking them beneath thick arms. Turgeis had not worn one, nor chain mail, like his companions.

"I am Ragnar Haraldsson."

Kristen had picked him accurately. A handsome man with gold hair tinged with red, and azure eyes—just like his sister.

"We know who you are," she called down to him. "I am Kristen of Wyndhurst."

"Aye, we know who you are as well, lady."

There was anger in his tone now, just for her, and it sounded new. She wondered if she had Turgeis to thank for that and decided she did. It was likely he had recounted what had happened outside Gronwood's gates word for word, deed for deed, whereas before Ragnar arrived, he probably had only a sketchy telling from those left behind.

"Does my sister still live?"

The question might have surprised her moments ago, but didn't now. And mayhap Turgeis had done them a favor by convincing his lord that she was as bloodthirsty as any man. It certainly couldn't hurt for him to think so if it came down to bluffing.

"Your sister enjoys good health—for the time being."

Thank God Royce could not understand her, for he would be yanking her up by the neck and shaking her for what was, in fact, a subtle threat. Ragnar, on the other hand, appeared to have expected no less.

He merely said, "I would see her."

"If you are willing to come alone, you may enter our gates. Otherwise, you must take my word for it that she has come to no harm here."

He was not pleased at all with that answer. "Where is your husband, that I might speak with him?"

"My Lord Royce stands beside me. Speak to him if you know Saxon. If not, you must speak through me."

He liked that answer even less. "You know why I am come, lady. You had no right to take my sister."

Her voice rose to more equal his. "Rights? You want to discuss rights? Firstly, my brother was on a mission for King Alfred to your king. He was sorely injured on the way and came to your Gronwood for aid. There he was accused of spying. The truth he offered was disbelieved. And he was lashed. With a raging fever and already in severe pain, he was lashed. He has the right to demand retribution for that, and your sister will answer to him for it."

"I have it from her man, Turgeis, that the lashing was ordered in anger because this Selig insulted her. I also have it from him that she was about to cancel the order when my son broke his arm and drew her attention to him instead. She made a mistake, but your brother made it first by trying to treat her as a common wench instead of the *jarl*'s daughter she is. I will not have her suffer for a mistake."

Kristen had heard from Royce about the "anger" that was supposedly responsible for the lashing. But she was to believe that lashing would not have occurred if Erika had not had her attention drawn elsewhere? When it took only a few words, given to any passing servant, to end or delay an order? She didn't think so.

And Ragnar's story did not account for the lady's laughter, which Selig clearly recalled. The amusement she had found in his suffering. She had to have been there to see it, which meant Ragnar was either misinformed by Turgeis or lying himself to save his sister. Kristen could not fault him for that, since she would have done the same thing. That it wouldn't work was because she was aware of more facts than he.

For his effort, she gave him a tight little smile that he could interpret as he would. "When my brother is satisfied that your sister has paid all she owes him, then will she be sent home."

"If all he wants is money—"

"He will not accept money."

There was a long silence while he considered the implication of that. "He has raped her?"

"If she is no longer a maiden, 'tis her own doing and no fault of ours."

"You are saying she is not?"

"I am saying I saw no reason to ask her if she is or is not, so how would I know? But she will not depart here without his leave, and he is not ready to give it."

Ragnar's horse reared, sensing his fury and frustration. "Lady, that is unacceptable. Send him out. I challenge him now."

"He is not recovered enough yet to accept any challenges. But I am the one who took her for him," Kristen reminded him. "Do you want to fight me?"

"From you I will have Danegeld for your temerity. From the one you took her for, I will have his life."

"If he is willing to fight you once he is well, so be it. But that will not be for some time yet. You might as well return to—"

"I will fight him now," Selig said behind her.

Kristen whirled around to block him from mounting the last few steps to the platform, silently cursing whoever had informed him that the Danes were here. And she did not quibble words. "Do you have your full strength back?"

"Enough of it—"

"But not all. And do not tell me you no longer suffer those headaches, because I know otherwise."

"This is not debatable," Selig insisted.

"Aye, you have that right. You will *not* accept the man's challenge unless he is willing to wait until you are fully recovered."

He understood her concern and loved her for it, but in this she could not interfere. "Kris, you have no say in this, so move aside."

When she did not, he leaned forward, caught her hand, and hefted her over his shoulder so he could mount the last few steps and put her aside. He then turned immediately to look down on the Danes—and started swearing when his eyes locked on Ragnar Haraldsson.

Ragnar was able to see Selig now as well and shouted up, "You!"

Selig turned his back on the Danes to face the hall. He was still softly cursing when he noticed the window to his chamber and saw Erika standing there, where she could see at least half of the army that had come for her. He had not rechained her to the wall. He should have.

"He sounds as if he knows you," Royce said quietly beside him.

Selig's voice was rife with exasperation. "Indeed he does. He is the Dane who saved my life when he mistook me for one of the Danish horde that your Saxons finally routed."

"I recall how amused you were afterward, though no less grateful," Royce replied, only to add what he and Kristen were both now thinking. "If you owe the man a debt, you can repay it by returning his sister."

"Nay!" Selig said emphatically and started back down the stairs. "I owe him, not her. And I will repay him by not fighting him." And then he swore yet again. "Thor's teeth, why did *he* have to be her brother?"

"Splendid," Royce mumbled as he turned toward his wife, who was still staring after her brother, a bit disconcerted by the irony none of them had been expecting. "So now we have a standoff."

"Mayhap not," she said and leaned over the wall again to tell the waiting Ragnar, "Selig is as surprised as you must be, Lord Ragnar, that you two should meet again this way. He acknowledges the debt he owes you, and because of it, will not fight you."

"There is no debt owing from deceit," Ragnar refuted angrily. "Never would I have aided him had I known he was my enemy. Now, either he accepts my challenge, or he sends out my sister."

Kristen was distinctly uncomfortable with the answer she must give to that. Her entire family had reason to be grateful to this man, whether he wanted that gratitude or not. And this was no way to show it. She had a strong desire to kick her dear brother.

"I am sorry," she finally said, and she meant it. "He still means to keep her—for the while."

"And I do not leave here without her. You want a siege, you shall have one." And he jerked his mount around to ride back to his men.

Kristen's expression was pure vexation. "Notice he left before I could make some threats of my own."

Royce frowned at her. "What threats?"

She sighed. "It matters not now."

"Then what are *his* threats?"

"You were correct, we have a standoff. He will not leave without Erika."

"So we are besieged, with the King of Wessex behind these walls?"

"God's mercy," she groaned. "I forgot about him."

Chapter 28

IT WAS UP to Kristen to relate to the rest of the family all that had transpired up on the wall, since Royce had not heard the whole of it. Unfortunately, King Alfred was there to hear it as well. But then, it was next to impossible to exclude him since he was involved due to the simple fact that he could not leave Wyndhurst until the dilemma was solved.

For the most part, Alfred didn't interfere in the discussions of what was to be done. Options were few, with Selig so against the obvious one, and so adamant that he lost his temper and stalked off.

His last words on the subject were, "I will agree to whatever is decided, as long as it does not include the loss of my prisoner. I'll even fight that giant Turgeis instead of her brother."

No one was willing to offer *that* option to the Danes. Waiting out the siege would have been the simplest choice, if Alfred weren't there to be confined with the rest of them. The men favored aggression, the women peaceful means. No one considered using a threat to Erika's life when they knew not how her brother might react to it.

In the end, it was Alfred who suggested the most logical solution, one that Selig's family would never have thought of themselves. And they greeted it with differing degrees of skepticism.

Royce simply laughed.

Garrick cleared his throat to say, "I would not wish that on my son, yet is he being unreasonable in his stubbornness to keep the girl."

"It matters not," Kristen insisted. "Selig will never agree to it. He would go out there and get himself killed first. And who is going to suggest it to him?"

"I will," Royce offered.

Kristen snorted. "You would not be able to stop laughing long enough."

"Nay, I am sure the rage he is going to exhibit will sober me—if he does not simply give me his fist." And he was off laughing again.

Kristen was glaring at him by now. "Would you mind telling me what you find so funny in this?"

"The irony," he said between chuckles. "The incredible irony."

Brenna had said nothing so far. Garrick, noting it, leaned near her to ask softly, "Why are you not pulling hairs and railing against this?"

Brenna shrugged. "Because I do not think he will mind so much—in the end."

Garrick lifted a questioning brow. "Have you kept something from me I should know about?"

The look she gave him was pure innocence. "You know what I know. He claims to detest her, yet does she appeal to him. I believe our daughter and son-in-law had this same difficulty at one time."

"Their circumstances were a mite different, my love. Royce was not seeking revenge."

"And Selig has a strange way of exacting his," Brenna replied.

He shook his head at her. "You are too much the romantic, to think his unusual behavior has more meaning than what it seems."

"Am I? Selig will be furious at the mere suggestion, I doubt it not. But let us see how long he protests before he concedes."

"You do not think this will force him to relinquish her instead?"

"Let us say I will be surprised if it does."

Garrick was not so sure, but he recommended they all find Selig to tell him what had been decided, since it would take a united effort to combat his stubbornness, one way or the other. And he still had two choices. The irony that had so amused Royce was that he had refused to give the Dane back, but the alternative was to be stuck with her for good.

They found him at the blacksmith's giving exact details on the sword he wanted made to replace the one lost during the thieves' ambush. He was forewarned by their number that he wouldn't like the reason they had sought him out en masse. He was right.

"*Marry her?* You have each lost your mind!"

Royce ended up sounding the most reasonable at that point. "Alfred wants to forge alliances through marriage. You knew that, were involved in it yourself. 'Tis not unusual that he would suggest it."

"And not unusual that I would refuse it," Selig shot back tersely.

"Tell *me* you do not find her the least bit appealing," Brenna said.

He knew it then, without a doubt, that she had indeed seen Erika beneath him in the corridor, naked, and had merely kept that part of the tale to herself. Stiffly, he told her, "That has no bearing. I am to marry a woman who hates me? Is that what you want for me?"

It was Kristen who answered, and indignantly. "Certainly not. We expect you to come to your senses and give her back to her brother, because it looks as if you must do one or the other."

And Garrick said, quite calmly, "We cannot be responsible for keeping the Saxon king here. He was to depart on the morrow. And if we just let the siege continue, the girl's brother could grow tired of the wait and attack instead, and he would unknowingly be attacking the King of Wessex. Do you want the responsibility of starting the war between these Saxons and Danes again, son?"

How was it fathers always knew how to pile on the guilt just so, so that there was no hope of digging your way out of it? And they were on his side? Mayhap he could put his honor aside and fight Ragnar Haraldsson after all—nay, he could not. He would have to give the lady up. He was not about to marry a woman he despised.

Alfred appeared in the doorway just then, tall, fair—regal. "I see you have found him," he said to no one in particular, then pinned Selig with his blue eyes. "What is your answer?"

Selig could argue all he liked with his family, but like most men, he found it extremely difficult opposing a king, even a Saxon king who held no exact allegiance from him. "I will marry her."

Alfred had expected no other answer. "Excellent. Then all that must needs deciding now is whether to invite the lady's brother to the ceremony or inform him after the feat is accomplished."

Royce suggested, "If we are to avoid an immediate assault, afterward."

And Kristen came out of her shock long enough to point out, "He is like to attack anyway. Think you he will not know she is forced?"

The word stung Selig to the quick. Any other woman he had ever known would be thrilled did he offer marriage. Anyone but this one . . .

"She will not be forced," he said tightly, only to know it for a lie and amend, "at least she will wed me willingly, and convince her brother of that."

It was his mother who cocked a brow at him. "How will you manage that miracle if she hates you as you say?"

He gave her an annoyed look. Verily, she didn't seem the least bit sorry for him, seemed almost *amused*. If anyone was being forced, he was, and his own mother should at least grieve a little that it was so.

"I will see to it," was all he said.

"Then you had better get to it right quickly," Brenna said. "If you mean to do this thing, it should be done this eventide, the brother told in the morn. He will need knowledge of a wedding night come and gone to keep him from thinking he can undo this match."

A wedding night? The thought was galvanizing—and chilling. A wedding night, with her—nay, there would be none. Without temptation thrown in his face, he did not want her. Revenge was all he wanted from her, had ever wanted—and would still have.

Chapter 29

BY THE TIME Selig reached his chamber, he was so furious he could barely contain it. It was in every line of his handsome face, and it was without direction. He wanted to blame Erika, the fates, even himself, but the rage wouldn't settle on any one person or thing specific—it was just there. And with it was the strangest exhilaration he had ever felt. If he did not know better, he would think it was pure joy, which, of course, it couldn't be.

Wearing her chainse, she stood before the window, from which she could see at least half of the army camped before the gates. He didn't doubt she had stood there since the Danes' arrival. She wouldn't even look away long enough to note who had entered the chamber, though he knew she had heard him, saw her tense, then force herself to relax.

He crossed the room, stopped just behind her, and could see the Danes for himself in the light of their campfires. They were impressive. They were deadly serious—at least her brother was, and he apparently led them.

She had tensed again at Selig's nearness, and did not relax this time. He didn't have to say a word for her to know it was him, yet she still wouldn't turn to confirm it. Not doing so, she was unaware of his fury, might not have said what she did if she could have seen it.

Her voice was soft, tired. "It is over. I will even apologize now."

He was amazed his own tone was moderate. "For having no heart?"

"For letting your insults provoke my temper into ordering that lashing."

His voice was sharper, though no less curious. "How did I insult you?"

It took her a few moments before she would say it. "You invited yourself to my bed."

He didn't recall it, but he would not be surprised were it true. It was his nature to court all women, and she was one of the lovelier ones. There

would have had to be something wrong with him for him not to try
to charm her—but there had been something wrong with him. And he
could do no more than curse that damn fever that had so muddled his
memory.

"Most women would consider that a compliment," he said. There was no
conceit in that, just a statement based on his life experiences.

"Then I must be quite different from most women."

He could agree with that wholeheartedly. Never before had a woman
played such havoc with his emotions. He despised her one moment, and
the next he wanted to bury his hands in her hair and ravage her mouth.
And he despised himself for that weakness of the flesh that she provoked
so easily.

Were she any other woman, he would have leaned into her. His mouth
would be on her neck, tasting her, his hands on her breasts, bringing them
to budding life.

The sensual habits of a lifetime were so ingrained, he had to make a
constant, conscious effort to keep his hands from her when she was this
close to him. But he didn't move back to make it easier.

He should have, but he didn't.

"You could have saved your apology, wench," he said now. "You still
do not leave here."

She spun around. "But my brother—"

"Has had no luck in dealing with my sister, so has decided to besiege
us. Since we have had ample time to prepare for it, who do you think will
last the longer, or lose patience first and attack?"

She was incredulous. "You would take this to war?"

"Not I."

"Most certainly you!" she snapped. "Just let me go home. I have suffered
enough—"

"How have you suffered? Have you marks to show for your lashings?
Do you ache from your labors?"

She was exasperated enough to yell at him. "I suffer from your presence!"

His color heightened at that, and she finally saw it, the rage he had
come in with, that she was provoking even more. A thrill of fear shot
through her. She stepped back, only to come up against the ledge of
the open window. For the briefest moment she thought of jumping. His
hand twisting in the chain wrapped around her neck took that option
from her.

"So you cannot stomach the sight of me, wench?" She wasn't about to
answer that now. "Then 'tis your misfortune that King Alfred was here to

offer suggestions for the settlement of this matter, and one he particularly favors. 'Tis the king's wish that we marry."

She gasped so hard she choked on it. He pounded on her back. She dodged his hand quickly before he dislocated something. She ended up glaring at him.

"That was not funny," she said.

"Do you see me laughing?"

He wasn't. What he was, was still seething with anger, and not even trying to contain it anymore.

She wailed almost desperately, "But you were not serious!"

"How was I not? 'Tis not healthy to ignore a king."

"Are you in trouble, then, for doing so?"

"You think I refused?" His laugh was hard, bitter. "Nay, wench, I am not that foolish."

Her eyes flared. The words came out breathless with shock. "You would marry me?"

"Aye."

She shook her head. "Lash me instead. Have done with it, then let me go."

"Are you finally begging?"

"*I am not,*" she gritted out. " 'Tis obvious you have not had enough revenge, or you would release me. I am offering an alternative to this madness."

"Madness? Nay, I think not, for it has just occurred to me that marriage puts you at my mercy forever, rather than for a short length of time. What better revenge?"

"But you ruin your life as well!"

"How so? My life will not change for having a wife. I will still go on as I have."

In other words, faithfulness did not come into this, not that she would have expected it from any husband. But she would have expected respect, discretion, a degree of kindness, none of which she would have from Selig. His life would not change, but hers would go from this hell to a worse hell, the humiliations endless instead of temporary.

He had let go of her to pound her back. She moved farther away from him now to say, "You will go on as you have without a wife—at least without this wife."

"The king's bishop awaits us below even now."

"The Saxon king is not my king," she reminded him. "I do not tremble at his displeasure."

"You are presently in his domain."

"Not by choice."

Selig ground his teeth together. He had been hasty in saying she would come willingly to the marriage. Prideful confidence that was misplaced. She wouldn't. Inducement would be necessary, something she would find more loathsome, something truly repugnant, something even he would find appalling. And fortunately, he was angry enough to make her believe it.

"You prefer pain to wedding me?" He crossed to her, taking her arm for once, instead of her chain. "Very well, come with me."

Her heart leapt into her throat as he dragged her from the chamber. "Where?"

He didn't stop to explain, had determination in his every step. And his voice was positively chilling. "I am taking you to the stable, where you will be staked out on the ground, naked, for the use of any man who finds you there. I would imagine you will gather quite a crowd in no time at all, and that crowd will grow rather than dispense."

They had just reached the top of the stairs when she gasped out, "I concede!"

That got her released instantly. She hurried back to his chamber, wishing she could hide, knowing she could not. He would have done it. The thought came again and again, and she trembled with that knowledge.

"Well?"

She turned to face him. His hands were braced one on either side of the doorframe. His eyes were a stormy, wintry gray. How could a man so handsome have such a devil's soul?

She dared to bargain. "I will wed you, as long as you do not touch me afterward."

He was angry enough to say, "Gladly will I agree to that—but I also have a condition. No one is to know you remain untouched—especially your brother."

She nodded curtly. Mischievous Loki could not have made a better bargain for them. But he was not finished. She had believed the other, and it sickened him how quickly she had believed it. But it was fortunate he had not mentioned the debt he owed her brother, or she would not believe what he was about to add.

He came before her again, slipping a finger through the ring on her neck shackle, forming a fist that lifted her chin. "My strength is recovered, wench. If you do not want to see your brother still die over this, you will not cry to him your woes when you are allowed to see him. You will, in fact, tell him how happy you are to have wed me."

She groaned at such an impossible task. "He will not believe it."

"Then you must think of a way to convince him."

"Loki must have exchanged one of his sons for you at your birth," she said bitterly.

That Loki's offspring were all reputed to be monsters made her remark a grave insult. He merely laughed now that he had gotten what he wanted of her.

She supposed she would have some time later to think of what she could possibly tell her brother, but right now Selig led her from the room again. To be married. To be married to him, and still bound in his damned chains. She hoped she could get through it without crying.

Chapter 30

THE BISHOP WAS to wait a while more for their appearance, because Selig's mother appeared at the top of the stairs before they reached the landing. And having asked Selig if Erika went willingly to the sacrifice—she did not use those exact words—Lady Brenna lost her temper. It took him a moment to figure out why.

"I will not have it!" she told her son, though it was at Erika's chains that she was looking so balefully. "Remove them. What you do later is your concern, but you have her consent for this wedding. You have agreed to it yourself. She will not go to it chained any more than you will."

Selig didn't argue, though it was a close thing, so annoyed was he. But with an expression of chagrin and not a little embarrassment at being so sharply upbraided, he simply slapped the key into his mother's hand and stalked off to await them below.

"Thank you," Erika said in a small voice.

Brenna gave her an impatient look before she started opening the shackles. "Do not thank me. You are as like to have them back as not. I wouldst suggest you learn quickly how to deal with my son. You will be the happier for it—and so will he."

Erika didn't expect to ever be happy again, but refrained from saying so. "I am not actually willing to marry him," she said instead.

Brenna sighed. "No one supposes that you are, child. But whatever means he used to gain your consent for this wedding, be glad for it. There would eventually have been bloodshed without it."

At the moment, Erika did not feel like being a martyr to save many lives. If her brother's was not one of them— Nay, she was forgetting what might have happened in the stable, what had frightened her so badly that she was willing to marry a man who hated her instead.

"Here," Brenna said as she stood up from removing the last of the shackles. She handed all three to Erika. "Put these away while I fetch you a gown. My daughter has suggested one of hers, since you are closer to her height than to that of any of the other women here."

Another shock, Kristen doing something nice for her, and that on top of Lady Brenna's taking Erika's side against her son—in the matter of the chains. It was the wedding, and the fact that however unwelcome she was, she was still soon to be part of their family. But she didn't expect these kindnesses to last beyond this day.

Brenna actually left her standing there alone while she continued down the hall to her daughter's chamber. And Erika held her chains in her fist. For the moment, she was as free as she had ever been here, as free as she was ever likely to be. Yet were there stone walls still between her and her brother. Freedom from chains didn't mean she could escape her fate. She was as trapped as if she still wore them.

She returned to Selig's chamber, taking wide steps because she could. But she didn't move to his coffer to put the chains inside it. She walked straight to the window and tossed them out of it. And she smiled with actual pleasure for the first time since she had been taken from her home.

"This will do nicely, I think."

Erika turned to see Brenna with a long-sleeved chainse draped over one arm, in a shade so light a blue it nigh matched her eyes. And over the other arm, a sleeveless outer gown of midnight-blue in the rare velvet prized by kings. It was trimmed in thick silver braid along the slit sides and hem, and across the deeply scooped bodice. There was also a gossamer headdress in the light blue, with a silver circlet set with sapphires to hold it in place atop her head. The girdle was wide, of brocaded silk, with more of the silver braid sewn to it.

"They are too fine," Erika said in soft appreciation.

"Not for this occasion. We have appearances to maintain, despite the circumstances. And I heard the Saxon king say he would escort you to the groom himself."

Why not, since he was responsible for this farce? But Erika didn't say that. She dressed hurriedly at Brenna's urging, and, surprisingly, with her help. Selig's mother even combed her hair and arranged the sheer veil, and pinched her cheeks to put some color in them.

Erika wanted to thank the lady again, and in an odd way she did by saying, "I could wish you had raised a less vindictive son."

Brenna actually smiled. "I have not raised *any* vindictive sons. When you finally see that for yourself, this battle between you and Selig will end."

Which made not a bit of sense to Erika, but nothing did today, especially why Selig would marry her when that was the last thing he could really want to do.

She was to be even more grateful for the fine raiments Brenna had picked for her when she noted the richly garbed court ladies who were to witness the wedding. And Selig would have had her wear those ugly and ill-fitting servant's garments—and chains. Her humiliation would have been extreme if not for the intervention of his mother and sister. Which was no doubt what he had hoped for.

Yet when she was led to him, he did not seem annoyed to see her dressed so. He was startled, certainly, before he concealed it beneath an inscrutable visage.

He waited for her, magnificent, on the steps of the small chapel which was in the bailey. The ceremony would take place there, allowing all to hear the solemn words intoned by the bishop, who stood with Selig. And the King of Wessex did indeed escort her.

Alfred was a surprise to her, as was his one remark. "You are the envy of every woman here, Lady Erika."

The words were Danish. She was not surprised he could speak her language, with as much contact as he had had with Danes for most of his life. His age surprised her, though, for he appeared no older than Selig. And he dressed no finer than his other courtiers. In fact, she would not have known who he was if she had not heard him addressed by name.

As for his remark, any comment she would have made to it would have embarrassed them both, for she did not feel very charitable at the moment. So she made none, and kept to herself that she would gladly let any woman there trade places with her. Envy? They did not know Selig Haardrad as she did. They knew only his charming side, which she could not deny she had seen, though not experienced, while she knew only what cruelties he was capable of.

And that would not change just because he could now call her wife. That designation merely offered him more opportunities to make her miserable.

The ceremony was over much too quickly. In fact, no more than an hour had passed from his telling her they would marry to their becoming, officially, man and wife. And she realized only afterward that she had been given no time to really think about what she had agreed to. Without such haste, she might have . . .

But it was done. She had a husband now. And examining that thought too closely would likely lead to hysterics.

The celebration feast that followed was a mockery as far as Erika was concerned. She had nothing to celebrate, and neither did Selig, yet they sat through it, side by side, enduring the good-natured jests and crudities that typically accompanied a wedding. In fact, everyone was enjoying himself, except the newly married pair.

Even Selig's family was in high good cheer, which Erika found strange, since she had come to understand that they all cared for him a great deal. It was the atmosphere, she supposed, and the fact that Selig didn't look nearly as gloomy as she did. Could they actually think he was pleased with the outcome of the day, and were happy for him? Obviously, he was merely putting a fine face on it for their benefit.

Selig downed yet another tankard of ale. He had given up trying to keep track of the constant swing of his emotions. And he had given up trying to ignore his *wife*.

She was not to have sat beside him until she called him master, yet here she sat. But she would be calling him husband now, and were they not one and the same, master, husband? They were supposed to be, but *she* would never think so.

He could have had any woman he wanted—anyone but this one. And yet he had this one. She was most definitely his now. He just didn't know what to do with her now that she had gone from slave to wife.

Had he really agreed never to touch his own wife? But he hadn't agreed to forgo his revenge. He would still have that. Wasn't that why he had married her?

Damned emotions weren't making sense today. She was beautiful, and miserable, and he found it difficult keeping his eyes from her. Yet the more dismal she looked, the more annoyed he became.

It was her wedding day. Brides were supposed to be happy on their wedding day. His bride should have been the happiest of all. It wasn't conceit that made him think so, but his experience of women and their reaction to him. Yet Erika would not even make a pretense of happiness for the benefit of their guests.

He finally told her, sharply, "This is not a funeral. If you are so uncomfortable, you may return to my chamber—and your place in it."

Erika flushed, though no one else had heard him say that. And even if he had been overheard, only a few knew that her "place" was a corner on the floor. She should have been only relieved, that that was where she was still to sleep. He was keeping their bargain. So why was she embarrassed and—and she wasn't sure what else?

That was a lie. She knew what else. But, Odin help her, how could she possibly be feeling disappointment? It had been her insistence that he not touch her—though made for reasons other than the obvious. She was simply afraid of the passion he had shown her, which she liked too much.

'Tis likely you will come to love him.

His sister's words had never stopped haunting her. She was afraid of that, too, because he didn't give her enough reasons to really hate him. He tried, but embarrassments were immediate and soon forgotten.

He has never hurt a woman in his life.

Was it true, then, his father's contention? And if it was, then what Selig had threatened to do to her today was a lie. He wouldn't have been able to do it.

She took his permission to leave the hall gladly. She needed to be away from his disturbing presence so she could think more clearly. That he let her go without an escort was a revelation. If the marriage had done nothing else, it had apparently given her back some freedom. And the damned chains were gone . . .

The damned chains were back on Selig's bed when she entered his chamber, retrieved by someone who knew exactly whom they belonged to—him—her. Selig probably wasn't even aware that she had given in to that act of defiance.

The chains went flying out the window again, and it gave her just as much pleasure to toss them out this time as before. Now if she could just find as much pleasure sleeping on the floor on her wedding night.

Chapter 31

RAGNAR MADE KRISTEN wait nearly an hour up on the wall before he answered her request for another talk between them. The discourtesy was the prerogative of a superior position, which he thought he still held. The only reason she didn't lose her temper or simply leave was because of the pleasure she was going to get from disabusing him of that notion.

Royce had less patience. He left and returned three times in that hour that they waited, and nearly dragged Kristen down from the wall the fourth time he stalked off, he was so annoyed with Erika's brother.

Her mother didn't bother to join them on the wall, since she spoke no Danish. But her father was there beside her, could have spoken with Ragnar himself, though he declined, knowing how much Kristen was looking forward to it this time.

And Selig, that sot, was no doubt still abed after drinking himself under the table last eventide. If he had been able to consummate his marriage after Royce and Ivarr had carried him up to his bed, it would be a miracle. But Ragnar wasn't going to know that. By the time Kristen was done with him, he would think his sister well and truly wed and bedded, with no recourse for undoing the marriage open to him. That is, if he ever bothered to make an appearance.

Turgeis came first, alone, to tell her that if she had nothing new to add to what had been discussed yesterday, Ragnar wasn't going to waste his time speaking to her again. He seemed embarrassed to have delivered that message. But Kristen showed none of the anger it was to have sparked. She felt it keenly, she just didn't show it.

But she did retaliate in kind by replying, "The only one who might have anything to repeat is your Lord Ragnar. The only thing I have to discuss is his sister—and her *new* situation."

She also added that she would wait five minutes more and not one minute longer, and if Ragnar hadn't come forth in that time, then *he* could wait until some other day to find out what had occurred to Erika since last they spoke.

Kristen pitied Turgeis's horse, having to support that kind of weight at that speed. But he did ride back to camp at a tearing gallop, and Ragnar was back with him in less than five minutes.

"I see now why you call Turgeis Ten Feet the 'giant,' but you should have taken pity on him," Garrick said beside her. "He only repeated what he was bidden to say."

"So?"

"So he is a man sick with worry over his lady, and with no control over what happens here."

"I saw Turgeis break a man's neck with a slight twist of his hands," Kristen replied. "Somehow, that does not inspire pity."

Garrick grinned at her droll tone. "Yet he is not the one you are annoyed with."

"True." She sighed. "I suppose I could apologize to him—afterward. That is, if I have the nerve to get anywhere near him ever again. I tried it once, and would not like to repeat the experience. Up here on the wall, with him down there on the ground, is close enough—"

She didn't finish, since Ragnar had arrived. He didn't come as close this time, which would force them both to shout. And he didn't look the least bit disturbed over the message she had sent back with Turgeis. Confident was how he looked, and arrogant in his possession of the upper hand.

"What say you, Lady Kristen?" Ragnar shouted. "And be quick about it."

She did say something, a few choice curses that he wasn't like to hear. Her father pointed out the obvious. "You are whispering."

"I know."

Ragnar could hear none of it from the distance he had chosen. "Speak up, lady!"

She put her hands to her mouth as if to shout, and whispered again—for her father's benefit. "If he thinks I am going to strain my voice just because he has a louder one and is comfortable raising it, he can think again."

Garrick had to put a hand to his own mouth to hide his chuckles. Below, Ragnar was holding a hand to his ear, but he still hadn't been able to catch her words. He tried twice more to get their talk going, but though her lips moved, no sound reached him.

At last out of patience, he moved his destrier forward, directly below the wall, to demand, "Can you hear me *now*, Lady Kristen?"

She leaned slightly forward over the wall so he couldn't miss her smile. "Certainly, Lord Ragnar. And it was good of you to come. After all, circumstances have changed somewhat since last we spoke."

"I thought they might." Smugness, which grated. "Is my sister being sent out?"

Kristen's smile didn't alter. "Nay, but you may come safely inside now and be welcome."

"And what makes that offer any more appealing than when I last rejected it?"

"We are now related—through marriage."

It took him all of two seconds to grasp the meaning of that and explode. "What have you done? If you have forced her to wed him—"

"On the contrary," she cut in, her tone still quite pleasant. "Erika looked quite willing to me. But you need not take my word for it. You can ask her yourself."

"Where is she?"

"Likely still abed." His face went florid at that. Kristen rubbed it in a bit harder. "Did I forget to mention yesterday that your sister and my brother have become enamored of each other?"

"You spoke only of his revenge."

"And would you not agree it was a fine revenge, making her fall in love with him? Unfortunately, he got caught in it himself."

"You are lying!"

"Actually, 'twas just yesterday, before your arrival, that my own mother caught them—well, let us say neither one of them was screaming for help."

"*Neither* one? You would have me believe your brother would object to—!" He could not finish. He was at that moment so exasperated by impotent fury that he could have pulled every one of his hairs out—and strangled Lady Kristen.

"You may discuss with your sister the how and the why, Lord Ragnar. The fact remains, she is a member of my family now, my own sister-in-law. She was wed last eventide, with much pomp and ceremony. The celebration lasted long into the night. Mayhap you could hear it?"

He was glaring up at her as if he would like to cut her into little pieces. "She would not marry without my permission," he gritted out.

"She did not need yours when she had permission from a king—his insistence, actually."

Ragnar flushed several shades of red; then, quite suddenly, all color left him with the implications of that last statement. "The Saxon king is within and you did not tell me?"

Kristen merely shrugged. "His presence here was unrelated to the issue."

Unrelated? He had besieged the King of Wessex. If Guthrum heard of it, Ragnar would know his wrath, and he had this vixen here to thank for that.

Kristen judged his expression accurately and added, "Alfred was to leave Wyndhurst today. As our two kings are presently on very good terms, I will assume you will likewise wish to keep him from becoming any more involved in this and grant him safe passage."

"Certainly," Ragnar said quickly and with obvious relief. "He may leave at any time."

"You might like to assure him of that yourself when you come inside. And I suppose I must repeat, you may do so safely now, because of our new relationship. However, if you are still distrustful, my younger brother Thorall has volunteered to come out to abide in your camp the while you visit with your sister. I would have offered to be hostage for you myself, but my husband is a jealous man. He would not permit me to go among so many Vikings. So what say you, Ragnar Haraldsson?"

"Open your gates, lady."

Chapter 32

"TELL ME HOW he forced you."

Those were Ragnar's first words to Erika after he had squeezed the breath from her in their mutual hugging. Hers had been, "I think you should not have left me home alone this time." But then, she was so close to tears, she had to say something that might make him laugh. It didn't work.

They had been given the privacy of the small chapel. She had joined him there immediately she was told of his presence. But she had never gotten around to giving any thought to what she would tell him. She had instead been so immersed in thoughts of her husband that she had even forgotten there was a possibility she might speak with Ragnar today.

The tears remained near the surface and likely would, because she was so happy to see Ragnar. She had begun to think she never would again. But there was her confusion, too, and she couldn't even speak of it to him. And there was his concern, so evident, and knowing she must lie to him. She had never had to lie to him before.

She led him to one of the pews to sit with her, and took his hands in hers before she said, with as much conviction as she could manage, "I was not forced."

"Erika—"

"Nay, hear me out. I considered many things, even that you wanted a strong alliance for me, and this one is indeed that. His brother-in-law is a warrior lord here, and a friend of the Saxon king. His father is a rich merchant prince. His uncle is a powerful *jarl* in Norway, and he himself commands many men, every one a Viking warrior. For an alliance, brother, you could not have hoped for better."

"I would not have sacrificed you for it!"

"I know, and I do not feel I have sacrificed myself. Ragnar, if I did not want to marry the man, I would have refused."

Sweet Freya, why did that sound so true? And why didn't he simply believe her, instead of still looking so doubtful? She found out why.

"Turgeis told me all that happened. This man took you to harm you."

"But he never did, and I—" She lowered her head, hoping he would just think her embarrassed to admit, "I have come to care for him."

"Why?"

The directness of that question caught her off guard. She almost laughed. She did grin. A woman would never have asked that.

She answered by asking, "Have you not met him?"

"Met him?" Ragnar growled. "I saved his miserable life in the last war."

Her expression turned incredulous, and rightly so. "How is that possible? He fought with the Danes?"

"He was with the Saxons," Ragnar said in disgust. "Helmeted, with Danish coming from his lips. I assumed—wrongly. Even when I saw that black hair of his after I had dragged him from the field and bandaged his wounds, I still thought him a Dane. And he let me think it. I knew no differently until I saw him again yesterday."

Yesterday. Selig knew yesterday it was her brother he owed his life to, and still he threatened him? Had that been a bluff, too?

It was on the tip of her tongue to tell all when it occurred to her that what could have been a bluff yesterday might not be one now. There was a very great difference, after all, between letting go a prisoner and letting go a wife. If her brother insisted on a fight, and he would if he knew the truth, Selig would meet him. And she hated to admit it, but Ragnar, even at six feet, was a much smaller man. Ragnar facing Selig would be like Selig facing Turgeis. The outcomes were almost guaranteed. She still had to lie.

He lifted her chin in his palm to draw her attention back to him. "What has my meeting him to do with your caring for him, Erika?"

"You must admit he is a fine-looking man. I find it difficult to take my eyes off him when he is near me." That much was perfectly true, which was probably why her cheeks started glowing when she added, "His attraction is quite powerful." That, unfortunately, was also true.

"You are saying you married the man because of his handsomeness?"

She hated putting herself in with that shallow group who cared only for looks, but Ragnar might better accept that as a reason for such sudden "caring." So she settled for merely elaborating on that point, and it helped that she could be truthful about it.

"His handsomeness began the attraction, which I felt when I first saw him at Gronwood. It was because of it that I was so rattled I lost my temper and ordered him lashed. You cannot begin to know how much I regret that." And *that* was especially true. "Now, did you find a wife?"

He frowned at her change of topic and waved it aside. "I cannot think of that now."

"But I need to think of something other than this. Did you?"

He pounced. "So you *are* upset?"

"I am upset by *your* upset," she insisted, and suddenly the words flowed from her without any difficulty. "I know you did not come here and expect to find me wed and willingly so, but, Ragnar, I simply could not help falling in love with this man. I tried to resist it. Selig tried, too. He wanted so much to hate me. And it endeared him to me, that he tried so hard, but could not. He wanted revenge, aye. That is the reason I was taken. But he found he is incapable of exacting revenge from a woman. Can you imagine his frustration, to end up in love with me instead?"

For a moment Ragnar did, and had the urge to laugh. With it came his relief, now that she had said something that sounded reasonable—and more like her.

Still, he had to ask, "Are you sure 'tis not guilt guiding you?"

She had stopped feeling guilty the day Selig put those damned chains on her, but she couldn't tell her brother that. What she still regretted was giving Selig a reason to despise her, because it didn't look like she was ever going to be forgiven for it.

So she lied again. "I am forgiven, so there is no longer guilt to trouble me."

His eyes searched hers for a long moment before he sighed. "Are you really asking me to leave you here with him?"

This was her most difficult answer to give. She wanted so much to go home. She wanted her life returned to normal. She was tired of the anger and confusion, and being attracted to a man she didn't dare love.

"Aye," she said, and swore to herself it would be the last lie she would ever tell him.

Chapter 33

SELIG CAME AWAKE at the third shaking. His hands went immediately to his temples.

"Thor's teeth, did someone hit me over the head again?" he groaned.

"You have yourself to thank this time—and my excellent ale."

"Is that you, Kris?"

"Why do you not open your eyes and see for yourself?" she queried.

"I would as soon not. I sense too much light even with them closed."

Kristen shook her head at him. Amusement was high in her tone. "So this is what marriage has led you to?"

Another groan. "How could I forget?"

His eyes did open now, the barest crack, but not to look at his sister. His head turned directly to the corner where Erika could usually be found. That it was empty did not cause any undue alarm—yet.

"Where is she?"

"Speaking with her brother in the chapel."

His eyes flared wide and came accusingly to Kristen now. "And no one woke me?"

He started to sit up, but something dragged him back down. Erika's chains, wrapped around his neck. He only vaguely recalled one of the servants telling him he had found them out in the bailey. Selig had hung them around his neck for want of somewhere else to put them, since he hadn't been willing at the time to go near his chamber.

"No one woke you because you were not needed," Kristen was explaining. "If she is to convince her brother that you are not the miserable wretch who has kept her chained nearly to your side, it cannot be with you standing close to intimidate her."

He didn't address the part about the chains, merely grumbled, "I do not intimidate her."

"Her brother would not see it that way."

He tossed off the chains and tried sitting up again. He couldn't move as fast as he wanted, not when the pain from his overindulgence was almost as bad as that first morning he awoke with the head injury. Yet what he was feeling could only be called panic.

"Did you at least place a spy to hear what she tells him?" he demanded.

Kristen's brows shot up. "When only you, me, and Father can speak their language? *You* might not mind asking Father to spy for you, but I would not be so daring."

"*You* should have seen to the task yourself."

"Me?" she exclaimed. "I did my part by getting the man well and truly furious with me. He ought to like you now in comparison."

He gave her a glare. She was just short of laughing at him. And the only effort she made to help him was to fetch his comb for him. He wasn't even going to try changing the clothes he had fallen asleep in.

When he was just about out the door, she ventured to ask, "Do you still hate her?"

He spared a moment to glance back at her. "Why do you ask me that again?"

Kristen shrugged. "Because you married her. That is carrying revenge a bit far, if you ask me."

"Stay out of it, Kris."

She tsked her tongue. "Gladly, just as soon as a certain arrogant jackdaw is gone from my home."

He winced. "I am not arrogant."

"I meant *her* brother, lackwit, not mine."

Selig found them still alone in the chapel, sitting side by side, their voices too soft for him to overhear, even though he eavesdropped for a while, hoping to hear something. Ragnar's arm was around her shoulder. Erika's head rested against his. This was her brother. Still, Selig had the urge to remove that arm from her.

"I trust you have had a pleasant reunion?"

Erika turned at the sound of his voice. Ragnar came abruptly to his feet. His expression revealed nothing, so Selig had no clue to what he had been told. Her expression was anxious, which could have meant anything, including she was still fearful for her brother.

Selig *had* stopped by the smith long enough to collect his new sword. He wore it now, though without armor, for he still wore the clothes he had been married in. Erika was likewise still in her finery. As he didn't recall getting to his bed last night, he didn't recall noticing if she had been in his chamber when he did, much less if she had removed her clothes or slept in them like he did.

Ragnar, of course, had entered Wyndhurst fully armed, though it was his left hand that rested casually on his sword hilt as he approached Selig, indicating that he didn't mean to use the weapon. A circumstance which could change at any given moment.

Ragnar stopped two feet away. His right fist landed before Selig saw it coming. Erika shot to her feet, crying, "Do not—!" but she cut off her words, for Selig had barely been moved by the punch. In fact, only his face had turned with it, and there was subtle amusement in his expression when he looked back at Ragnar.

To give Ragnar his due, he was annoyed rather than distressed that he had done so little damage. Erika, however, was absolutely frantic, because she was sure she held no power over her husband, and so would have no luck in persuading him not to retaliate. She didn't get the opportunity to try.

"That was for the worry you put me through," Ragnar told Selig plainly.

"Ah," Selig replied, as if that made perfect sense. He fingered his cheek before adding, "Then 'tis not your wish to fight me?"

"Not at the present, though I reserve the right to alter that decision in future."

"Certainly."

Selig's smile had Ragnar close to losing his temper again. "Understand me, Haardrad. I do not believe much of Erika's tale, yet is she sincere in her desire to stay with you. I like it not, but I will grant her wish. However, I leave her man Turgeis with her. If she comes to her senses and wants to return home, he will bring her, and Odin help you if you try to stop him."

That took care of Selig's amusement, replacing it with something quite unfamiliar—possessiveness. "*This* is her home now. She will have no wish to leave Wessex."

It was Ragnar's turn to smile, and not very pleasantly. "Or you?" And he scoffed, "She is enamored of your face, man, but more than that is needed to sustain love—if there be any. Bring her to Gronwood in six months and we will see if what she feels for you has a chance of enduring. If so, then I will be pleased to call you brother."

Selig wasn't going to worry about what might or might not happen six months away. Ragnar was conceding, would leave here without his sister. Selig had been able to diffuse the situation without killing the man, or rather, Erika had managed to do it. He would give anything to know exactly what she had told her brother, aside from the fact that she thought him handsome. Did she really? He shouldn't be so pleased to know it, but he was.

Ragnar turned to find that Erika had come up behind him. He hugged her now, and Selig again experienced that ridiculous urge to tear them apart.

Her voice held dismay as she asked her brother, "You are not leaving yet, are you?"

"Nay, Rika," he assured her. "But I must inform my men of what has occurred. We will not depart until the morrow, so I will return to spend the time with you."

His promise relieved her enough that she even smiled. "And you must tell me more of this great heiress who refused to marry you."

"She refused, but her father did not. Yet am I reconsidering the offer. Thurston needs a mother who will give him the care you did. But we will speak of it later."

He had already assured her that Thurston was fine, his arm healing apace. He had also mentioned that the thefts Gronwood had been plagued with had abruptly ended with Wulnoth's death. Turgeis had saved him the trouble of hanging the man, apparently, and she was not really surprised to learn that Wulnoth had been responsible for the thefts. It explained why a man so eager for victims had not come up with one for that crime.

Ragnar turned to leave and caught Selig staring as if mesmerized by Erika's smile—which vanished the moment she noticed his perusal. Ragnar frowned and told Selig in parting, "She and I share the same father with a score of other siblings, but Erika is the only one of them who shared the same mother with me. Besides my son, she is the only family I acknowledge and is very dear to me. You have wed her without my consent. If you hurt her, I will take back the life I saved."

Selig said nothing to that. He liked ultimatums no more than he liked subtle threats. Blatant threats were usually answered immediately and in kind. But for her brother he had to make an exception. He wished he didn't understand so perfectly how the man felt, but he did.

He nodded curtly and Ragnar left. It was a moment before Selig turned to gaze at Erika again. He didn't like the wary look she returned.

And then the truth occurred to him with no little amazement and relief. "You actually lied to him?"

The wariness left abruptly, replaced with something akin to annoyance. "You doubted I would? We had a bargain. You kept your part, so I could do no less."

Mention of the "bargain" brought some annoyance of his own. But before he could react to it, another joined them.

Erika saw him first and beamed with pleasure. "Turgeis! Ragnar did not mention you were—"

She ended on a gasp as Turgeis reached for Selig to turn him around. Ragnar's punch hadn't moved Selig. Turgeis's punch knocked him flat on his back and unconscious.

"Nay!" Erika cried and fell to her knees beside Selig. "You cannot hurt him, Turgeis!"

His voice was a growl. "Why can I not?"

"He has suffered enough at our hands."

"And you have not suffered at his?"

"Not at all."

He lifted her to her feet. "Do not lie to me as you did to your brother."

She flushed. "In this I am not. Truly, Turgeis. All he did to me was try to embarrass me, and make threats that never came to pass."

"He still means to have his revenge."

"Mayhap," she allowed, "but you cannot interfere. He *is* my husband."

"Husbands can be gotten rid of."

"Do not even think it!"

Selig moaned then. Erika bent to him again. It took a moment for his eyes to focus on her.

"I believe you know my friend Turgeis," she said hesitantly.

Selig looked beyond her to the giant standing at her back. "Did you also hit me for the worry I caused you, or are we not finished?"

"My lady says we are finished—for now."

Selig's eyes dropped back to Erika. "You were wise to call him off. My family would not take it kindly were I to leave here all mangled, and neither would I."

Erika grinned and glanced over her shoulder. "You see, Turgeis? Naught but threats."

Turgeis and Selig both grunted in reply.

Chapter 34

RAGNAR ASKED TO see Selig's home and was taken there that afternoon, after the king's departure. Erika was in a fine state of nerves the while they were gone, because she had not been invited to accompany them, and they left before she got up the nerve to invite herself. And they went alone, which made her anxiety that much worse.

She remained in the hall, since no one told her she couldn't. But the only ones who spoke to her at all were Selig's parents, and that just briefly. From the rest of the hall, at least from the women, she received nothing but hostile looks. She had dared to marry *their* Selig. They weren't going to forgive her for it.

She could have cared less right then. All she could think about was her brother and husband killing each other, and no one around to try to stop them.

Anything could have happened, but amazingly, nothing did. Ragnar and Selig returned before dark, both without wounds, and Ragnar certainly in better humor than when he had left.

He had only good things to say about Selig's home—from a man's point of view. "He has a few very *accommodating* slaves whom a wife might want to get rid of, but other than that, I think you will do well there."

The emphasis he put on that word told her that Ragnar, at least, had been "accommodated," which would account for his relaxed mood. Her brother always was unusually mellow after fornicating. She looked for the same signs in her husband, but he was no different than when she had seen him before in the midst of many, quick to smile at all the women and quick to laugh, even at himself.

Not that it would bother her had he availed himself also of those accommodating women. He could and would do as he liked, as all men did, and she was expected to say nothing, not just because of their unique relationship, but because wives rarely if ever interfered in their husbands' doings. A wife would be lucky if one or more of her husbands' lemans didn't live under the same roof with her.

Erika wasn't going to break tradition and complain if she wasn't one of the lucky ones. She would have to care to do that, to actually love her husband and expect more from him. Not likely on either account.

While her brother's mood had risen to pleasant, Erika's had decreased to just short of simmering. She could blame it on the day and all the lies she had told, even on the worrying she had done. She certainly didn't blame it on Selig's possible unfaithfulness.

"He has an amusing sense of humor, Rika," Ragnar told her before they sat down to table. "But then, I am sure you have already discovered that for yourself."

She had done no such thing, and was not likely to. Selig? Amusing? About as much as a frothing wolf.

Turgeis had gone back to Ragnar's camp for the afternoon, but he returned for the evening meal. As was his custom, he sat with the retainers at another table. The seats around him were empty, the men here wary of getting anywhere near him. Even the servants were extremely nervous about serving him. Two accidents occurred because of shaking fingers.

Aware of it, this, too, annoyed Erika. Her friend had given these Saxons no cause to fear him, but they saw his size and looked no further. It did not help, of course, that he did a lot of glowering in Selig's direction, and when Turgeis glowered, he looked quite fierce. It didn't seem to bother Selig, however, so it shouldn't bother anyone else.

But it recalled to Erika a conclusion she had reached and worried over in the past. Turgeis was a lonely man. The people of Gronwood had come to accept him, which meant they ignored him. None had ever befriended him.

Erika was, in truth, his only friend, which was sad indeed. She had tried to rectify that before. She had assigned Turgeis a squire, but the boy had run away. She had involved him in tasks with men his age, but nothing had come of it. She had even tried to interest the women of Gronwood in him, but they had either looked horrified by the notion or laughed it off. He was nigh two score in years. He ought to have a wife and family of his own.

She had one small hope that it might be different here in Wessex, with new people, including Norwegians like himself. Even the women here were already accustomed to Selig and Royce with their extreme height, and Turgeis was only a half foot taller than they. But from what she was already seeing, the hope was not strong.

At her own table, she sat between her brother and husband. For Ragnar's benefit, Selig's arm came around her shoulders quite frequently in a show of husbandly affection. He even leaned close at one point and kissed her neck, setting off all sorts of pleasant reactions in her body—which she didn't appreciate one bit. It wasn't as if he were going to do anything about what he was thoughtlessly causing her to feel.

She was ignored for the most part as the two men spoke around her of subjects she had no interest in, or with the others at the table. Selig's family also made Ragnar feel welcome, which she was grateful for. It could have been an extremely uncomfortable meal for them both, but Ragnar enjoyed himself. So did Selig, for that matter. He laughed a lot. And he didn't drown himself in ale as he had the previous night. Only Erika could wish she were elsewhere, though for her brother's sake, her demeanor said otherwise.

When she was finally able to leave without undue notice, she was surprised to hear Selig make his excuses to depart with her. Not only that, but his arm went around her waist as he escorted her from the hall, again for Ragnar's benefit but there nonetheless, and she was painfully aware of it, the fingers spread wide on the side of her ribs, holding her tight to his side. Nor did he release her once they reached the upper hallway and were no longer under scrutiny, though she made a subtle effort to move away from him.

"You must admit, wench, this serves nearly as well as your leash," he said to her as he opened the door to his—now their—chamber.

She was able to jerk away from him then. After that remark, she would likely have clawed him to see it so. And she would have made a scathing reply if the clothes on the bed had not caught her attention and drawn her to them.

He had come right up behind her, though he didn't touch her again. "My sister is generous," he said.

She was indeed. There were three gowns there with matching chainses, and not one could be considered ready for charitable donations.

"Her generosity is for you, not me," she replied a touch bitterly.

"How so?"

"So you will not be embarrassed by a wife wearing rags, of course."

"And how would that embarrass me, wench?"

She heard the laughter in his voice. She turned to see it in his gray eyes. "So I am mistaken." She shrugged. "As it matters not to me either, you may return these to your sister. My brother will be sending my own clothes, but if you prefer I not wear those either, you may lock them away, or give them away."

"Or throw them out a window, as you did to my property?" he queried.

Immediately she looked for the chains he referred to, hoping she wouldn't see them. She found them in a pile in her corner of the room, and her temper rose at the sight.

"I refuse to wear those again," she said softly, but no less furiously.

"If I want you to wear them, you will."

"Then you will have a fight on your hands," she promised.

He actually laughed. "We already know the outcome of that, do we not?"

She met his gaze, one brow arching. "Do we? I was not referring to myself, Selig, but to Turgeis. He will go berserk if he sees me enchained."

His amusement ended right there. "That damned giant—"

"Stays with me if you do not want to undo all that has been done today. My brother saved your life. I saved Turgeis's life. But unlike you, he has made it his life's endeavor to repay that debt."

"I repaid your brother," he growled. "I refused to fight him."

"The outcome of which was not guaranteed, so that hardly suffices."

He glowered at her for a moment; then he said, very softly, "To provoke my temper is to risk provoking my passion. If you do not want to be acquainted with the latter again, I would suggest you say no more."

He turned away, dismissing her. Her question came in raised tones, unexpected—and unrelated. "Did you dally with your slaves today as my brother did?"

He swung back around, his look incredulous for all of two seconds. Then the amusement was back in spades, and he gave her that smile she detested.

"And spoil the illusion that we are newly in love? Certainly not. My dallying will have to await your brother's departure."

She turned her back on him and marched to her corner, determined to ignore him. She couldn't believe she had asked that question of him. Just because he had mentioned passion, which reminded her of her earlier thoughts about his unfaithful proclivities . . .

She was mortified. She had sounded jealous! And the handsome wretch was amused by it!

She thought of offering an excuse. Surely she could think of something to explain her curiosity other than jealousy. She was *not* jealous.

"I am not jealous!" she shouted at the wall in front of her.

"That is a relief," he said behind her, just before Kristen's gowns were all dumped on top of her. "Do something with these. You can wear them or not, but they will not be returned to my sister until you have your own clothes to replace them. She would be hurt to have her generosity scorned."

"Is that supposed to influence me?" she shot back.

"Our bargain is very shaky, wench. I would not put it to the test any further this night, were I you."

She said not another word.

Chapter 35

HER NAME WAS Lida. She had been stolen from her village five years hence because her Slavic people were horse breeders, not warriors. They hadn't stood a chance in the raid that decimated her village, and she was not the only woman to be carried off by she-knew-not-whom. She had been sold west herself, and had known three owners before the last died and she ended up in the Hedeby slave market on the neck of the Jutland Peninsula.

She had learned much in her years of slavery, learned that she had powers that went beyond ownership, and learned how to use them to her advantage. It was almost too easy, for she was not just beautiful with her sloe-black eyes and long black curls, she was all things sensual. Sensuality could have been her middle name. She exuded it in her every movement, her every glance. She knew how to drive men wild to have her, and how to enslave them once they did. It was so much a part of her that she didn't have to make a conscious effort to entice. It was natural. It was inevitable. She had yet to meet a man who didn't want her for his own.

She might be branded a slave, but she had not experienced the drudgery that went hand in hand with the distinction. She was too smart for that, and too lazy to do other than work her way to a position of favorite.

Each of her previous owners had succumbed to her allure, giving her power even over their wives, who were helpless to supplant her. Fine gowns and jewels had been hers for the asking, servants to wait on her, her own slaves if she wanted them. No, slavery was no drudgery for Lida. It was, in truth, an ideal life. Her only complaint was losing everything and having to start over again if her owner should die, which had been the case with all three of the men who had previously bought her.

Only once had she suffered for it, in the case of her first owner, whose wife had regained her power at his passing and had had Lida nearly beaten to death before being carted off to the slave market again. Lida had taken steps to see that that didn't happen a second time with her next owner, getting him to send his wife away. But that wasn't as much fun. She did so enjoy lording it over a lowly wife. So with the third owner, she found it was a simple matter to have protection arranged for her in advance.

She didn't want her freedom and so never asked for it. Freedom was without protection, and Lida liked being protected and cherished. Nor did she want a husband of her own. Wives had too many duties, whereas Lida enjoyed having none. They also had the appalling chore of producing children, which Lida wanted no part of. It was much nicer to usurp a wife's powers without the attendant responsibilities. And Lida had no doubt that here in Wessex she would rise to the privileged position she was accustomed to.

Her only competition was no competition at all as she saw it, merely the two other female slaves who had sailed with her here. Golda was a robust, matronly sort with nothing to recommend her, except she knew how to run a household, which was what she had been bought for. She had nondescript brown hair, though her eyes, her best feature, were the color of golden oak. They were wasted in a face that was just short of homely—except when she smiled. When she smiled, she was actually pretty. But she was at least a score and ten years, was used to hard labor, and wouldn't know how to entice a man if she tried.

Magge, on the other hand, was a lusty, red-haired Scot who enjoyed men and was prone to laugh for no good reason, finding humor in anything and everything. She was pretty in a loud sort of way, her coloring so vivid, but she couldn't hold a candle to Lida's sultry looks.

Lida had cultivated a relationship with the Viking Ivarr, until she found out he had bought her not for himself, but for another. She had been disappointed, for he was the most handsome of the men she had set out to seduce. At least she had been disappointed until yesterday.

Her first sight of her new owner had been a shock. She hadn't known men could be as beautiful as Selig Haardrad, hadn't in her wildest dreams ever imagined a man like this Viking. Another shock was that he barely gave her a second glance, spent his time with Golda instead, discussing the responsibilities that would be hers—and the authority. Lida had cajoled Ivarr into giving her the position of overseeing the servants, and he had done so, though he had warned it would only be temporary, that the final decision was not his to make. Yesterday, Selig had taken just one look at his three new slaves and made that decision.

Lida was not discouraged, merely annoyed. Ever since her arrival, she had done little or no work, delegating it to others. Until she could get Selig to give her back the authority he had so thoughtlessly taken from her, she would be under Golda's supervision.

Without authority, Golda was as meek as a lamb; with it, she was a veritable dragon. At least she was not a vindictive dragon. She didn't retaliate for all the extra work that had been hers under Lida's direction. She merely doled out the work equally, which was, of course, unacceptable to Lida, who abhorred menial labor of any kind.

This was only a temporary setback, though, which would correct itself just as soon as she shared the master's bed. And based on her experience, that would be almost immediately he moved back into his hall.

Word had already been sent that he and his new wife would be taking up residence this very day. So Lida did not have long to wait to get everything she wanted. And one of the things she would insist on was a larger household, which she was more accustomed to. There were ample male servants, but with only three women, or rather two, tasks were likely to come to Lida due to necessity. That simply wouldn't do.

That Selig had a new wife gave Lida no worry at all, for she had already been told that he despised the lady, and had only married her at the Saxon king's insistence. But even had he been in love with her, Lida wouldn't have worried. She knew her own appeal, knew the power of it, and her confidence had never been daunted.

Still, there was risk involved with a man like Selig Haardrad, a risk that she might become as enslaved to him as he would be to her. She had always remained detached in her involvements with men, her emotions her own to control. But for such a man, it was a risk she would gladly take.

Chapter 36

SELIG LED THE stallion from the stable. It was not his horse, but one borrowed from Royce, his own favored destrier in the hands of thieves now, as well as his prized sword. He had thought often of pursuing those ambushers during his recovery, if not to lay waste to them all, then to retrieve his property. He was still considering it. Mayhap after he settled in his own home . . .

He had not picked the best time to leave Wyndhurst, what with the activity in the bailey greater than usual with the arrival of more visitors. Royce and Kristen were busy with a group of men he didn't recognize, but then, half the men from the king's party he hadn't known either. His brothers ignored all with a test of arms in the south corner, which garnered a small crowd, including their father. His mother was having words with Turgeis Ten Feet, who stood some fifteen feet distant from Erika, not far—her shadow, he had heard him called. He wondered what his mother could find of common interest with the giant. She looked like a child standing next to him, but not the least bit wary.

Erika waited for him just outside the hall, where he had left her. Only a few hours earlier she had said her good-byes to her brother. Selig had thought there might be tears afterward, so he had taken her immediately back up to their chamber to pack her belongings with his, thinking that might distract her. More fool he.

His thoughtfulness had received a scathing remark that she had no belongings to pack. He had retaliated by picking up her chains from the floor and tucking them into his coffer. She had been looking daggers at him ever since, which he found vastly amusing.

Kristen waved to him and approached. She was all smiles, telling him either she was delighted that her home was about to return to some semblance of normalcy now that he was departing for his own, or she had thought of some mischief to bedevil him with.

"My son will complain mightily if you do not await his return," she told him. Both children, along with young Meghan, had been sent to Royce's cousin Alden as a precaution, because of Ragnar's anticipated arrival. "They should be here shortly."

"I am only changing where I sleep," he reminded her. "With all the family here, I will, of course, ride over each day, or at least every other."

"With your wife?"

He frowned, refusing to answer that. Kristen's teasing wasn't so easy to take when it concerned one woman instead of women in general. Easiest was to ignore it.

To that end, he remarked, "I thought all of the king's party had left with him."

Kristen followed his gaze to the group of strangers Royce was still talking to. "Those are new arrivals who have business with Alfred. They were directed here; now we have directed them elsewhere."

His eyes narrowed on one of the men. "That one in the middle looks somehow familiar to me. Has he ever been here before?"

"Lord Durwyn? Mayhap he has visited in the past, since Royce does seem acquainted with him, but not since I have lived here."

Selig shrugged it off. Staring at the man was giving him a definite headache, and he had thought he was done with them for a while.

He continued to the front of the hall where Erika waited, Kristen falling into step beside him. Her thoughts went in a new direction as well.

"What is bothering your wife, that she is scowling at you so? Does she not want to leave Wyndhurst?"

Selig's humor returned. "Nay, she just objects to taking her chains with us—ouch!" Kristen had punched his shoulder. "Now, what was that for?"

"For smiling when you said that," Kristen grumbled. "You know how I feel—"

"Odin help me," he cut in. "Do not start that again, sister. She is not wearing them, is she?"

"Which does not mean you will not force them on her again, does it?"

"As it happens—"

He didn't get to finish his sentence, the new commotion at the gates drawing both their attention as the children and their escort arrived. Young Alfred was off his pony first and racing to his father, then his grandfather; then he came tearing across the bailey to throw himself at Selig. His mother was the last to be greeted, but she understood that he had reached that age where men came first.

Selig was laughing all the while, and the more so when Thora was brought forward by her nurse, and it was Selig the little girl reached for, not Kristen. He couldn't resist the angel, of course, and drew her into his arms.

Not for the first time, he wished he had a daughter just like her. That his eyes happened to fall on Erika as he had the thought gave him a jolt, though. A wife, whose main duty to husband and church was the bearing of children. But not *his* wife, who was as pagan in her beliefs as he, and who had extracted a promise from him not to touch her. No children would be forthcoming from *that* bargain.

"Mayhap it *is* best you are leaving."

It took a moment for Selig to tamp down the irritation his thoughts had caused, and to realize what his sister meant. "Now, do not be jealous, Kris." He grinned at her. "Alden's wife likely smothered Thora with so much affection, she wants naught more to do with women, even mothers."

"I never noticed *you* having that problem."

"How fortunate for me."

She laughed then, because his look was so intentionally lecherous. He had not changed, her brother, just because he had a wife now. She wondered if that would be a problem for Erika. She knew it would have been for her.

Selig played his game of buzzing kisses with Thora for a few minutes, making her giggle and shriek with delight, before he turned her over to her mother. He then bade Erika come to him. She did so slowly, and ignored his motion for her to mount his horse.

"I will ride with Turgeis," she said stiffly.

Her tone dictated his own. "You will ride with me."

"Were there no other horses?"

"I saw no need to borrow more when 'tis just a short ride. Or mayhap you would prefer to walk—again?"

Her eyes flashed with the reminder. "What I would prefer is to never—"

"Now, children, enough bickering," Brenna said, coming up behind them. "You are setting a bad example for my granddaughter."

Having said that, Brenna took Thora from Kristen and went into the hall with her. Red-faced at being chastised, Erika mounted the horse. Just as red-faced, Selig did the same. Neither said another word, nor did Selig do more than nod to his sister before heading for the gate. Turgeis, of course, was not far behind.

Erika deplored being this close to Selig. As so frequently happened, it did strange things to her senses that she would rather not feel, especially since she couldn't get the scene of Selig and that baby out of her mind. *His* baby. There was no doubt of that, and Lady Brenna had confirmed it with her remark about being the grandmother.

Her new home was within sight when the questions would remain silent no longer. Still, she began hesitantly. "This is not your first marriage, is it?"

"It is."

"Then who is the mother of your child?"

"What child?"

"The little girl."

"You mean Thora? Aye, of course you do." He chuckled. "She *does* look like me, does she not?"

"Exactly," Erika almost snarled.

He glanced back at her, amusement still in his eyes. "If you think you will be asked to raise her, rest easy. Her mother is doing a splendid job of that."

"And I repeat, *who* is her mother?"

"My sister."

Kristen? If the resemblance between Selig and the little girl hadn't been so strong, she would have realized that for herself.

Her urge was to laugh and hit him and she started to do both, until she recalled that she didn't have that freedom with him. The wretch had been teasing her, but she couldn't respond in kind. She suddenly wished she could, and the thought amazed her. This marriage was not turning out as she had imagined it would. And she had to do something about these ridiculous spurts of jealousy that he found so entertaining. How could she be jealous when she didn't even like the man?

Chapter 37

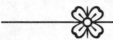

RAGNAR HAD BEEN right. Erika was not displeased with the home that was to be hers. It was mayhap half the size of Wyndhurst, which made it quite large, yet still in the same design, with two stories, giving it ample rooms for sleeping. Unlike Wyndhurst, it had a kitchen that had been built outside, right next to the hall, to eliminate much of the inside smoke, at least in summer. There were other outbuildings that she would discover later, including a separate sleeping hall for those men who followed Selig, but had yet to build their own homes.

The lack of defense was appalling, outer wooden walls barely begun, but then, she understood that the buildings were only recently finished. The outer defenses in wood would not take long to complete with the great many servants she noted. And she had overheard Selig's father mention that he intended stone walls like Royce's to eventually replace the wood, though at a much later date.

There were, indeed, many servants about, and all of them were men. The few females were inside the hall, but when Erika had her first sight of them, she could have wished there were not so many.

Golda she knew she was going to like. The older woman introduced herself and the others, and gave Erika a long dissertation on what had been accomplished since her arrival and what she felt still needed doing. There was nothing subservient about the woman, was instead a brassy forthrightness that said she was accustomed to command, yet was she completely respectful in her manner.

Magge, now, seemed a good-natured girl, if a little *too* good-natured. The smile she wore never faltered. And she wisely kept from looking directly at Selig while in Erika's presence. If the girl knew him intimately, she didn't want the wife to know it.

182

Lida, of course, had to be the one Ragnar had felt Erika would want to get rid of, and rightly so. The girl was incredibly lovely, but more than that, her sexual appeal was blatant in the extreme. Even her clothes were revealing, an outer gown split down the front and tucked back into a wide V, and a chainse that was scooped so low the girl's breasts threatened to spill out. But more than that, her eyes spoke volumes in the way of invitation, and since Erika and Selig had entered, Lida's eyes had not left him except for a brief, dismissive glance sent Erika's way.

To give him credit, Selig wasn't paying the girl any attention—which meant absolutely nothing as far as Erika was concerned. Ivarr was there to greet him, and he'd moved off to speak with his friend, leaving her alone to meet the women of what was, theoretically, her hall.

The trouble was, she doubted she would have much say in this hall. There was even the possibility that she would be made to wear those damned chains again, which would leave the servants in no doubt as to how little authority she possessed. But until that happened, or her husband said otherwise, she would go on as if she had a normal marriage, with the normal responsibilities that came with it.

"Here, now, out with those muddy boots," Golda was suddenly shouting. "Clean them or take them off, but you will not be tracking that filth across *my* fresh rushes."

Erika turned to see who the culprit was, and was a little shocked to find that the only one who had just entered the hall from outside was Turgeis. He was late because he had taken their horses to the stable, and it was likely in the stable that he had picked up the filth Golda objected to.

Turgeis merely gave Golda a hard look, then proceeded to do as he had been told. What Erika found amazing was that Golda had not been the least bit intimidated by him, had actually *ordered* him; to Erika's recollection, no one besides her had ever done so before.

Selig had also witnessed the scene and was just short of laughing over it when his eyes caught Erika's and he kept his humor to himself, deciding she wouldn't appreciate it about her friend's scolding. Why he should consider her feelings on the matter he wasn't sure, though mayhap it was because he was suffering a little guilt over what he had almost done.

He had planned to free one of the women to be his housekeeper, with authority over the others, and he had done so. He had a wife to supervise the servants now, but this wife he had had no intention of giving any authority whatsoever, or at least that had been his plan. Now he felt uncomfortable with the notion of denying her the rights that were her due. So he decided to say nothing on the matter and see if Erika would take up the reins of the household without his leave. Golda certainly assumed she would do so.

If he still wanted revenge, and he was not exactly thinking along those lines now, he could keep it on a more personal level. The fact was, the more time that passed since his marriage, the less Selig was able to retain his anger. His good humor was returning instead, in abundance, to the point where he even found Erika's displays of temper amusing, and he was having more fun teasing her about what he might do, rather than doing it.

As he watched her mount the stairs, one of the women escorting her, he was glad he had not set the stairs behind a wall, where they wouldn't be visible from the hall. Her lifted skirt revealed slender ankles and once, twice, a portion of the shapely legs he had come so close to having wrapped around his hips. She was a woman of volatile passions, with fires easily kindled by a man's touch. How many men besides him had found that out? The thought was absolutely infuriating.

"Is it revenge you married her for, or do you just want her?"

Selig turned at Ivarr's teasing question, prompted because Selig had been unable to take his eyes off her. He was embarrassed to be caught ogling his own wife, and the more so because he had no answer to give his friend. He simply didn't know anymore.

"You do not care for your husband?"

Erika stiffened at the question, which drew her from her perusal of the large bed. She would learn that, like many of the other furnishings, it had recently come from Hedeby. But the bed, suitable for a lord, was not the only thing that told her she had been shown to Selig's chamber. His coffer was also there, the one that had been carted ahead by one of the Wyndhurst servants, the one that contained his clothes and hers combined—and those damned chains.

Golda had asked Magge to show her to her room. Lida had interrupted to say she would do it. Neither of the other two women had objected. Erika had thought nothing of it either, though she should have. A woman like Lida never did anything without an ulterior motive, and Lida's motive could be guessed at. Erika wasn't inclined to oblige her.

"Your question is impertinent," was all she said, intending to say no more.

" 'Tis obvious you do not," Lida continued, undaunted, her tone almost purring. "Anyone can see that. And we know he was forced to marry you."

"*He* was forced! If anyone was—"

Erika cut herself off, furious now that she had taken the bait, despite her resolve not to. She was not going to discuss her husband with this woman. But another reason for Lida's boldness suddenly came to her.

"My brother, Ragnar, was here yesterday. Did you make his acquaintance?"

"Nay. I am saving myself for Selig."

Erika's face reddened. So much for her second assumption. The first had been accurate, and there wasn't much she could do about it when her own position was so in doubt.

Still, she was the mistress here, for the moment. "That is *Master* Selig to you."

Lida laughed and couldn't resist bragging a little. "You will find, lady, that I can call him anything and he will not mind. You will also find that he will be spending his nights with me."

To say something like that to the lord's wife guaranteed some sort of punishment—unless it was true. "Get out of my sight."

Lida just smiled and sauntered to the door. There she stopped to glance back, not at Erika, but at the room. Her look was positively possessive.

"Enjoy this chamber for the while, but know that I can have it for myself whenever I like. Whatever I ask for will be given me by your husband. Do not doubt it."

Erika didn't doubt it. And now she knew how Selig planned to further humiliate her.

Chapter 38

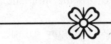

SELIG WAS TRYING to honor their bargain, he really was, but it was becoming more and more difficult with each passing day. He had given up his room to Erika, knowing he could no longer sleep with her near and not touch her. But he was getting tired of finding other places to sleep.

And that damned wench Lida was becoming a nuisance with her stalking him and caressing him at every given opportunity, when all he had done was smile at her once in the way he smiled at any woman. He had actually had to tell her he was not interested. And it was true, though it didn't end her pursuit, since she chose not to believe it. But her sensual brazenness reminded him too much of himself.

She was lovely, certainly, exceptionally so, but he had known too many lovely women for beauty to make a difference. And he might need a woman desperately, or so his body kept trying to tell him, but Lida's hair was not sun-kissed gold, her voice did not remind him of the north countries and home—she was not the woman he wanted.

And you are the greatest fool to want your own wife when she happens to be Erika No Heart.

He could not recall the exact day he had given up denying to himself that he wanted her. What else he felt didn't bear close scrutiny, for the anger was still there and came at the oddest moments, particularly when he brooded about a future with a woman who didn't possess any tender emotions. Did he want them, then, tender emotions from her? Certainly not. Just her body would do. Then why, when she ignored him as she had done since he had brought her to his home, did her attitude cause him such frustration?

After a week had passed, Selig reached the conclusion that he would simply have to brazen his way out of the bargain he had made. He could worry about the rest of his problems later, but this main one had to be eliminated.

He waited until the hall had quieted down for the night, hoping that Erika would think twice about starting a shouting match that would wake the servants. Golda had been allowed one of the rooms abovestairs; Turgeis had been given another. Yet he found Turgeis asleep on a pallet outside the door his wife was behind.

Selig had not been abovestairs himself this week to know if this was a typical arrangement or not. He was simply infuriated that tonight he would have to go through the giant to reach his wife. There was no thought of turning around and forgetting about it.

He nudged Turgeis awake with his boot. "If you think to keep me from my wife—"

"Be easy, man," Turgeis cut in as he sat up, then stood up. "I am here to protect her as I have always done. If her husband slept with her, then he could protect her and I could find my own bed."

Selig was amused by what was clearly reproach. "Just who do you protect her from?"

"Anyone who would do her harm. *Anyone.*"

Selig flushed at the implication. "I have never harmed her."

"So she also claims, but there is harm that is not physical," Turgeis replied, then shrugged. "Your mother asked me to give you time, saying all was not as it might seem between you and my lady. But Erika is not happy here. If you can change that, do so and quickly. Otherwise—"

He left that threat open, to be interpreted however Selig liked. But he also gathered up his pallet and entered a room down the hall.

Selig watched him go with some disgruntlement. So he was to be trusted? He doubted it. If Erika called for her giant, Turgeis would come running, and he'd already had a taste of what the man's fists could do.

Without further thought on the matter, he entered his chamber, expecting to have to wake his wife. But the men's voices had disturbed her sleep. She was sitting up in bed, wearing a chainse for modesty, just as she had done every night they had spent at Wyndhurst. He would have to see about having some comfortable sleeping robes made for her. Nay, that was a stupid thought. He would prefer she slept in nothing at all, just as he did.

She seemed surprised by his appearance. "What do you here?"

"Is this not my room?"

"I have not noticed that it is." The dryness in her tone grated, but the indifference that followed was much worse. "But if you wish to use it as such, I will, of course, sleep elsewhere."

"Nay, you will sleep here as well."

She thought about that for a moment, before her expression turned mulish. "Then you can make use of the floor this time. I have grown used to the bed."

That brought a smile to his lips. She didn't understand yet why he had come. He was pleased to explain. "And I have yet to try the bed. We will share it."

He took a step toward the bed. She threw back the covers and jumped out the other side of it. "Just what do you mean by 'share it'?" she demanded.

"You will sleep on one side, I will sleep on the other, and occasionally we will find ourselves in the center of it—together."

She didn't grasp his meaning immediately, but when she did, she gasped. "Nay, we will not!"

"You married me," he reminded her.

"With an agreed bargain," she reminded him back.

"That bargain has been satisfied in full."

Another gasp. "My part has, but yours has not. You would break your word?"

He sighed in exasperation. Brazening was not so easy against such stubborn tenacity.

"Recall your own words, wench. Your demand was that I not touch you afterward. You did not say *forever* afterward. Afterward was only directly after the wedding and not a day more than that, yet have I given you much more than that. But no more."

She was growing alarmed, and her voice rose accordingly. "You twist my words to suit yourself!"

"Nay, I merely interpreted them differently."

"You do this for more revenge. Admit it!"

His voice turned soft, his expression sensual. "I do this because I want you, Erika, heart or no heart. We can at least have this between us."

"You think making love will make things different between us? Do you forget *why* I am here?"

He was trying to, but she wasn't letting him. He didn't say that, though, didn't answer her question at all. "Turgeis claims you are not happy."

"Ah, now I see. 'Tis your exalted opinion that making love with you will make me happy."

He grinned despite the derision in her tone. "It will not make you *un*happy, wench."

She was afraid he was right, and that was the problem. She had been furious with him all week for flaunting his leman beneath her nose. And now he expected her to forget about that, to lie down and play wife to his husband? Not likely.

She had spent each night imagining him with that slut Lida, and waiting each morn to be told to move out of his room so he could share it with another. That she hadn't been displaced yet meant nothing. It could still happen. Or mayhap he thought to share the room with them both now.

She was seeing red before her thoughts had finished. "I am not interested, so go back to your other women."

"I have known no other women since we wed."

Since they had met, would be more accurate, but that would have sounded too absurd coming from him, was absurd, especially as he had had ample opportunity. He just hadn't taken it—because of her.

"I am to believe that," she scoffed, "when every time I turn around, that black-haired wench is practically in your lap? Hah!"

Contempt now, and it had him flushing when he was not at fault. "I never slept with Lida. Ask her—nay, do not," he amended. "She might lie. You will just have to take my word for it."

"Hah!"

That second "Hah!" got him angry, enough to say, "As it happens, the other wenches are unavailable this eventide. 'Tis not a good time of the month for one, and the other is already taken for the night."

"So abstain," she raged at him. "Can you not go without for one damned night?"

He hadn't meant to admit it, it just came out. "As I have gone without for every night since I met you, nay, I cannot go without for even one more night. I am your husband, like it or not. Tonight you will be my wife in every way. So get you in that bed, wench, to await me. Do *not* make me put you there."

He had never taken a woman in anger and wasn't going to start now. It was not in his nature to be aught but tender with a woman, but he wasn't taking any chances with Erika. His temper had to cool first.

He sighed and moved to one of the two windows that flooded the room with light in the daytime. A stool was before one, and he rested his foot on it. Did she sit there often, pining for the life she had left behind?

The silence thickened behind him. She had not gotten into the bed.

After a while more, he said, "This can be a new beginning, do you let it."

She didn't answer him, but he did hear the bed creak under her weight. He turned around to see her sitting there watching him. And as he gazed at her, she lay back against the pillows. He sucked in a sharp breath. His heart began to pound to a new drum-roll. His body thickened and filled to the passions of the moment.

His step was hesitant as he approached the bed, fearful that he mistook her actions. Yet she waited; she didn't move. But he was still nervous, never so nervous, not even with his first woman so many eons ago. He knew not why this was so important, just knew that he didn't want to frighten her with the feelings that were overwhelming him.

He should have extinguished the candle by the bedside, but he didn't. He wanted to see as well as feel again the body that had consumed so many of his dreams. She was so lushly made, his wife. And as he joined her on the bed and gathered her into his arms, he could feel every curve against his own body and knew ecstasy.

For a while all he did was hold her to him. He was in a ravishing frame of mind, unique for him, but he had it under control, prayed to keep it so. He was afraid to speak; words had never been gentle between them. But without words, he knew not if she lay there resentful, in mere acquiescence, or because she did, in fact, want a new beginning. He could pretend it was the latter.

Erika didn't know what to think when he just held her. He was allowing her too much time to reconsider. She shouldn't have given in like this. It was crazy to hope for something better out of her marriage when there was so much bitterness behind them.

Yet his anger had reached her. If he hadn't shouted at her, she wouldn't have believed him. But she did believe him, and the long abstinence he had claimed made a world of difference to what she was feeling.

That "I want you" had affected her more strongly than she had realized. Her own anger had masked it, kept it from taking over. But once her anger dissolved with his confession, she was helpless against those feelings.

She wanted him, too. It was that simple. She didn't want him sharing his nights with another woman, she wanted him in her bed. As his wife, she had a right to have him there, a right to know his body, a right to know his passion, a right to bear his children. Sweet Freya, she wanted her rights, all of them.

There was nothing to reconsider.

He began so slowly, touching her, and so carefully, she barely felt it— at first. His hand moved along her side, her back, over her hip where he squeezed gently. He lifted and bent her leg against him so he could caress its entire length without moving his cheek from her breasts. He explored her feet, her ankles, behind her knees, which made her shiver. He rolled her on top of him so he had full access to her backside, which he kneaded, pressing her loins more firmly to his.

His hands moved into her hair, spreading it, smelling it. His fingers caressed her cheeks like the softest whisper, teased her lips, circled her ears, and skimmed over her neck, causing more shivers. No part of her escaped his notice—arms, shoulders, hands—and when he rolled her onto her back, her breasts knew full discovery, blossoming, filling, and bringing her first moan; all without removing their clothes, all without him kissing her.

But when she did know the first taste of his lips on hers, it was her undoing. The care he had taken, the slow arousal of her senses, converged in a burst of fiery need that was met and surpassed. It was a kiss of ravishment, and she experienced both sides of the coin, taking as well as surrendering, tongues sensuously thrusting, kindling fires all along her senses. She didn't want it to end, yet did. She wanted to know the rest, yet hated to relinquish any part of the now. He had disturbed her from the first, and now she knew why. Her body had known all along.

Her chainse came off in one swift tug. His clothes took longer, but she didn't lose contact, was able to caress his body as it was bared. Touching him in certain places brought groans from him and he would stop to kiss her again. She didn't mind this delay. Learning his body was a revelation. He was thick and hard, his muscles in prominent display. As he had been before his near starvation? She was sure of it, for his was a body perfect in every way.

When his manhood was revealed, so swollen with need, she felt a virgin's fear. It didn't show. The fear was there, but her own need was now greater.

He came to her again, this time with scorching heat wherever their bodies touched. She opened for him, but only his hand came to rest between her thighs. Gently, so gently she knew his touch there, soothing what he had caused to heat.

And then he drove her wild by starting over.

By the time he joined his body to hers, Erika was almost mindless with wanting him. There was a moment's pain, so minor it was come and gone before it was even noticed. But he noticed. She saw the surprise in his eyes, however brief. And he kissed her deeply, holding still the while, so that when he did finally begin to move in her, there was only pleasure drawn from each thrust.

Somehow it lasted forever, yet was too brief. And the pinnacle they reached was glorious, ecstasy flooding all senses, leaving awe in its wake.

For once, she didn't mind that sensual smile of his. For once, she thought she might be wearing one of her own.

Chapter 39

THE HOUR WAS late, yet Erika found it impossible to sleep. She never dreamed she could lie against her husband and be comfortable, let alone at ease, but she was both. A new beginning? It certainly felt like it.

Selig wasn't sleeping either. He had an arm around her waist, holding her to him, and every so often his hand would move in a roaming caress. He hadn't spoken. Neither had she. They both knew that to speak would shatter the pleasant mood they shared.

The last she had known, he had still hated her. He had said so. Did his wanting her change that? It was not a question she could face. But if he really wanted a new beginning, if that had not just been meaningless words on his part to gain her compliance, then there was one thing, at least, that she had to know. Yet she put off the asking of it, wanting to savor the pleasantness as long as she could. She waited, in fact, until it seemed he was about to fall asleep.

Then, hesitantly: "Would you really have staked me out in that stable?"

He sat up abruptly, running both hands through his hair in an aggrieved manner. "Thor's teeth," he complained. "If you have been lying there all this time pondering that, I think I will beat you."

It was amazing, the difference their having shared passion made. Because of it, she didn't take the threat seriously. She was even amused by his disgruntlement.

"What was I supposed to be thinking about?" she asked innocently.

He gave her a suspicious look before he turned to lean over her. "Shall I remind you?"

She put up a hand to hold him back. "Nay, that will not be necessary. And you will not avoid my question."

He sighed. "I would not do that to any woman, even you."

That was what she had hoped to hear, but it still sparked her temper to hear it. "Another trick?"

"Call it whatever you like, it worked to avoid a war. Yet I would still like to apologize to you for that, have wanted to since the words came out of my mouth. It was my anger—"

"Say no more, or I will perish from shock."

He frowned at her. "Is that to imply you think me incapable of apologizing when warranted?"

"To me, aye."

"To you I owe no other apologies."

She hit her pillow and turned her back on him. He lay down and did like-wise. She was now simmering. So was he. So much for new beginnings.

When Erika came down to the hall the next morning, she was ready to do some apologizing herself. She had ruined what had been an incredibly beautiful experience last night; at least for her it had been. Her question could have waited for some other time. She had even gotten the answer she wanted, and still she had let her temper spoil things.

Did she prefer the hostility between them? So Selig must think. She wasn't sure herself. She had let passion take over yesterday, let it disregard all that had passed between them and made it seem of little import. He had despised her, still might. He had wanted revenge against her and never really got it. Did she honestly think he could forget all that and what he had suffered because of her? For that matter, how was she to forget the chains, the humiliations, and the worst, being tricked into marriage?

For all she knew, he could have let his passion guide him last night just as she had, and now regretted having come to her. Still, she did owe him an apology, at least for last night. But as for a new beginning, she didn't think it was possible. As had happened last night, the past would continue to resurface and get in the way of any progress made.

On the other hand, her marriage had now been consummated. She had been shown one of the benefits of marriage, and it was an extremely nice benefit. Which left her with a new dilemma. Did she accept this unexpected benefit—the *only* one, as she saw it—and hope that children might come of it? She was not, after all, much different from most women, married to men for expediency and never really happy about it. Could she forget that she could have had much more from a marriage if she had not been forced into this one?

Her only recourse would be to hug her resentment to herself and deny Selig his marital rights—if he would allow that. That was supposing, of course, that his regret was not so great that he wouldn't come to her again. And verily, why should he when he had women like Lida available to him?

Mayhap she wouldn't apologize after all.

Turgeis had waited for her in his chamber, leaving the door open so he would hear her, spending the time sharpening his weapons. He followed her down to the hall now with no more than a grunt in greeting. Typical, yet had she expected more from him this morn, since he was aware that Selig had come to her last night, just as he was aware that he had not come all those other nights.

The hall was nigh empty, the hour was so late—she had overslept. As usual, Turgeis went to a different table to break his fast. Erika, preferring to have company today, even silent company, broke their custom and joined him.

"You should not," was all he said.

She ignored him. Golda, who had also heard him, did not. "She is the lady here," she said with sharp scolding. "She can do as she likes."

That wasn't exactly true, though it certainly sounded nice to Erika. Turgeis made no comment, just glared at the woman until she moved off.

Erika hid a smile beneath her hand. She had noticed that Golda seemed to single Turgeis out for complaints or ridicule, and by the look of him, he was getting mighty annoyed by it. That he never said anything to her in reply or defense was just his way.

He caught Erika watching him and grunted. "That woman is a harridan."

She revealed her grin now, teasing, "Mayhap she just likes you, to single you out so."

He blushed at the suggestion. She didn't think she'd ever seen her friend blush before. And his eyes sought out Golda again and somehow looked at her differently this time. Erika's own eyes widened. She had been teasing, but what if she was right?

She looked at Golda again, too, and wondered if she ought to try, one more time, to speak to a woman on Turgeis's behalf. Nay, she had enough troubles of her own. And Golda's attitude wasn't exactly encouraging. Besides, Turgeis could do something about it if *he* was interested.

When they were near done with their meal, she asked him, "Do you know where Selig is this morn?"

"Working on the wall."

She should have guessed. If Selig was not over at Wyndhurst, then he was working on the defenses here, and so it had been all week.

She had been told that the feast he had planned to celebrate the completion of his hall was now being put off until the outer wall was finished. At the rate the wall was going up, that feast might be sometime next week.

She was not looking forward to it herself, not being certain of her role in it, and certainly not having anything she wished to celebrate. But everyone else here was, which gave both servants and warriors alike the incentive to get the wall finished the soonest; in fact, everyone was working on it, even Turgeis, as long as Erika remained outside where he could see her.

She didn't do so often, at least not when Selig was there, for the simple reason that the weather was so warm, the men would strip down to their leggings by midday. And it didn't matter that there were dozens of bare chests to look at—the sight of Selig's bare chest always disturbed her. It was no wonder she had succumbed so easily last night. She had been primed for it without realizing it.

But the hour was still early enough that she didn't expect to see any bare skin yet, so it was safe to seek out her husband and, depending on his own reaction to her appearance, request a private word to tender her apology for losing her temper last night. If his regret was obvious, however, then she would say nothing. That would, after all, be the end of it, and today would be no different from yesterday, when she had assumed he was sleeping with Lida and could have cheerfully murdered the unfaithful wretch.

She waited until Turgeis finished eating, because she knew he would follow her outside, and so he did. And Selig was easy to find, not actually working on the wall with the rest of the men, but on the gate, which was being put together in the center of the yard, the master builder on loan from Royce standing there directing. But there was one other there helping, if what Lida was doing could be called help.

Selig, bent over the frame of the gate, hammering, seemed not to be paying the woman any mind, yet how could he not? She was bent over him, actually leaning against his hips and back to reach his shoulders, which she was apparently massaging. But it looked to Erika like she was doing no more than caressing him—with both her body and her hands.

Had she witnessed this yesterday, she would simply have turned around and returned to the hall, keeping her feelings to herself even had she choked on them. But after last night, she didn't feel like keeping quiet. The man had lied to her to break down her defenses. One woman was not enough for him—even a dozen were not enough. He had to bed his wife, too, and lie to do it.

She couldn't contain herself. She screeched at the top of her lungs, turning heads and stopping all work. Then she picked up her skirts and ran to the hall, not to retreat, but to find a weapon. She was going to geld that bastard she was married to, then pin his leman to the rafters by her hair.

"Erika!"

She didn't stop, though it sounded as if Selig had given chase. She was sure of it when he called again, much closer, and although she had just entered the hall, she knew she would never make it up the stairs to Turgeis's store of weapons before he reached her. Those damn long legs. She needed an immediate weapon, but there was nothing in the entire hall suitable to ward him off. All the tables had been cleared already, except the one where she and Turgeis had eaten.

She rounded that table now to put it between them and grabbed whatever came to hand. She threw what remained of the meal, both wooden bowls that still had dregs of porridge in them, a smattering of bread and cheese, the spoons, the saltcellar—all went sailing through the air toward Selig's head. If she could have lifted the bench, she would have thrown that, too.

He managed to dodge or block most of her missiles, except for the ground salt, which ended up showering him with grayish-brown crystals. It went well with the few splatters of porridge on his cheek. He looked comical, but she was too furious to appreciate that. It was his expression, so incredulous over what she had done. He thought her mad.

He said as much, yelled it, actually. "You are mad, woman!"

"Am I?" she yelled back.

She was looking around for something else to throw. He vaulted over the table before she found it and started shaking her. Some of the salt fell from his shoulders with his movements, but most of it was still clinging to him from head to toe.

A low rumble sounded near them. "No shaking."

They both turned to see Turgeis standing there, arms crossed, fully prepared to intervene. His expression was deadly serious.

Selig demanded of him, "Do you see what she has done to me?"

Turgeis couldn't miss it, but still he maintained, "No shaking."

Selig growled in exasperation, but he nonetheless dropped his hands from Erika. She swung at him when he did, but only managed to connect with his upper arm. No damage to him, but more salt fell.

"What in the name of all the gods has got into you, wench?" Selig roared.

"You are a liar, Viking!" she told him. "A despicable liar. And a lecher. You should be fourscore years to be such a lecher as you are."

He didn't know what he might have lied about, but lecher was clear enough, and he was incredulous again. "You are jealous?"

"I am disgusted," she corrected him.

"You *are* jealous," he insisted, and suddenly he was grinning.

She jabbed a finger into his chest. "I care not how many women you service, but you will not include me in their number and then go back to them. That is not jealousy. That is what I will not tolerate as your wife."

Had she been thinking clearly, she would have known she was overstepping her bounds. A wife did not dictate; a wife was dictated to. But Selig happened to come from a family whose women were notorious dictators. He wasn't offended or even angry at her display of fury. He was, in fact, delighted that she was demanding her rights, because of the reason she was doing so. She was jealous.

He was still grinning. He couldn't help it. "Since you are not jealous, but only disgusted, might I ask what brought about your . . . disgust?"

"So you would play the simpleton as well as the jester? I am not blind!"

"Ah, her."

"Aye, *her.* And as long as she resides under this roof, I will reside under my brother's."

"Nay, that is not an option."

"Then get rid of her!"

As it happened, Selig had already decided to do just that. Lida was a definite nuisance in that she refused to accept rejection. But now he pretended to consider the matter for the first time.

"That is not a bad idea. I will ask my men if one would like to take Lida to wife." Then he reconsidered. "Nay, she was expensive. I doubt one of them would be willing to pay her price."

"Then lower her price."

He thought his wife mad again, or so his look said. "And take a loss, just because you are jealous?"

"I . . . am . . . not—!"

"I will pay it."

This came from Ivarr. He was trying not to laugh, he really was. The rest of the crowd that had gathered with him wasn't nearly as tactful. Smiles, chuckles, guffaws, backslapping. Thorolf was sitting down on the floor, he was laughing so hard.

Erika wasn't amused. She might have gotten what she wanted, exactly what she wanted, but it had come one day too late, as far as she was concerned. Already proven was that her husband would never be faithful. He found the very subject laughable. But she didn't.

She slipped away while he and Ivarr were haggling over Lida's price. She caught sight of Lida before she mounted the stairs. The girl was avidly watching the proceedings, pleased to be the subject of so much contention. There was no alarm or even disappointment that she was being sold to another.

But Erika realized, with despair, that her own reaction would have been much different were she in Lida's shoes. Erika would have been devastated if Selig were getting rid of her. Sweet Freya, had she been foolish enough to fall in love with her own husband, just as his sister had warned might happen?

Chapter 40

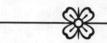

Selig waited until the sun had nearly set before he sought out his wife. He found her in the kitchen, overseeing the last-minute preparations of the evening meal. He had been there earlier himself, to fetch the makings for a private meal, which he already had stowed on his horse.

He had also had to explain to Turgeis what he was about so the giant wouldn't follow. He hadn't exactly got his wholehearted approval, but Turgeis did seem to feel that as long as Erika was with Selig, she was safe.

Though the incident had happened that morn, Selig still wore a fine coating of salt. He hadn't washed it off for two reasons. He enjoyed the reminder of what his wife had done. And he wanted an excuse that he could blame on her to talk her into joining him for a swim. He would need the excuse. The one time he had seen her again today, she had given him a look meant to freeze him on the spot. She had not calmed down yet.

Nor did she look any more amenable now. But one other thing in his favor was that after spending time in the kitchen, she appeared as hot as he was, though she could not feel as sticky. Yet the heat was going to aid his cause, too, or at least it should have. Of course, knowing his wife, he realized she could let a little thing like her temper get in the way of her own preference.

Mayhap he wouldn't ask her after all, but just take her to the lake and throw her in. They could discuss if she would like to swim after that.

His teasing nature favored the latter course, and to accomplish it, he feigned a stern expression to throw Erika off guard, which would hopefully, also, keep her from arguing with him.

He motioned her outside, and as soon as she came through the door, he said, "Come with me," and started off to where his horse waited.

She didn't budge farther. "Where?"

He had to come back to get her, and he took her arm this time to start her forward. "We go for a short ride," was all he said.

She still dragged her feet. "But the meal—"

"Can wait."

He tossed her up onto the horse. She was scowling at him by now, so after he had settled in the saddle himself, he relented enough to offer, "You will not mind this ride, Erika. 'Tis something I thought to share with you, and you will find it pleasant if you will but—relax."

She said nothing, and the ride to the small lake was indeed short. By the time they got there, Selig thought better of throwing her in. He dismounted and helped her down. Dusk was full upon them, with just enough light left to see the wildflowers in bloom and the tranquility of the setting. He had chosen the evening to come here; that way, her modesty would be less disturbed if he actually managed to get her in the water with him.

"My sister loves this place and comes here often with Royce," he said. "For that matter, my parents also swim here frequently when they are visiting."

Erika couldn't quite picture his parents swimming in this lake, but his telling her so somehow put her at ease. "What do we here?"

He grinned before he said, "I am going to wash off the fruits of your temper. Notice I am not going to make you do it for me, though by rights I should. You might enjoy a swim yourself, after such a warm day."

He didn't wait for her answer, but turned his back on her and dove into the water, clothes and all. She was surprised enough by that to put her suspicions aside for the moment. He came up laughing, and shaking water from his hair so that drops reached her even on the bank. He was like a playful child in the water, and when he wasn't looking at her, she smiled at his antics.

The water *did* look inviting, deliciously so, but she would not, of course, swim with him. To do so would be to forgive and forget, and she wasn't going to make that mistake again. She wasn't even going to thank him for selling his leman, because he hadn't actually gotten rid of the woman. Lida would still be around, albeit Ivarr's now. But who was to say Selig wouldn't still make use of her with his friend's blessing? And in that case, what he had done was no more than a meaningless gesture, and she had accomplished nothing by making a fool of herself over it—except to amuse her husband.

She had also wondered about that, his amusement, yet could she make no sense of it. Any other man would have been furious over what she had done today, especially since she had done it in front of his men. Another man might have beat her then and there. Of course, Selig couldn't do that with Turgeis there to stop him. Yet he could have punished her in some lesser way, and even Turgeis had to draw the line at interfering when she *was* in the wrong.

Part of her continued anger was defensive for that very reason. She shouldn't have attacked him and reviled him so publicly. She had been wrong to do that, and worse, for such a stupid reason. It was no wonder his friends found it so entertaining. Husbands were *never* faithful. Why should Selig be any different? But she still couldn't figure out why he had found her "jealousy" so amusing.

She was still watching him when he began to remove his clothing. Tunic, cross-garters, leggings, boots, all were tossed up on the bank near her. It was dark enough, and he was deep enough in the water, that she didn't feel she had to look away—yet. But this was what she had expected to begin with. Where he was concerned, she couldn't help but be suspicious of his every action, and in particular, his attempts to use that potent charm of his on her. And his smiles. His smiles had to be most suspect.

Damned Viking. Why did he have to be so different from other men? Why did he have to be so desirable?

It is not in his nature to hurt women.

Nay, just those who were foolish enough to love him.

"I like it not, swimming alone," he called up suddenly in a coaxing tone.

"Then you brought the wrong woman with you," she called back.

"I brought the right one."

His answer started a glow inside her that she refused to acknowledge. Aware of her feelings now, she feared it was going to be even harder for her to resist his charm. Yet she had to. He was a man born to seduce women. Nothing he said could be taken seriously.

She moved back to find a spot where she could sit comfortably among the flowers. He tried once more to get her into the water before he gave up. Yet he took an inordinately long time at his "washing," and she was growing warm, watching him.

Finally she asked him, "Will they not hold up the meal until we return?"

"Not tonight, for we eat here," he replied. "If you are hungry, you can start without me. You will find the food in my saddle."

It was on the tip of her tongue to argue with him. She didn't want to stay there any longer. The place was too—romantic, the breeze warm, the scent of flowers heavy in the air, the water lapping lazily at the bank. And so private. Entirely too private.

She fetched the food just to distract herself, and the wine she found she started on right away. But it didn't soothe her nerves as she had hoped, or rather, it did too much, because she didn't even think to look away when Selig walked out of the water a while later.

The moon had come out by then, and it was a bright one. Before she had drunk the wine, she would have considered that unfortunate, but now all she could think was what a magnificent, pagan sight her husband was, emerging from the water, a veritable gift from the gods. She had the strangest urge to reach out and touch him, just to be sure he was real. And then the urge was to touch him for other reasons.

She jumped to her feet when she realized what was happening to her. The wineskin was grasped in her hand like a weapon, though she wasn't even aware she held it. He hadn't said a word, hadn't touched her, and yet she was seduced.

She swung around so she couldn't see him. And all she could think to say was, "You will become ill, wearing those wet clothes."

"I brought clean ones."

"Then put them on."

" 'Tis the first time I have felt cool all day," he replied. "You would deny me that when there is no one here to see me but you, and you are already acquainted with my body, clothed or not?"

Put like that, it would have been unreasonable of her to do so. "Aye," she said anyway.

His chuckle was deep and sounded wickedly pleased. But no sooner did it end than his hands slipped over her breasts, pulling her back against his wet chest. Her gasp was silent. Her senses whirled.

"What is it you fear, little Dane?" was whispered at her ear. "What you make me feel, or what I make you feel?"

Both! her mind screamed, but actual words were lost to her already. His one hand stayed at her breasts, but the other had slid over her belly and somehow worked its way between her legs, despite her chainse and gown being in the way. And his mouth had fastened on her neck, was moving slowly upward . . .

Across the lake, Royce moved back from the bank and put a finger to his lips to caution his wife to be quiet. Those lips were grinning.

" 'Tis a good thing we saw his horse," he whispered to Kristen, who had stayed back with their own mounts at his direction. "I do not think your brother would appreciate our joining him just now."

"You mean . . . ?"

"Exactly."

"So you were right. He cannot even hate a woman with any real conviction."

He laughed at her disgruntled tone. "I did not say he was with his wife."

"Nor did you have to, after Thorolf came by to relate what happened today—and Selig's reaction to it. Do you ask me, my brother does not know *what* he wants."

"At the moment, I would say he does."

At the end of the lake, it was Brenna who was amused, and Garrick who was annoyed that he wouldn't be cooling off in the lake, at least not tonight. Unlike Royce and Kristen, who had been at the Wyndhurst village and thought to swim before they returned home, Garrick and Brenna had come straight from the hall. So they had each approached the lake from different directions, the reason that they had not seen one another. Yet both couples had seen Selig's horse.

As Garrick helped Brenna back into her saddle, he wondered aloud, "Do you suppose he might be done quickly and we should wait?"

"If he is anything like you, love—"

"Never mind. And do not say, 'I told you so.' I would have preferred some other way of finding out that he likes his wife more than he would have us think."

Brenna just laughed.

Chapter 41

THE DREAM WOKE Selig, causing him to sit up so abruptly, he disturbed Erika. It was not the first time he had had that dream, but it was the first time he recalled it so vividly. Even the pain in his head was back, as if he had just received the blow.

"What is it?" Erika asked sleepily.

"I have remembered where I saw Lord Durwyn."

"Who?"

He threw off the covers to leave the bed. "I must speak to my family," was his only answer.

Her eyes opened wide. " 'Tis the middle of the night," she pointed out.

He was already dressing. "This cannot wait."

Immediately, her eyes narrowed on him. "You do not need an excuse to leave this bed. Just go."

That got his full attention, the words as well as the caustic tone, and he would have had to be dense not to realize what she thought. "You are the most suspicious woman I have ever met."

"With you, there is ample reason to be," she retorted.

"Nay, there is no reason to be. Contrary to your opinion, dear wife, I do *not* make a habit of lying. If I tell you I had no interest in Lida and never laid so much as a hand on her except to set her away from me, you can believe it. If I also tell you I have known so many women that I cannot possibly name them all, you can believe that. So why would I deny having one woman out of so many?"

"Because this one you had *after* you married!"

He gave her a long, exasperated look before he said, "Get dressed."

"Why?"

"Because you are coming with me. And I tell you now, I am seriously considering putting you back on a leash and keeping you with me for every hour of the day. Then, by Thor, you will not accuse me further of what I have not done."

Considering that last threat, and that it was uttered with notable heat, Erika chose not to argue with him any further on the subject, or about going with him. She got dressed, and hastily, then met him out in the nearly enclosed bailey. She had only one more comment to make when she saw him lead just one horse forward.

"I have been in your stable, Selig. I know you have a great many horses available. Am I never to be permitted to ride one?"

That got a smile out of him at last. "I am a lecher, remember? Lechers prefer to have women cuddling next to them whenever the opportunity presents itself."

"I do not cuddle," she snorted, yet the urge was there to laugh.

Her brother had been correct about him after all, she was learning. When Selig wasn't pursuing revenge, he could be very amusing and enjoyable to be around. And he had started using his sense of humor against her, just as he used those sensual smiles.

He had made love to her at the lake. He had made love to her again when he came with her to bed tonight. Obviously, he was still intent on a new beginning—or he was just enjoying the novelty of a new woman. There was even a worse possibility, that this was merely another form of revenge for him, that he wanted her to love him because that would give him new ways to hurt her once he was sure she did.

Whatever his motive, she was going to stand firm against him for her own protection. She was not going to let her feelings grow any deeper than they were. And she was going to try, desperately, to ignore those feelings she had already discovered. Hopefully, he would grow tired of having to coax her each time he wanted to bed her. And hopefully, she would not go berserk again when he did finally give up and seek out others instead.

There were a few hours yet before dawn when they arrived at Wyndhurst. Selig had changed his mind by then about waking his entire family. Only Royce was summoned, and they waited for him in Selig's old room so the servants sleeping in the hall would not be disturbed by their talk. Several candles had been lit by the time he joined them.

"You decided you like it better here?" were Royce's first, dryly uttered words.

For once, Selig did not reply with a sally. "I regret waking you, but I felt you might want to act immediately on what I have to tell you."

Royce's expression turned instantly serious. "Then tell me."

"The day I moved back to my hall, I noticed a man here who seemed familiar to me, yet could I not recall where or when I might have met him before. Kristen said he was Lord Durwyn, but the name meant nothing to me."

Royce nodded. "He does not live near here, but I have known him for many years. Durwyn and his wife used to follow the royal court, until she died some seven or eight years ago. Durwyn retired to his estate after that, though he left his son at court in his stead. As I recall, the son, Edred, died in that last battle with the Danes, the one that also saw you wounded. Edred closely resembled his father. Mayhap 'twas he you remembered."

"Nay, 'twas the older man, and only recently that I saw him. Royce, 'twas the day of the ambush. I saw Lord Durwyn cut down that old bishop we escorted, just before I received the blow to my head."

"You must be mistaken."

"Nay. I dreamed of the ambush tonight. It brought the day back to me clearly, as well as Durwyn's part in it. He was the only one there I *did* get a good look at that day. I even recall noting that he was dressed finer than a thief ought to be dressed."

Royce ran an agitated hand through his dark hair. "God's mercy, do you know what this suggests?"

"Aye. 'Twas not thieves who ambushed an unsuspecting group of travelers that day. 'Twas a planned attack against the *king's* party, to put an end to our mission. What I need to know from you is, do you tell the king of this before or after I kill the man?"

Royce's lips curled upward despite the seriousness of the subject. "I doubt me you will get the opportunity. Alfred will want to deal with this matter himself. But be assured that if you are right, Durwyn will hang."

"I nearly died, Royce, and the pain I lived with for weeks will never be forgotten. I want the satisfaction of challenging the man responsible."

"Aye, and so will your father want it, and your mother, *and* my wife. You, my friend, may well have to get in line do you handle it the Viking way. But you reside in Wessex and Alfred does have strict laws, so better to let him see to it. The crime *was* against him, after all."

Selig only mumbled to that, not exactly an agreement, but Royce chose to take it as such, and so continued. "Now, I know Alfred's direction. In fact, he had planned to visit here again on his way back to the royal estate at Chippenham, but I do not think this should wait until then. I will go now to send a messenger to him."

Selig nodded. The urgency that had brought him here with such haste was relieved, if not put to rest. He was vexed, though, that the matter could have been done with if he had just made the connection with Lord Durwyn the day he saw him at Wyndhurst. But everything about that harrowing time was fading in his memory, except for the pain and Erika's part in it, and he wished *that* would fade as well.

Royce stopped at the door to say, "You might as well stay here until this thing is settled. Alfred moves quickly sometimes, and sometimes not. 'Tis not likely, but he could conceivably arrive on the morrow, and he will want to see you immediately."

"Fine."

"Then go back to sleep. I intend to, after I send the messenger."

Erika had sat patiently throughout their talk, even though she had not understood a word of it. She would have been annoyed if she had been excluded deliberately, but that was not the case, since Royce and Selig could communicate only in Celtic. Yet she decided then and there that if Selig was not going to learn Anglo-Saxon to put an end to this difficulty, she would learn Celtic, and likely quicker than he, as new languages came easily to her.

"Do we leave now?" she asked, drawing his attention to her at last.

He seemed momentarily surprised that she was even there. "Nay, we will remain here until the king comes."

Her brows rose. "You are to become involved in the king's business?"

He realized then that he had not actually told her why they had come here in the middle of the night. Amazing that she had not harangued him for every detail. His mother and sister would have, and still would, as soon as they heard of it.

He explained briefly, ending with, "We will sleep here for a few days." And then suddenly he grinned, glancing around at the room they had shared before they wed. "Do you want the floor or the bed?"

Her scowl was immediate. "That is not funny."

"You will think so if you pick the floor and we end up making love on it."

Her mouth dropped open, then snapped shut. "I assume you mean on the morrow?"

His grin grew wider. "Actually, now that it has been mentioned—"

She gasped, mostly in surprise. "But you cannot possibly . . . you have already . . . twice . . ." She didn't try to finish when he started laughing— and walking toward her.

"Verily, Erika"—that sensual smile was fully in place now—"how little you know your husband."

But she was learning, and, sweet Freya, sometimes *most* pleasantly.

Chapter 42

THE WYNDHURST PATROL brought advance word of the king's approach late the next afternoon, giving Royce the opportunity to ride out to meet him. He went alone, since a discussion on horseback was easier between two people rather than three or four, and he wanted to gauge Alfred's mood on this matter before he met with Selig about it. Though the very fact that Alfred had come so quickly and ahead of his entourage, with only a small escort, said a great deal.

"I had hoped our next visit would be without incident," Alfred began.

Royce winced. "My in-laws do keep things from becoming boring around here."

Alfred acknowledged the sally with a brief smile, then got to the heart of the matter. " 'Tis a grave accusation your brother-in-law makes. Of course, Lord Durwyn will be allowed to face his accuser."

"He denies it, then?"

"He has yet to be told," Alfred admitted. "I thought it best to see to the matter all at once, and I did not want to arouse his suspicions by inviting him to ride ahead with me. An element of surprise would be helpful in this so he has no opportunity to device a defense if he has none, and 'twould be best if your brother-in-law springs it."

"He will be glad to, but he may also challenge Durwyn at the same time."

"Nay, you must prevent that."

Royce had known Alfred would say that. But stopping a Viking intent on revenge was well nigh impossible, as he knew from firsthand experience.

Alfred considered that subject settled, however, and went on to the next. "I have tried to reason why Durwyn would do this. He hates the Danes, of

208

course, nigh as much as you. He lost his only child to them. But I do not think that can be the only reason."

"I agree," Royce replied. "This attack was not against the Danes, but against you—or rather, against your plan to strengthen the peace."

"Exactly," Alfred said. "And if you consider the nature of that plan, then mayhap you can discern a logical reason for Durwyn's interference."

Royce frowned. "You know something I do not?"

"Something I wish I had recalled the sooner, that one of the offered heiresses is a neighbor of Durwyn's, the very girl who would have wed his son, Edred, if the lad had not died beforehand."

In Alfred's defense, Royce said, "Lord Durwyn does not know you as well as he knew your brothers. 'Tis likely he assumed you would put the good of the peace before the concerns of one single lord."

"He would have been wrong, inasmuch as wedding a Dane to that particular girl would have led to outright battles eventually, with neighbors such as Durwyn. How, then, would that have strengthened the peace? Nay, he should have come to me with his rancor. There are other heiresses who could have served in lieu of this one. Instead he took matters into his own hands and resorted to outright murder—assuming your brother-in-law has not made a mistake."

"Aye, assuming that."

Alfred sighed. "I fear he is not wrong, and this is a nasty business that I do not look forward to. I can only guess that Durwyn resides with the court now so he will have notice of the next delegation I would have sent, which he would have attacked as well. I was even informed that he came to court with a large party of men, but because he never presented them, I gave it no further thought—before this."

"How many men?"

"Enough to attack a small number and be assured of leaving no survivors. And they do not travel with us directly, but they always camp near. I have grown lax in not suspecting vipers so close to home."

"How could you know?"

Alfred was not as forgiving of himself. "That is no excuse. With so many losses to the Danes, Durwyn cannot be the only one who does not embrace the peace. But in his case, we will know for certes on the morrow, when he arrives with the rest of the court—or at least by the next day. Verily, I do not expect them all at once. How your wife ever rode to East Anglia and returned so quickly, I cannot imagine. It would have taken my entourage five, mayhap ten times as long."

Ending on that lighter note put them both at ease, and no more was spoken of the matter that day, other than the questioning that Selig had to be put through. Alfred did, however, reiterate to Selig that if Durwyn was found to be guilty after the confrontation, then his disposition was a royal prerogative, though he relented enough to add, "If it comes down to your word against his, with no proof in the offing, I would not find it amiss if I heard a challenge issued," which put Selig at ease on the matter.

While the men had their discussions, Kristen prepared for the return of the royal court, and Erika, with nothing to occupy her here as she had at home, offered to help. It was a mistake. This was the first time she had actually tried talking to Selig's sister since the journey to Wyndhurst, and she quickly found that nothing had changed.

The clothes lent to her by Kristen were as she had thought, not for her sake, but for Selig's. She herself was barely tolerated. In fact, Kristen's manner toward her was an extension of the other women's, purely hostile, but for a different reason.

Erika, however, was no longer as meekly accepting of circumstances as she had been. Her guilt had kept her from fighting back before, but she had exonerated herself of that. She was no longer willing to accept total blame, and besides, she was the man's wife now. They had all seen to that.

So she did not hesitate to confront her sister-in-law's frosty manner when she finally found a moment alone with her in the smokehouse. She didn't even warm up to the subject, asking baldly, "If you still hate me, why did you not protest this marriage?"

Kristen was caught off guard, yet her manner was still stiff in her reply, and she didn't mince words either. "I do not exactly . . . hate you. But I doubt me I can ever forgive what you did. Mayhap Selig can in time, since that is his nature, at least where women are concerned. But I cannot."

"Has it not occurred to you that if my brother had been at Gronwood at the time, Selig would likely have been hanged instead of lashed? I am sick of feeling guilty for something *he* instigated with his insults. Sweet Freya, I even suggested excuses that he could have used, so that I could simply let him go, but he ignored them, insisting on a truth that was highly suspect and only made him appear more guilty. And do not say again that it *was* the truth, because what he claimed was *not* believable at the time."

"Are you finished?" Kristen asked frigidly.

Erika sighed. "Certainly, and as usual, what I say makes no difference."

"Mayhap because the lashing was not what I referred to, is no longer even an issue, with him healed from it. What I find unforgivable is that you were so vindictive that you laughed at his suffering."

"I did *what?*"

"Do not try and deny it, Erika. He has mentioned it more than once to me." And Kristen repeated his words with rising anger. " 'It amused her to see me in pain. Her laughter I will never forget.' "

Erika gasped. "That is a lie! I never laughed during the interrogation. Ask Turgeis. He was there."

"I said naught about the interrogation. 'Twas the lashing Selig referred to."

"But I was not even there for it!" Erika cried. "Had I still been there, it would never have occurred. Had my nephew not broken his arm, I would have stopped it in time. But I was called away. And I did not see your brother again until you did."

"So your brother tried to tell me, but think you I would believe you over Selig? If you say it happened differently, then discuss it with him, but do not try to convince me—"

"To what purpose?" Erika cut in, her own anger mounting. "He does not believe me in what I say, any more than I believe him, any more than you believe me." And then she added with scathing derision, "But thank you for telling me this. I had not realized I was so—vindictive."

Having said more than she had intended, Erika returned to the hall, leaving Kristen annoyed, yet thoughtful. One of them was lying, and, of course, it had to be Erika. But curse her eyes, how was it she could sound so very convincing—and innocent?

Kristen might have dismissed the subject entirely from her mind if Selig had not confronted her with it the next day in a direct complaint about his wife. Apparently Erika had not mentioned to him anything about the talk she and Kristen had had, yet was Erika still angry about it, enough for Selig to catch the brunt of it—without knowing why.

Storming out of his room, where he had been unable to get a single word out of his wife to explain her newest pique, he nearly collided with Kristen in the hallway and took his confusion out on her, demanding, "How can she hold a grudge so long for one little insult when I have already forgiven her for what she did to me, which was much worse?"

"Did you tell her that?" Kristen asked.

"What?"

"That you forgive her."

The question annoyed him. "I have shown her. I asked her for a new beginning. Must I actually say the words when they are likely to be thrown back at me? She still hates me. She does not care that I no longer hate her."

"When did *that* happen?"

"What?"

"Your no longer hating her."

He waved a dismissive hand as they continued down to the hall. "What does it matter when?"

With a sigh, she led him straight to the ale barrels and, pouring them both a healthy draught, sat him down at the nearest table. "So tell me."

His expression turned morose. "What is to tell? She will not talk to me now."

Kristen couldn't resist grinning. "Some husbands would consider that a boon."

"Save your teasing for another time, Kris. I am in no mood for it."

"I can see that. What I cannot see is how you two can be married and not discuss what you each find most important—except with other people." And then she saw Erika come down the stairs and, noticing them, head in their direction. But instead of warning Selig, she asked deliberately, "Would it interest you to know that she does not recall laughing, at any time, while you were at Gronwood?"

He snorted. "I do not blame her for denying it. She is a woman, after all, and what woman does not try to deny shameful behavior?"

Erika had stopped upon hearing that, but Kristen was too disgusted by his remark to quit now. "With an attitude like *that*, 'tis no wonder she will not confront you about it. And yet it was her laughter that so infuriated you that you wanted revenge. So tell me again what you recall of it."

He scowled at her. "I am trying to forget that. But I recall now what she claims was an insult, and it was no insult, or was not intended as such. I needed help. I wanted you there, but you were not. She was. My head ached. My sight was blurred. My thoughts would not stay with me. One moment I knew who she was and why I was chained to a wall, the next I did not. I told her I needed a bed, hers if she liked. I was not insulting her. 'Twas what women have always wanted of me, and I merely offered her the same. That was all I had to offer just then."

Kristen did not expect the stricken look on her sister-in-law's face, or to see her turn and run from the hall as if the damn rafters were about to fall on her. She felt rather contemptible for playing such a trick on them, no matter that she had hoped for a confrontation that would put an end to the lie, whichever one of them was responsible for it.

She decided not to mention what she had done to Selig. It was bad enough that Erika knew.

Chapter 43

ERIKA WOULD HAVE run through the gate to leave Wyndhurst, except the king's entourage had just started arriving, and the passage was too crowded just then to get through. She moved back against the wall instead, out of the way. Leaning against the cold stones, she squeezed her eyes shut, trying to block out the noise. She was so close to tears, it was all she could do to keep them from falling. Her guilt was back, and it was ripping her apart.

No insult intended—his way of paying for help. Did Selig really use himself like coin? Had women taught him to do that? Ah, sweet Freya, it was all a mistake; his fever and the head injury had made him act as he had. Why had she not seen it? Why couldn't she have helped him, instead of losing her temper and hurting him more?

And why did he think she had laughed at his suffering? He really did think it. She recalled his words: *I mean to see you never laugh again.* She had thought, at the time, that that promise was significant, and so it was. Had that, too, been because of the fever? Had he imagined her laughter, and now thought what he remembered was real? *Erika No Heart.* He believed it, so how could he bear to touch her, thinking that of her? And with him believing it, how could she convince him it wasn't true?

"You there." She was startled from her thoughts. "Who is that Celt standing with King Alfred?"

The tone was imperious. So was the man's expression. He was one of the king's party, with two others by his side, all three of them waiting for her to answer. And there were now so many people, horses, and baggage wains in front of her, she had to go up on tiptoe to see whom he referred to.

But she should have known by the description of "Celt." "My husband, Selig the Blessed, and only half Celtic. His other half is pure Viking."

"You are both *Danes*?"

Revulsion, as if the word were the foulest curse. Erika was too numb to care.

"He is Norwegian," she said, pushing herself away from the wall. "I am the only Dane here."

She returned their rudeness with her own, walking away from them, but they were immediately forgotten. She had to get away from this crowd to decide what she should do. But with Selig in the bailey and apt to notice her wherever she went . . . She pushed her way through the gate after all.

Lord Durwyn watched her leave with narrowed eyes. "I do not like this," he said, turning to one of the men with him. "Find Ogden and tell him to follow her. He can take one other with him, but they are not to lose her. Tell him Aldwin will bring word if they need do more than that."

The first man slipped away to locate the three others who had entered Wyndhurst with Durwyn. Aldwin, who remained with him, asked, "What is it you suspect, my lord?"

"You did not recognize that black-haired Viking with Alfred? You should have, since we left him for dead last month. Ogden wears his sword even now."

"One of the king's delegates?" Aldwin gasped. "Nay—a twin mayhap?"

"When Alfred cut short his business in the west to return here, and there stands a man with him who should be dead? I think not."

"Then we must leave—"

"Do not be a fool. If I am to be accused, I must know it. If I am, then it will be that Viking who will do it. So do not associate yourself with me or come near unless I bid you, for it will be up to you to take the woman and use her against him, to get him to withdraw his accusations. You know where to hide her?"

"Certainly."

Durwyn nodded. "I have a feeling we will know one way or the other as soon as I show myself, so stay near enough to hear what transpires. You can judge for yourself if the woman needs be taken. You can do so, I trust?"

"Aye."

"Good. Then let us find out now." Durwyn started to leave, but turned back to add one more thing, almost as if he had forgotten. "And, Aldwin, if I do not leave Wyndhurst by, say, late this afternoon, kill the wife."

Durwyn made his way through the crowd then, not to approach the king, but to make himself visible. As he had guessed, both Alfred and the Viking moved toward him as soon as he was noticed by them. He was not worried, though. It would be his word against the other man's, and the other man was a *Viking*. Who, after all, could trust the word of a Viking?

It went exactly as he had supposed it would, except that Lord Royce had to translate for the man, since he didn't speak Saxon, and Durwyn didn't bother to admit that he spoke Celtic. But this merely added to the confusion, and in his favor, so he was not displeased by it.

As Durwyn had expected, he was accused of the very crime he had committed. Of course he denied it. His feigned disbelief and then outrage were worthy of applause. And Alfred's frown said clearly he didn't know whom to believe. There was no proof, after all.

What he had *not* expected was for the hotheaded young man to backhand him, and before he could even get up from where the blow had landed him, he'd heard Royce explain, "You have called him a liar by your very denials, Lord Durwyn. For that he challenges you."

"This is an outrage! I cannot be expected to fight a damned heathen—"

" 'Tis my brother-in-law you speak of, so be careful what you call him, or my challenge will follow his. And frankly, my lord, I am inclined to believe him, particularly since I know you had good reason to keep a Dane from wedding the girl your son should have wed. You were a fool not to bring your objections to Alfred."

"And I would have if I had even known such was in the offing. But I was not aware of it, I tell you! I knew naught of it until I but recently joined the court."

"So you say. His contention says differently. Yet are you challenged now, so it really no longer matters who is telling the truth, does it? So do you accept, or do you let him cut you down where you lie? And I assure you, he would not hesitate to do so."

Durwyn got hastily to his feet and said shakily, "I accept—but I need time to recover from my travels first. I am no longer a young man."

Royce heard the snorts clearly, two of them, and knew without looking that they came from Turgeis and Garrick, both older men than Durwyn, who was not yet twoscore years. Durwyn's flush said he had also heard them. Yet was it Alfred who decided the matter.

"Three hours hence, my lords. Lord Durwyn may rest during that time, break his fast, sharpen his weapons. What he may not do is depart Wyndhurst without my leave. And there will be no wergild accepted in lieu of this challenge. Unless I hear a confession in the interim, the challenge will go forward as issued and accepted."

Chapter 44

"MY LADY, YOU must come with me."

Erika turned from tossing pebbles in the lake to see a short, dark-haired man-at-arms at the top of the bank. She didn't recognize him, but then, Wyndhurst had so many soldiers, and she would know by sight only those she had traveled with from East Anglia.

"Who are you?"

"Ogden, my lady. Your husband has issued a challenge and would like to speak with you before he fights. He has men searching for you every—"

"*Who* is he fighting? That Lord Durwyn who masquerades as a thief?"

She was rushing up the embankment too quickly to note the man's clenched jaw and baleful stare. "Aye, Lord Durwyn," he answered tightly. "You will have to ride with me. We must make haste."

Haste? Her heart was already racing. She would have run all the way back to Wyndhurst had it been necessary. And in fact, she did run past Ogden to the waiting horses. Another man stood with them. Still another was already riding hell-bent back toward Wyndhurst, obviously to inform others that she had been found.

"Well, hurry!" she snapped at the two who had been left to escort her, trying to mount one of the animals without assistance.

She was boosted up to the saddle before she had managed it herself, and Ogden mounted behind her. They set out immediately, and at a gallop that matched her state of urgency. She was frantic with dread. *Why* would Selig want to speak to her before he fought? Did he think he might not survive? Did he have things to tell her that she had longed to hear, but would be hearing too late?

At the speed they were making, it took only a few minutes for Erika to

216

realize that they weren't riding toward Wyndhurst. "Where do they fight, if not at the manor?" she turned to ask Ogden.

"We are almost there," was his only answer.

No sooner had he said it than she saw the camp in the distance. She didn't bother to wonder why this place on the edge of a woods had been chosen for the challenge. She would find out in moments, and in fact, it was only another minute or so until they burst into the camp, retaining their speed until the last second.

Erika was practically thrown from the saddle, the horse had stopped so abruptly, and then she was tossed down, literally, and just barely caught by one of the men on the ground. When she regained her balance, she started to upbraid her escort, but didn't get the chance, his orders issuing first.

"Bind her and put her in the pit. I trust you have had time to finish it?"

" 'Tis almost done," replied the man who had caught Erika and was still holding her arms.

"Then that is done enough," Ogden said. "She is a woman, so it does not have to be as deep as the others, and we cannot take the chance of someone coming by and finding her. See to it immediately."

Erika tried to jerk loose of the man at her back, but he was a stocky fellow and too strong. His hold only tightened to a painful grip.

"What means this?" she demanded, glaring up at Ogden. "You lied?"

"Only about who sent me to find you. My Lord Durwyn *was* challenged, and if your husband cannot be made to retract it for your sake, you die."

"Is your lord such a coward, then, that he fears to fight in single combat?"

"You jest, lady. I was told your husband is nigh a giant, and a Viking berserker besides. Any man would be a fool to face him in battle."

It was amazing that she could feel pride in those words even as impotent rage rushed through her. Her being here was *her* fault, for going down to the hall this morning without stopping by Turgeis's room to tell him, for leaving Wyndhurst alone, for being so gullible that she had come right along with her kidnappers, had even urged them to hurry—so she could be thrown into a pit. A pit! Odin help her, she was afraid theirs would have no resemblance to the one at Gronwood, but would be an actual hole in the ground.

Having said all he intended to, Ogden rode off, back to Wyndhurst, she assumed, to tell his cowardly lord that she had been captured as ordered. And Erika was dragged over to the start of the tree line, where, a few feet beyond, two men were pouring dirt into a crate that another man waited to carry off into the woods to dispose of, thereby leaving no evidence that a hole had been dug.

The pit was there, three feet long by two feet wide. Near it was a plank of wood the same size, and on top of that, the grass that had been carefully cut away from the top of the hole, so that when it was replaced, there would be little or no evidence that a hole was beneath it—or anyone inside it.

"You heard?"

"Aye," one of the diggers replied, the one standing hip-deep in the hole in the ground.

"Then get out of there," the man holding Erika said, then called loudly over his shoulder, "I need some rope over here and something for a gag."

Erika fought to keep from trembling. They were going to put her in that pit. There were at least twenty men in that camp. She wasn't going to get away. And she could conceivably die in that hole if she was never let out.

"You dig pits everywhere you make camp?"

She said it to be sarcastic, to take her mind off her mounting fear, but the one holding her took her question seriously. "Always. We have found them most useful, and they are never discovered."

"But how can you dig it so quickly? Your lord just came this morn."

" 'Twas started last week when we stopped here briefly while Lord Durwyn sought the king at yon manor. There was no time to finish it then."

"So you have finished it now. Then you must kidnap people everywhere you go?"

He shook his head. "It is sometimes necessary to hide one or more of us. With these pits, a man can completely disappear from sight, in the middle of the day, with no trace or clue left for his pursuers."

"Ah, so you *have* become thieves as well as murderers under your brave lord's guidance," she sneered. "Now do I see the necessity for these pits."

Her scathing contempt infuriated the man, so that he shouted at whoever had come up behind them with the requested items. "Gag her!"

It was done with swift efficiency, her binding. She managed half a scream before cloth was stuffed in her mouth and tied off. She was then pushed to the ground, her knees bent to her chest, a rope wound tight around her to keep her in that scrunched-up position. It was not even necessary to bind her hands separately, the rope looping around her so many times keeping her arms tight at her sides, yet still her wrists had been tied at her back, merely to add to her discomfort, no doubt. And they had tried to deny doing this before with other victims? Craven churls, the lot of them.

But the moment she was dropped into the pit and the cover was pushed into place, sealing out every trace of daylight, she no longer thought of Durwyn's men. Pitch blackness. The air was so thick with the scent of newly cut earth that she could barely breathe. And it was cold. Who would have thought a tightly enclosed space could be so cold? Or was it her own blood, freezing with fear?

How long? Surely if a challenge was issued, it would be seen to right away. But they wanted Selig to cry off. She was being used to that end, but at what success? His compliance was certainly not guaranteed. The revenge he had been unable to extract from her he wanted out of Lord Durwyn, and he wanted it badly. She had realized that when he told her about Durwyn. So what would a man do who didn't love his wife? See to his honor first, then merely hope he could find the wife before she was murdered?

She was so afraid that Selig would do just that, she already counted herself dead. And not another thing needed to be done to have Durwyn's threat carried out. Why bother to drag her out of the pit just to cut her throat? Leaving her there with no escape and no hope of ever being found was just as effective and much crueler. This pit would be her grave and she would die knowing it.

Chapter 45

"WHAT DO YOU mean, you cannot find her?" Selig asked, sitting up from his slouch against the wall, where he had been staring at Durwyn on the far side of the hall, savoring his anticipation of the coming fight. The man had only one hour left to live. "Where have you looked?"

"Everywhere," Turgeis replied.

It was the look of worry that was revealed, just briefly, in Turgeis's expression that was responsible for the panic that burst on Selig without warning. "Where in Loki's realm were you?" he demanded. "You are her shadow! I trust you to always know where she is when I do not!"

"She did not let me know she was leaving her room. I have not seen her at all this morn."

Selig's raised voice drew Royce and Kristen. Kristen asked her brother, "Have you seen her since you came down?" When Selig shook his head, she added, "I did, briefly. She was on her way out to the bailey." Then she asked Turgeis, "Did you check Selig's hall? She could have gone there."

"She would not leave Wyndhurst alone," Turgeis insisted. "She is not that foolish."

"If she were . . . upset . . . she might not have been thinking of caution," Kristen replied hesitantly.

"For what reason would she be upset?" Turgeis demanded, a growl entering his tone.

"She is *always* upset," Selig answered before Kristen could, relieved now that Erika's whereabouts had been guessed at. "Why would today be any different?" Then he turned to Royce. "Would you send someone to make sure she has gone home? I will not be able to concentrate on my fight with Durwyn unless I know she is safe."

"Do you want her returned here?"

"If she left early, she may not even know that I fight. She can be told, but the decision will be hers if she wants to return for it. I would not force her to watch if she has no interest—"

"God's mercy, spare us such self-pity," Royce cut in, laughing now. "You know very well your wife would want to be here."

Kristen's conscience would not let her remain quiet any longer. She opened her mouth to confess why Erika had likely left, and her part in it, but she didn't get the chance. One of the servants was shouting for Royce as he raced toward them, and when he arrived, out of breath, terrified, what he had to say made her confession irrelevant—for the moment.

Only Selig could not understand what Royce was told, and demanded, "What?" when he saw so many grave faces turning in his direction.

Royce answered, "The message he was given is for you, and you will not like it."

"Tell me."

" 'You will claim you are mistaken in your accusations against Lord Durwyn, or you will never see your wife again. And the king is not to know of this, or you will never see your wife again.' "

Selig lifted the servant up by one hand. "Who gave you that message?"

Royce had to repeat the question in Saxon, and after listening to the man's frightened response, he told Selig, "Put him down, man. He did not see who it was. He was approached from behind, told exactly what to tell you, then pushed into the crowd. When he turned, there were too many men about to know which one had spoken to him."

"But I know who *sent* the message," Selig said and started across the hall with deadly purpose.

Royce went after him and grabbed his arm, but was thrust aside. Durwyn saw him coming and leapt to his feet, but to no purpose. Selig was on him, his hands closing around his throat. It took five men to pull him off, and he let go of Durwyn only long enough to throw off those restraining him, which he did right quickly.

It took his father to step in front of him and push him back when he went for Durwyn a second time. "Are you mad?" Garrick demanded. "What has happened that you cannot wait to end him properly?"

"He has taken Erika," Selig replied furiously. "He threatens her life if I do not retract the challenge and claim I was mistaken in accusing him."

"But he has not left this hall," Garrick pointed out.

"He does not have to. He has men aplenty with him to do the deed."

At that moment Durwyn rallied sufficiently to cry, "What does the heathen accuse me of now?"

Selig didn't understand him, but Garrick did and rounded on the man. "You should have taken your chance at fighting my son, because you prove your guilt by taking his wife to tie his hands. And if he withdraws his challenge because of it, be apprised that you now have one from me."

Durwyn said nothing at first, was staring in horror at King Alfred, who was near enough to have heard every word. Then he yelled, " 'Tis a lie! All of it! If someone has taken the Viking's wife, 'twas not done by my order!"

At that point Royce pulled Selig away and pushed him toward the front of the hall. "You will get nothing out of him," he hissed. "The bastard will die swearing innocence. But you were a fool to attack him, proving his guilt. You should have closed the gates first. Whoever works with him has now been given the opportunity to leave—and to carry out his threat."

Selig was running toward the door before Royce had finished speaking, though Royce kept up with him. They both stopped, however, upon reaching the bailey and seeing the gates already closed and Turgeis standing in front of them, his own horse and Selig's at the ready.

"At least someone was thinking with his head instead of his heart," Royce said wryly. "Go ahead. It will take me a few minutes to send out my men in a wide enough sphere that a call can go out and be heard as soon as she is found—and to make sure only my people leave."

There was no longer a need for such tearing haste, now that Durwyn's henchmen were contained within the walls, except to get Erika freed the sooner. And that was all the reason Selig needed to continue with all speed.

He did spare a moment to say, "Thank you," to Turgeis when he reached him.

The giant merely said, "You were too fraught with emotion to think of it. Did the lord tell you where she is?"

"Nay," Selig replied bitterly. "But he has men camped somewhere near here. That much I already knew. Royce is gathering his men now to spread wide the search. Whoever finds the camp first will call out."

"They can call out, but I will not," Turgeis said as they both mounted. "I will see to the matter myself."

"Then I ride with you."

Chapter 46

THE CAMP WAS easily seen from a distance. No effort had been made to conceal it, though a woods was right there and could have been used. It was even in the first logical place to look, west of Wyndhurst, the direction from which the king's party had come.

Turgeis spotted it first and galloped in that direction. Selig, so anxious to have Erika rescued and safe again, overtook him. Unfortunately, the way they both charged into the camp gave every indication of attack, and not one man scattered or tried to run, but drew his weapon instead. There were twenty against two. Durwyn's men considered the odds too high in their favor to lose, despite the size of the Vikings. So they attacked en masse.

For Selig and Turgeis, that meant every blow they struck had to be a killing blow, with none wasted, which had not been anticipated, but was the only way to keep from being felled themselves. Selig would not have killed them all, yet it looked like they might have to. He tried to locate Erika in the camp, but there was no opportunity to see beyond the next sword thrust. Yet until they were assured she was there and not taken elsewhere, someone had to be alive to answer questions when this was done, but the bodies were already piling up.

He shouted to Turgeis, who had an equal number of men coming at him from all sides. "Leave at least one alive to tell us where she has been taken."

"You see to it," Turgeis called back. "My Blooddrinker does not leave wounds that might heal."

Not long after that, Selig cut down two of the last three men attacking him with a single lucky stroke. The third man, realizing that he now stood alone, started backing up, terror in his eyes.

"Tell me where the woman is and you can go free," Selig promised him.

The fellow didn't understand a word he said, turned to flee, but one of his downed comrades tripped him up and he fell face-forward. Selig moved in swiftly to apprehend him, prepared to beat the information out of him if necessary, but the man didn't get up. When Selig turned him over, there was a spiked mace embedded in his forehead. He would be answering no questions.

Selig looked immediately toward Turgeis, but the giant had already finished off his share of the attackers and was wiping his great ax on one of the dead bodies lying next to him. Selig then quickly scanned the area, his heart starting to beat harder than the battle had caused it to, but Erika wasn't there. No one else was there. There was not even a cart she might be hidden in.

He groaned, and started checking bodies for signs of life, yelling at Turgeis to do the same. Minutes later he gave up hope and dropped to his knees, his belly gripped with fear and rage. Too much hate, too much lust, now too much fear. Everything he felt for this woman was in the extreme, and now he knew why; now, when it might be too late.

"What did they do with you?" he shouted at the sky.

Erika heard him. She had been screaming already, repeatedly. Her efforts to twist out of the ropes had dislodged dirt on her head and shoulders. Bugs now crawled on her, what kind she didn't know, but her throat was raw because of them. Yet she yelled again, yelled with what strength she had left. Still, whatever sound got past her gag would not penetrate the wooden plank and grass above her head. Selig was there, he had come for her, and yet he couldn't hear her.

"Come," Turgeis said, helping Selig to his feet. "There is no more to do here."

"Come where?" Selig snarled bitterly. "I was so certain she would be here. Now where do we look?"

"Lord Durwyn will tell you naught, but he was not alone at Wyndhurst. We still have his messenger to find, and I will rip the answers from his throat if I have to."

They rode back to Wyndhurst with no less speed than before. Royce was encountered on the way, and Selig informed him, "We found the camp, but she was not there, so leave your men to still search for the while."

"And where do you go?"

"I fear looking for her will produce no results. We will have to be told where she was taken."

"Durwyn will not do it," Royce insisted. "His only hope is to protest his innocence to the bitter end."

"But his messenger will know," Selig said. "And his messenger is still at Wyndhurst. Turgeis plans to rip the answers out of him."

"Do you set Turgeis on him, the man will die of fright," Royce predicted, and not entirely in jest.

Selig repeated that for Turgeis's benefit. The giant merely grunted. Selig's expression hardened, though, when he added for Royce, "I *will* have answers, one way or another. And I would ask that you stay near me, to speak for me. I would already know where Erika is if Durwyn's last man had understood me when I promised him freedom. Instead he fled and died anyway, but by accident."

When they reached Wyndhurst and entered the bailey, they found it twice as crowded as it had been that morning. Near the hall, Durwyn stood with two guards on either side of him. As Selig rode that way, the guards both reached for their swords in warning.

" 'Twould seem Alfred is now convinced of his guilt. You must let the king have him, Selig," Royce said.

"He can have him as long as I can find my answer elsewhere. What goes here?"

Since Royce had no idea, he shouted for his wife. She was not far away and came running. "Did you find her?" she asked first.

"Nay, but what is going on?"

Kristen quickly explained. "If Durwyn had men here, Alfred wants them as well, yet will they not give themselves up. So everyone is to account for his own people, and those accounted for, separated from the rest. Whoever is left unclaimed had best have good reason for being in the king's party, and be able to prove it."

"How much longer will this take?"

"It has only just begun. Those accounted for are being moved over there." She pointed to the far side of the bailey. "I have been sending our own people over, one by one. Now you are here, you can help."

"That may not be necessary," Royce said as he stared into the crowd, then suddenly nudged Selig. "There, the man in the leather jerkin. If I am not mistaken, he was with Lord Durwyn when he stopped here last week. Give me a moment and I may be able to find the rest."

Selig stared at the man; then his eyes widened. "That one wears my sword!"

"Proof positive." They started toward the man. "Do you interrogate him, or cut him up some first?"

"You can offer him his life," Selig replied. "If he gives me back Erika, he need not bleed at all. He can even keep my sword."

Royce grinned. He just couldn't help it after a telling remark like that. "When did you start loving her?"

"Odin only knows." Selig sighed.

Ogden was already in a state of terror, with guards pushing him closer and closer to the line of separation. The king was there to identify his personal household and his lords and ladies. And those lords and ladies had to identify their own servants and retainers. Anyone unclaimed was in dire trouble, and one luckless thief had already been taken away by the king's guards.

His fear kept him from thinking clearly and coming up with a logical reason for being there, one that could be verified. That was the rub, and that damned Lady Kristen had suggested that proof be required, so that a good liar couldn't talk his way out of this.

And then he saw that the Viking was back with Lord Royce, and his terror turned to panic when he saw them staring directly at him, and then starting toward him. The end, then. He was going to die—nay, he would finish what had begun last month first. If he had done his job properly the first time, this wouldn't be happening. The Viking should have died with the others. He would see to it now.

Ogden waited until Selig was almost upon him before he drew his sword and attacked—with *his* sword. The jest was on the Viking, that he would be killed with his own sword. But the man dodged Ogden's first swipe and drew his own blade. Ogden swung again and again, but met only the steel of the other blade each time.

"Desist, man," Lord Royce shouted at him. "Tell him where his wife is and he will let you go."

Ogden did not pause in his attack, though he shouted back, "You lie. If he does not kill me, the king will have it done. Think you I would aid a damn Dane when I am to die anyway? You will never find her, yet she is right beneath your nose." And he laughed—just before Selig's sword hilt slammed against his head.

He collapsed, unconscious. Royce retrieved his sword and handed it to Selig.

"That was your wisest move," he said. "For he was determined to let you kill him—and without telling you where Erika is. We will question him further when he comes around, yet do I doubt we will get any more out of him."

"Any more?" Kristen questioned as she and Turgeis joined them.

"He said we will never find her, yet she is right beneath our nose. There is a clue in that, if we can but discern it."

"Beneath our nose would be right here, or so near we should stumble over her," Kristen replied. "Yet I have already had the servants search every container, crate, trunk, even the barrels, anything big enough to stuff a body into. She is not hid within these walls."

"What does she say?" Turgeis asked Selig.

Selig repeated it, and the clue they now had—and made up his mind then and there that he was going to learn Saxon if it killed him. His sister was grinning at his exasperation, for only Royce was excluded from the conversation, now they had switched to Norwegian.

"If we eliminate Wyndhurst, then that leaves the immediate area beyond," Kristen pointed out. "Where was their camp located?"

"Near a woods."

"Then mayhap they found a cave or a tunnel."

"Or a pit," Turgeis added.

Selig frowned at that suggestion, reminding him, "Your pit was a four-walled shack."

"First it was a hole in the ground. Is there anything like that in the area?" Turgeis asked.

"Not that I know of," Selig replied.

"Could they have dug their own?" Kristen wondered aloud.

Both Selig and Turgeis stared at her incredulously for a moment; then both suddenly ran for their horses.

Chapter 47

THE PIT WAS not easily found. It took an hour of moving bodies aside to cover every inch of ground, then working their way outward. It was Turgeis who discovered it and threw off the grass covering, but it was Selig who was determined to lift Erika out. She was not conscious, could not help even if she were, but her condition absolutely terrified him. And he couldn't reach her far enough to grasp more than her head, nor was there room in the pit for him to climb down. In the end, Turgeis had to lower him by his feet, then drag them both out at once, luckily an easy task for him.

She woke before she was laid on the ground, putting their worst fear to rest. Selig ran his dagger along the length of her side, cutting all the loops that bound her, but that was all he did before he yanked her up into his arms, crushing her with his emotion.

"Thank the gods you are all right! *Are* you all right? If they hurt you, I will kill them again, every one of them. Ah, sweetling, I love you so much. I have never been so frightened in my life! And if you *ever* go off alone again like you did, I swear I will put you back in chains."

Behind them, Turgeis cleared his throat. "You might get a response from her if you finish untieing her and remove that gag."

Selig laughed. His relief was making him almost giddy. And Erika *was* trying to say something through her gag, seemed somewhat urgent about it.

He cut away the last two restraints. Her arms were stiff, but she still managed to raise them to pull the gag out, then immediately started yanking at her clothes.

"Help me," she gasped out, "get them off!"

"What off?"

"My gowns! I am crawling with bugs!"

228

Her hysteria communicated itself to him, and with each helping, her clothes had never come off so fast. And although he could see no more than two insects on her, she was slapping and rubbing at herself everywhere. He helped her, though much more gently, smoothing her skin with his hands, soothing her panic with the calmness of his voice as he uttered nonsense to put her at ease.

"My hair," she cried, and meticulously, he examined every inch of it for her, until he could tell her the bugs were all removed.

She collapsed against him then, hugging him, thanking him, crying, and suddenly he was too aware of her nakedness—and that they were not alone. He looked toward Turgeis, but the giant was paying them no notice, had turned his back and was sitting on the ground, calmly doing to Erika's clothes what Selig had done to her hair, examining every inch of them, inside and out, until every insect had been removed. The sight was so incongruous, of that fearsome Viking sitting there plucking bugs from a lady's gowns, that Selig wanted to laugh. He didn't. Turgeis had today earned his friendship for life.

Not until Erika was reclothed did her thoughts turn to her rescue and the conclusion she drew that would explain their finding her. "You withdrew the challenge for me?" she asked Selig in wonder.

He was chagrined to have to admit, "I would have if I did not go berserk instead."

"He attacked Lord Durwyn with his bare hands," Turgeis added.

"And no one was sent to kill me?"

"Turgeis immediately closed the gates to prevent anyone from leaving."

She walked over to the giant and hugged him. "I can always depend on you, my friend."

"Always."

"You will not be angry with me for very long, will you, for going off without you?"

"Not too long."

Selig carefully parted them and drew Erika possessively back to his side. She raised a brow at him.

He explained, if evasively, "We need to return to Wyndhurst."

Turgeis just laughed, a deep barrel sound. Selig gave him a sour look. But they did return to Wyndhurst then, and even with all the extra horses about, Selig still insisted she ride with him. She didn't object this time. She doubted she ever would again.

Selig's whole family met them just inside the gate. The bailey had been cleared, or at least it was back to normal, since Royce had been able to identify the rest of Durwyn's men, and the lot of them were chained to the prisoner post.

"So *that* is Lord Durwyn?" Erika asked, staring in that direction.

"You know him?"

"He saw you with Alfred and asked me who you were, but he did not introduce himself, and I was too upset to wonder at his interest."

Selig frowned, remembering. "We are going to have to discuss this upset of yours that made you behave so foolishly."

"Oh, we will," she promised, only she did not sound the least bit upset at the reminder. "But how *did* you find me, if you were not told where to look?"

"Kristen figured it out."

Erika looked at her sister-in-law and smiled. For the first time, Kristen smiled back. A silent apology extended and accepted. They were not friends, but the possibility was now there that they might be eventually.

And then Selig surprised them all by saying, "We came here first to assure you that Erika is unharmed, but I am taking her home now. It will take me a while to get over nearly losing her. Until I do, I am not letting her out of my sight, and you are not like to see us for a while. Verily, as I need to recover myself from this harrowing day, I doubt me we will leave my chamber for at least a week."

Since he was grinning outrageously as he said it, Erika blushed furiously. Garrick and Royce laughed heartily. Brenna teased, "Mayhap I should come with you, to assure you are cared for properly the while you recover."

"Not if you want me to keep my sanity, Mother."

There were a few more jests that caused Erika's cheeks to grow even hotter, but then they returned to the peace and quiet of their own home. Only there was nothing quiet about it when they entered their hall with Turgeis, and Golda immediately started in on him.

"Covered in filth again, and blood this time," Golda sneered. "Can you never manage to stay clean, Viking? Or do you do it just to annoy me?"

Turgeis said not a word as usual, but he didn't ignore Golda this time. Far from it. He lumbered toward her, hefted her onto his shoulder, and, as casually as if he didn't now have a shrieking woman pounding on his back, mounted the stairs to his room.

"Should I do something about that?" Selig asked Erika.

Erika closed her mouth, which had been hanging open. That he was serious made her want to laugh. "Nay, I think it would be best not to interfere. I do not know what he means to do with her, yet am I sure he will not hurt her."

Selig grinned. "Ah. So that is the way of it."

"I did not say that."

"Nor did you have to," he replied. "And I would not find it amiss if you would like to carry me off like that."

A single giggle escaped her before she cut it off, yet the laughter remained in her eyes. "If I ever have the urge to, I will remember that I have your permission."

He sighed with dramatic disappointment. "Then I suppose I will have to do it for now."

He bent over and up she went, firmly planted on his shoulder. She didn't shriek or pound as he started up the stairs with her, said merely, "This is not necessary."

His hand came to give her backside a gentle caress. "But I am enjoying it."

So was Erika, truth be known, so she said no more about it. There was something very . . . romantic . . . about being carried off to a bedchamber, even if it was over her husband's shoulder rather than cradled in his arms. As they passed Turgeis's chamber, they heard laughter, both a man's and a woman's. Erika made no comment, but she smiled to herself, so very pleased for her friend.

In their own chamber, when Selig set her on her feet, he was immediate in demonstrating what he had in mind to do. Her own intentions were forgotten momentarily as she savored the taste and feel of him pressed along her length, and returned his kiss wholeheartedly. But when he reached to lift her gown, she put a hand over his to stop him.

One of his dark brows arched in question, but she was suddenly shy of beginning. She had to discuss his mistaken beliefs with him and try, somehow, to convince him that he *was* mistaken. But what she was most interested in was what she was sure she had heard him say after he had pulled her out of that pit. She wasn't positive he had said it. She had been too frenzied at the time because of those damned bugs and not paying attention. But a single question would clarify the matter for her.

She asked it. "Did you—say you loved me today?"

"Did I? I do not recall."

"Then mayhap I am mistaken."

His finger ran along her cheek. "Mayhap you are fishing to hear it again."

A bit of stiffness. "If 'tis not so, then I certainly do not want to hear it."

"And if it is so?"

"If you continue to tease me about this," she growled, "it will not matter if it is so or not. I will—"

"Throw some more salt at me?"

She burst out laughing. The man was absolutely impossible, could not even be serious about what was so very important to her. She didn't notice how still Selig went, though, hearing her laughter, but she saw his confused frown, which ended her amusement abruptly.

"What is it?"

" 'Tis not the same, your laughter. 'Tis not as I remember it. Let me hear you laugh again."

She understood. They were going to discuss the other first, after all, whether she wanted to or not. "I cannot laugh at will, but—"

He was suddenly gripping her shoulders. "Please, Erika, you do not understand."

"I do. 'Tis not the same, because you never heard me laugh before. It was your fever, Selig, that made you imagine it. I was not there for your lashing. I meant to stop it, but I was called away. Ask Turgeis."

She saw his stricken look just before he dropped to his knees and wrapped his arms around her legs. He was groaning as he buried his face against her belly, and the sound tore at her heart.

"Nay, get up," she beseeched him. "You are not to blame for what the fever made you believe."

"Why did you not tell me?"

"I never knew what you thought. Your sister told me only yesterday."

"But how can you ever forgive me for what I tried to do to you?"

She had to smile at that. "Tried, Selig. You never actually managed to get your revenge. You simply could not hurt me."

"I put you in chains!"

"My own guilt allowed it, or be assured, I would have protested more than I did."

"I tried to humiliate you."

"Aye, well, that you managed, and for that I will let you make amends."

"Anything. Just tell me."

"Nay, you tell me. Do you love me?"

"So much it frightens me."

Her breath caught in her throat, those words caused her such joy. And since he wouldn't get up, was determined to wallow in his own guilt now, she went down on her knees to cup his face in her hands.

"You are the most gentle man I have ever known. You wanted to hate me, but you could not. You wanted to hurt me, but you could not. I should feel sorry for you that your very nature defeats you, but I must be glad for it instead, because it has given me a truly remarkable man to love. And I do love you, Selig. So do not ask me for forgiveness again. 'Tis I who must still beg yours."

He grinned suddenly, and then he laughed and hugged her until she cried out for breath. "We make a fine pair, you and I, with so much to be sorry for. And yet I am too happy just now to feel very sorry. Do you think *now* we can begin anew?"

Her nod brought more laughter from him, and it was infectious this time. If Erika was not mistaken, and she was sure she was not, she was going to have a great deal of laughter in her life from now on—and more love than she had ever counted on.